# FIVE FINGERS

BY

TONY H. LATHAM

Cover design by Jay Griffith

# Acknowledgments

I've heard it said that it takes a village to raise a child. In hindsight, I think it took a village to turn this book into something readable. English was not my favorite class.

Thanks to my pre-readers for finding the story holes and associated problems. And special gratitude to my editor (and sister), Jane Griffith for the hours she put into this tale.

To my partner and love, Stephanie Smith; thanks for putting up with my reclusive writing moods and finding a far-off corner of our house that she's designated as my *writing growlery.*

And a final thanks to my confidential source on drug use; he/she's been off the chemical and away from the glass pipe for many-many years, but lived it every hour for a year, and somehow managed to run away from the addiction for the love of family.

# Epigraph

*"If the Blue Meanies are going to get me, they'd better get off their asses and do something."* -The (never-arrested) Zodiac Killer

# Chapter 1

His mouth tasted like burnt plastic; it'd been that way for three days. He pulled off the gravel road, killed the engine, rolled the window down, and listened. A few snowflakes swirled back into the pickup's cab, and he felt their bite on his hollow, unshaven cheeks. The only noise in the darkness was the metallic pinging of the engine block. The yard light from a lone ranch house burned far off in the valley. Swiveling around, he looked behind him. No lights. Nada. He sat listening and looking. Satisfied, he reached down to the hump on the truck's floor and felt for the rubber shifter boot, pulled the base up, reached in, and fished out a Crown Royal bag. He set it on his lap, letting his eyes adjust to the blackness while absently feeling the lumps inside the velvet bag. After a few minutes, he looked around and confirmed there were still no lights moving in the valley. He pulled a pipe out of the bag, held it by the stem, and felt for the vent hole on the bowl with his ring finger. Pulling a Bic lighter out of his shirt pocket, he lit it and held the blackened glass pipe bowl in front of the flame, illuminating the emptiness inside. He stared into the bowl, looking for the ghostly effigy he'd seen time and time before. Suddenly, the heat of the lighter started to burn his thumb and he shut it off. His eyes had lost their edge, and he couldn't a see thing. Still grasping the pipe, he caressed the rifle sitting next to him with the back of his hand. Again, he scanned around the valley and stared back through the rear window of the truck. Nothing but the far off ranch light. *Time to chase the dragon.*

He flicked on a flashlight that was lying on the seat, giving him just enough vision to see what he was doing, but not enough to expose him. Reaching back into his Crown Royal bag, he pulled out a small plastic baggie containing a loose crystalline jumble. Sticking his thumb and forefinger in, he grasped a rock-salt sized crystal and carefully dropped it into the vent hole in the pipe's bowl. After returning the baggie to the Crown bag, he snapped the lighter back on, held the flame under the bowl, and gently rotated the stem with his thumb and forefingers. He brought the pipe up to his lips, keeping the flame under the vaporizing crystals, and slowly inhaled its breath while maintaining the back and forth roll of the pipe's orb over the Bic's tongue. His lungs burned with a hot itch as the methamphetamine vapors entered his bronchi, passed into his alveoli, and transferred the molecules into his blood. Slumping into his seat, he felt the shit's effect squirting through his brain like hundreds of sparks mimicking a game of three-dimensional billiards. He held the burning fog as long as he could and finally exhaled. He sat and reveled in the meth's god-like pleasures.

Tweaking had seduced him in his youth. Now three days into his binge, each hit from the dragon smacked him with the remembrance of that first tryst.

After five minutes, he turned the flashlight off and snapped the lighter's flame back on. He reheated the bowl and inhaled his second lungful, holding the scorch, letting it come home. Exhaling, he felt his capillaries tightening and the worms beginning their long crawl through his veins. Laying his head back on the seat, he rolled it slowly back and forth, mimicking the movement of the pipe's bowl. *Gawd,* he mused, *this shit is somethin'.*

After a few minutes, he placed the pipe back in its velvet bag and hid it under the rubber shifter boot. He started to reach for the ignition but stopped. *I know you're out there.* Again, he looked into the darkness for vehicle lights. Still just the one yard light at the distant ranch house. He fired up the truck's engine, turned the headlights on and flipped a dash mounted toggle switch that turned on the dual overhead spotlights above the cab, illuminating the snow-covered sagebrush that paralleled both sides of the road.

He pulled onto the roadway, reached past the rifle, and grabbed a can of Keystone beer from its half-full cardboard box. Popping the top while steering with his leg, he took a long deep swig, washing the garbage-fire flavor from his mouth. He felt the liquid run down his throat into his belly as the cold air rushed in through the open window. Looking out the windshield, he saw a thousand twinkling stars staring back at him from the snow. Breathing deep, he inhaled the pungent turpentine emanating from the sagebrush. His senses were on the run. *Jesus,* he thought, *this shit's lightin' my wires!*

The road was covered with an inch of snow and more was falling, each flake illuminated by the truck's lights. A line of small tracks dotted across the road and he jerked the wheel to the right. He brought the truck to a stop, the lights cascading out into the sagebrush. *Fuckin' coyote. Where you at?* He stared into the sage, looking for the reflection of the animal's eyes. Nothing. His hand left the rifle as he reached over and killed the lights. He looked around big-eyed and thought, *YOU ain't gonna leave me laying scalped and bleeding in the snow.* He shut the engine off, held his breath, and listened from the open window. Nothing. Exhaling, he tasted the air—still nothing.

He'd cut the distance to the ranch house by about half, but it was still a good mile away. *You watching me?* For a moment, he thought he could feel the snow crystallizing on his skin, but he realized it was the meth worms slithering around. Scratching at the parasites, he started the engine and turned the lights back on. He continued his slow weaving while looking for eyes staring back from the darkness. He pulled the can of beer from his crotch, finished it off, and dropped it on the floor. His toes played his old keyboard through his boots, trying to recall an old song. Giving up, he reached over and turned on his CD player. A guitar hit a few chords and Hank Williams, Jr. began singing, "That Ain't Good" with a pissy twang. Listening to the singer, he looked down at the Keystone box, thinking Hank was right—*it ain't good to be out of beer*—and grabbed another.

And there they were. On the left, maybe fifty yards up ahead, four eyeballs shined back at him from the sage. Bringing the truck to a stop, he angled slightly towards them and felt his wires snapping. As Hank chorused what wasn't good, he turned off the ignition and killed the music. While the truck's lights flooded into the foot-high brush, he eased the rifle out the window. Through the scope, he could see that the animal on the right was a four by four Mule Deer buck. The one on the left was a doe. His mind flashed back to the redheaded girl he'd seen walking in town. He flipped the safety off and put the crosshairs on the doe's head. The worms started squirming as he eased back on the trigger. The shot woke up the night like a bomb. The doe dropped like a rock. The buck bounced back a few yards, stopped, and looked into the lights. *Dumb-ass muley,* he thought, as he racked the rifle's bolt. The buck started to walk off and the crosshairs found the animal's back. A second explosion and the buck collapsed.

He reached over, grabbed the flashlight from the seat, and stepped out into the fresh snow, leaving his door open. The truck's lights illuminated the sage and he walked to the doe with his shadow leading the way. Dark blood oozed out of the deer's smashed head like a bucket of spilled paint, pushed by the last quivers of her heart. He heard a noise back where the buck had been and shined the light. The deer was trying to get up on its front legs, but fell back, still staring at the shooter, and not understanding why its hind legs didn't seem to exist. He started to pull the .357 from his cross-draw holster and thought, *Fuck it, it ain't goin' nowhere.* His brain shifted back to the redhead wearing those fine Levi's. *Goddamn, she fits 'em good.* He grinned, and his tongue rubbed back and forth across his lower lip as he turned back to the doe and dropped to his knees. His meth-fueled heart started to pound, the worms squirmed under his skin, and he felt the blood burning inside his skull as he rolled his head back and forth.

# *Chapter 2*

The ringing broke into Charley Cove's brain. He fumbled for the cell phone and glanced at the red glow of his alarm clock; it was 3:34 a.m. Shifting his focus to the phone's display, he recognized the sheriff's dispatch number, flipped it open, and answered. "Yeah, what's going on?"

A female voice gave him the news. "Sorry to wake you, but I just got a call from a rancher. He heard some shooting and saw a truck. I thought I'd better let you know."

"Who was it?"

"Bob Harris, up the Pahsimeroi."

Cove thought through the fog for a moment, rubbed his neck and stared at the digital clock. "He say how many shots?"

"I didn't ask," she said. "But he said he looked out and saw taillights below his place heading back down the valley."

"What kind of truck?" Cove asked.

"I asked the same thing," she said. "All he saw were the taillights. Sounded like he was assuming it was a truck, and I'd assume the same thing out in that country."

"Did he say how far from his place?" Cove asked, struggling to find the right question.

"He said it was down on the BLM ground. Does that mean anything to you?" The dispatcher asked.

"Yeah. I know his ranch. 'Puts it at least a quarter mile from his house, maybe more. I don't think he's got any cattle that far out, they're probably shooting rabbits or deer," Cove said, and thought about how long it would take to get to Harris's place–at least thirty minutes down the highway along the Salmon River and then another thirty or forty minutes up the Pahsimeroi. "I'll roll that way... have you got a deputy working north of town?"

"Nobody's on graveyard right now. You want me to call Fred out for some backup? He's been off since the bars closed."

Cove hesitated, "Naw, it's probably just kids, if they're still around, it shouldn't be any big deal." *Maybe,* he thought. "Don't apologize for the call-out, Sarah. I'll let you know when I'm mobile." Cove snapped the phone closed, turned on his nightstand light and squinted his eyes. *Maybe,* he thought, *maybe it's my deer shooters.* Grabbing his long johns off the floor, he slipped them on. *I oughta buzz that reporter, see if she's serious about tagging along on a call-out for a story.* He picked up the phone, hesitated and then selected her number.

While it rang, he thought, *this isn't a good idea.* On the fifth ring she gave a groggy answer. "Hello?"

"It's Charley Cove. Were you serious about wanting to go along on a call-out?"

"Who's this?"

"Charley Cove, the game warden. Sorry about the late call, but you said you wanted to go out on a run sometime." *This is stupid,* he thought. *She doesn't even remember me.*

"Oh, Charley! Yeah, yeah! Sure!" She said.

"I'll be at your front door in ten, then. Wear something warm. We're headed for the Pahsimeroi," Cove said, and hung up.

He put on olive green Wranglers, slipped his ballistic vest over his T-shirt, and covered it with his gray long-sleeve uniform shirt. It had a silver and gold shield-shaped badge above the left pocket, a silver name tag over the right pocket and emblems on both shoulders. He slipped into his lug-soled insulated boots and quickly laced them up. Cove buckled his gun belt, snapped the keepers that held the rig to his pants belt, reached for his .40 caliber semi-auto Glock sitting by his alarm clock and holstered it. Besides the firearm, the heavy nylon belt held two loaded pistol magazines, a collapsible steel baton and two sets of handcuffs. His chocolate lab was up, wagging her tail and watching him with her flopped ears cocked and head canted. She had the same badge Cove wore attached to a silver chain around her neck. Her dark brown hair was set off by a bit of premature gray showing on her muzzle.

"Time to go to work, girl." The two walked to the back door and Cove pulled his dark green coat off the rack, slipped it on, and exited into the night, feeling the cold swirling snow hit his face.

Charley Cove stood five-foot-ten and carried a solid torso. His skin was a light chestnut color and his hair was the color of strong coffee. He had high cheeks and a strong jaw. His beard showed a day's growth of dark stubble he'd normally have shaved off if he were having an ordinary day, but few of his days could be called ordinary since he didn't have an ordinary job. An eight-to-five day or even something resembling a shift was rare. On some days Cove was able to set his own schedule, but most of it was set in play by a variety of factors: lawbreakers, wildlife, weather, and geography controlled his days and nights. His official title was Senior Conservation Officer; locally he was called *game warden* and Cove was proud of both the moniker and his profession.

He'd been awake for five minutes. The phone call had charged his body and cleared his head better than any pot of home-ground coffee could have. He was focused, eager and anxious to roll.

There was an inch of fresh snow covering his patrol truck, which was a dark-brown GMC four-wheel-drive heavy-duty club-cab pickup truck. On its door was the shield-shaped insignia of Idaho Fish and Game, consisting of a graphical representation of a bull elk, a leaping fish, and two mountain peaks all outlined in gold. Smaller versions of the shield were on his badge and uniform shirt. Cove pulled an old broom from the truck's bed and heard his dog jump up on the tailgate. Brushing the snow off the windshield, he exposed an owl tail-feather hanging inside the cab from the rearview mirror. Giving the roof a quick cleaning, he added an extra sweep to the low-profile high-intensity emergency blue light centered on top. Walking around the truck, he closed the tailgate and brushed the snow off the taillights. His dog sat watching him from her covered kennel. He set the broom back into the bed, turned to his dog and said, "Annie, let's go get the crooks."

Cove drove down his driveway, engaged the four-wheel drive, and pulled his seatbelt across his chest while turning onto the fresh snow of Garden Creek Road, and was shortly on the main drag of Challis. The town was dead quiet. The only thing moving were the falling snowflakes that looked like popcorn in his headlights.

If there was ever a sleepy little town, this was it. Challis, Idaho sat in the middle of nowhere on the edge of the largest chunk of wilderness south of the Canadian border. A thousand folks still asleep in a town set around a twelve-block main street. Not a stop light for sixty miles. Challis had started out as a gold mining town and had evolved into a combination cow town and modern day hunting, fishing, and whitewater-rafting destination, but still relied on a nearby molybdenum pit for its bread and butter.

Turning right onto Third Street, Cove drove two blocks, and parked behind Julie Lake's Subaru. The porch light was on and she met him at the door, bundled in a bright blue down coat. She flashed an eager smile. She was a slender, long-legged athletic looking young woman with long flowing hair, fair skin, striking facial features, and intelligent green eyes.

Cove spoke, watching for a reaction. "Sorry about calling you so late, but you did say 'anytime, night or day'?"

"And I meant it—this is great," Julie said smiling. "I'm very serious about writing a story on poachers. What's happened?"

"Jump in and I'll tell you."

They both climbed into the patrol truck. Cove noticed a different aroma in his rig. It wasn't the normal atmosphere of his well lived-in truck cab. He couldn't put a finger on it, but it wasn't perfume—it was something fresh and womanish.

He fired up the engine and pulled onto Main Street's coat of untrodden snow. "Look," Cove said. "I don't know if there's a story here or not. I hope I didn't get you outta bed for nothing. A rancher called the sheriff's office saying he'd heard some shooting. Might be some kids partying and killing jackrabbits, but it could be something bigger." Cove's brain was turning during the conversation and he realized that Harris must have heard the shooting from inside his house from a quarter mile a way. *'Had to be a big rifle, not a twenty-two,* he thought, *maybe my deer shooters?*

Julie interrupted his ruminations. "I started out in photo journalism. Sometimes you get the shot and sometimes the light's bad, or it just doesn't happen. You just never know." Julie put her gloves on the dash and looked at Cove. "Is it legal to shoot jackrabbits?"

"The season's open year 'round for jackrabbits. The landowner could give them permission to shoot them at night, but I know this rancher; he wouldn't have called if he'd given somebody the okay. In fact, I think he woulda talked to me about it first. Most of the land below his place is public BLM ground. You can't hunt out there with artificial light anytime." He glanced over at her, saw she had turned her head and was looking at him. He looked back down the street. "We get spotlighting problems in the Pahsimeroi a lot. It's wide open wild country and a long ways from anything," Cove continued. "Somebody killed a beef cow up there a month ago, the sheriff's department worked it. I'm sure it was done at night. This could be guys trying to fill their freezer with venison too, but I doubt it."

"Is that legal here?" She turned and asked.

*She's not a hunter,* he thought. "No, the season's been closed for a month and it isn't legal to shoot deer frozen by a light. Besides, it's dangerous firing a rifle in the Pahsimeroi in the dark. Spotlighters can't see beyond their light tunnel and there are ranches scattered up and down the valley. Last year we had a bullet smack into somebody's washer."

"In somebody's house?"

"Yeah," Cove replied. "Their garage. It was stopped by a load of wet clothes. If it'd been empty, the bullet would have gone into the bedroom where there were two kids asleep. I never did figure out who the shooter was." Cove thought about the incident, felt a flush of anger, and recalled the copper-jacketed bullet still sitting in an evidence envelope.

"Do you think they shot the cow by accident?"

"Just a sec, I've gotta give dispatch a call before we lose cell coverage in the canyon." He pulled his phone out of his pocket, and speed dialed the sheriff's office. "Hey Sarah, I'm just turning onto the highway. You might give Harris a call and let him know I'm headed out there. Tell him to call you back if he sees those lights again."

"I'll do that."

"And please don't call me on the radio unless you can't get my cell—in case these guys got a scanner."

"Knock the shit off, you know me," Sarah said. "You sure you don't want some backup? I'd love to get Fred's ass outa bed to come help you out."

"No, but thanks," Cove replied. "I'll call you when I get close to Harris's."

He hung up and turned back to Julie. "An accident? No, I wasn't the one that investigated it, but I'm sure that cow was looking right at the road, right into the light when somebody shot it in the head."

"Why would somebody do that?"

"Good question," Cove paused and looked back at the snowflakes still falling into the sphere of his headlights. "These guys doing this kinda stuff aren't deep thinkers. A lot of spot lighters are drinking and some are smoking pot; two or three guys sitting in the front seat of a truck. It's usually a party on wheels; driving around laughing, drinking, and shooting stuff. They're not contemplating the meaning of life. Spotlighting is like shooting pool in a bar, it's a social activity. Most of these yahoos aren't real bad," he said, glancing at her. "But once in a while we'll get a ringer."

"So a lot of these people are poaching?" Julie asked.

"All of this night hunting is illegal, so yeah, it's poaching. We call it spotlighting or shining; the codebook refers to it as 'hunt with the aid of artificial light.' Every year we get several deer and elk shot and left laying where the shooter fired at them. Some wardens call it thrill killin'. Sometimes they cut the head off if it's got antlers and sometimes they'll take some meat, they high-grade the choice cuts and leave the rest. Once in a while they'll take the whole carcass, but I don't see that a lot when the season's closed like this. The thrill killin' thing seems to be on the rise. I've worked two does that were shot and left in the last two weeks and don't have a clue as to who's doing it."

"What do you mean by thrill killing?" Julie asked.

Cove glanced over at her. "Kids out driving around and shooting anything with eyes. It's not sport and it's not for the meat. It's just for the fun of killin'. When ever you see road signs with bullet holes, it was done at night."

"How often do you get called out like this?" Julie asked.

"During hunting season, I work about every other evening and take radio calls from the sheriff's dispatch when something gets called in. Once the season's over and the days get short, I think these people catch cabin fever and I'll get a call-out two or three times a month. I think they get bored. I'm surprised this call came in so late, though. Most guys are ready to crawl in bed by now."

"Do they eat the jackrabbits?" Julie asked.

"No. They were an important food for the people many generations ago, but no, these guys just leave 'em in the sage."

By the time they hit the Pahsimeroi Valley they still hadn't seen any traffic on the thirty miles they had covered on the highway. Cove turned onto the county road leading up the west side of the drainage that would take them to Harris's ranch. He studied the one set of tracks as he drove. Whoever had made the tracks had been on the road during the storm. The tires had impressed into two inches of fresh untracked snow and those tracks had been snowed over with another half inch. Cove couldn't tell if the tracks were going up or down the valley. There was a distinct back and forth pattern left by the vehicle. Cove's first take on the track pattern was that they might be following a drunk, or someone driving with a passenger running a spotlight. Some  spotlighters used their headlights to find something to kill, but most of them consist of a driver and another person running a handheld spotlight out of the passenger window. The vehicle would wander back and forth because the driver spent more time watching the spotlight's illumination than the road. The weave of tracks Cove saw in the snow appeared to be more of a consistent, consciously repeated pattern.

"I'm guessing these guys are still up here," Cove said. "The tracks aren't old. They coulda crossed over to the other side of the valley, and turned down towards Salmon and beat us out," Cove added, thinking out loud. "Obviously we didn't see 'em headed back into Challis on the highway. I suppose they could live up here someplace, too."

"Are you going to arrest them if we find them?" Julie asked.

*Can I transport a prisoner while I've got a civilian?* "Well... first of all, we don't know if a crime's been committed. If we find a vehicle moving out here before we get to Harris's ranch, I've got enough suspicion I could stop 'em and it'd hold up in court. I'd want to listen to their story and look into the rig for a spotlight and rifles. At least find out who they are." Cove thought for a moment, moved his jaw a bit and said, "The prosecutor isn't gonna like it, but I think the judge would rule it a legal stop. If they're running a spotlight I can issue tickets and seize the guns and light and it's a slam dunk."

Julie turned back and looked at him. "What do you mean about the prosecutor not *liking* it?"

"I've got to have probable cause to stop a vehicle. It's cut and dried when a deputy catches somebody going over the speed limit with his radar or if we actually catch them running a light, but this is a different deal if they aren't. I have to be able to articulate 'reasonable suspicion' that they are involved in something illegal. With what the rancher told the dispatcher, it's sensible for us to assume, or have suspicion, a crime's been committed." He glanced at the dash clock and saw it was 4:33 a.m. "We haven't seen a vehicle since we left town, there's this lone track we're following, and there isn't any good reason for someone to be up here in the middle of nowhere at this hour in a snow storm—but to answer your question, the prosecutor isn't a big fan of wildlife cases."

Julie glanced at Cove and squinted her eyes. "What's he got against wildlife?"

"Challis is a small town. Everybody knows everybody. I've pinched a couple of his buddies in the past and I think it's caused him some problems. Critters don't vote and they can't write letters to the editor. Wildlife doesn't have a voice." Cove hesitated and asked what he was wondering. "Speaking of letters to the editor, how'd you end up as a reporter in a town in the middle of nowhere, three hours from the nearest box store?"

"Good question," Julie answered. "I was working for a newspaper in Detroit and doing freelance stuff on the side. I grew up in a small town in Wisconsin and hated the city. I'd been in a bad relationship that I'd broken off from. He kept badgering me. I wanted to get as far away from him as I could. The Custer Chronicle was advertising online and here I am." She looked over at him, smiling. "I've always wanted to live in the mountains and I'm smitten by this country around here."

"A daily to a weekly. Quite the career change, eh?" Cove asked, wondering if he was stepping into murky water.

"Yes, it has been. Covering a bowling tournament doesn't get my journalistic brain going, but I do find it fun. Most of my income is from my freelance pieces, not from the Chronicle. I like Challis and there are several papers I write for around the country. I've got an editor back east I'd like to pitch a poaching story to." She paused and added, "If I can put one together."

"Hopefully you'll get one tonight and not a wild-goose chase," Cove said, turning off the main road. "I need to take a look around the valley; there's a good lookout hill right over here. See if there's some lights moving." He turned off his headlights and used his parking lights to stay on a two-rut road that cut into the sagebrush. As he approached the top of the hill, he flicked the parking lights off and stopped. The truck's interior was dimly lit by the dash lights, but everything outside was black. "This is a great place to sit and watch for spot lighters. We'll be here just a minute or two," Cove said. "I'm going to grab my night vision goggles and take a quick look around." He reached up and made sure the interior cab light switch was in the off position and stepped out into the night. Compared to town, the Pahsimeroi was bone chilling cold and Cove zipped his coat up. *At least I don't have to worry about snakes,* he thought. Reaching towards the rear of the truck cab, he opened the half-door and retrieved the goggles from a Pelican case on the seat. He closed both doors, turned the goggles on, and brought the green-glowing twin oculars to his eyes, holding the third-generation device by the mono tube protruding from the front. It had quit snowing and the NVGs played their magic, turning the black-masked night into a bright chartreuse landscape. The base of the Lemhi Range stood out several miles across the valley floor. He could see a few scattered yard lights from ranch houses glowing in the valley floor. There was no vehicle traffic. He studied the side drainages across the flats, turned around and looked at the convoluted terrain of the Lost River Range behind him. *Where'd you guys go?* He didn't expect to see a vehicle, but even taillights five miles away would have popped. A match light would have been visible miles away enhanced by the device. Pulling the goggles from his face, he felt the chill of the night, got back inside the truck and turned up the heater. "I didn't see anything moving. Take a look with these." He handed the NVGs to Julie. "They're pretty cool."

She took the goggles, brought them up to her eyes and looked out through the truck's windshield. Cove took the opportunity to look at her with the green glow illuminating her face. Long curling hair framed her lean features. She was wearing small silver earrings and her lips formed a slight smile in front of a strong angled jaw. Her skin looked soft and she had graceful neck.

"You can see the line of cottonwoods in the middle of the valley. That's the Pahsimeroi River. There's the Lemhi County road on the other side of the river that parallels the Custer County road on this side that we've been working up. There's three or four lanes that connect the two roads." She caught him staring, and she turned back and looked into the goggles smiling.

"Wow," Julie said. "My boyfriend's going to be jealous when I tell him about these things!"

Cove looked away with a flush hidden by the night and silence took over the cab's interior.

After a bit Cove broke the dead air. "If anybody's working a light in the draws or side canyons, you'll see a glow coming from it that you can't see with your naked eyes."

Julie took the goggles down and passed them back to Cove. "Thanks. The view through them is breathtaking. It's easy to forget how big this valley is when it's so dark."

Cove took one more look around through the NVGs, turned them off, and placed them on the seat. "Lets go see what we can find," Cove said. Starting the truck up, he flipped the lights on, drove off the hill through the sage and turned onto the main road, following the lone set of tracks covered with a half-inch of fresh powder.

*****

The poacher was sitting in his darkened truck, watching the other vehicle move up the valley through an old pair of binoculars. His toes tapped an imagined keyboard through his boots. *It's got to be the goddamn warden,* he thought, and finished his Keystone. *Maybe the sheriff.* Dropping the beer can on the floor, he

scratched his flattened nose and spoke to himself.
"Fuckin' rancher must have heard my shots."

Setting the binoculars back on the dashboard, he
reached down for his Crown Royal bag and fished it out.
He leaned his head back on the seat and rolled it back and
forth.

\*\*\*\*\*

Charley Cove drove for another five minutes and
found the Furey Lane Junction, where you could cross
over to the other side of the valley, or continue along the
route they had come up. There was another set of tracks
coming from the new road that joined the tracks they were
following. Cove stopped the vehicle and pulled out a small
SureFire flashlight from his gun belt. Getting out, he
turned the flashlight on and studied the new track. *Either
another vehicle going up the valley,* Charley thought, *or
they've already come down and are gone. Bob said he
saw the taillights heading down.* The new track had less
snow in it than the one they had been following. He
shined his light on the older set and compared the width
of both tracks. They appeared to be the same.

He looked at his watch—it was 4:46 a.m. Harris had
called at about 3:30 and they were at least ten minutes
from his ranch. *If this is them,* Cove thought, *these newer
tracks are over an hour old.* He got down on his knees,
leaned over the freshest track and blew the powdery snow
out of it. Shining his light at an oblique angle exposed an
interlocking Z shaped pattern. Cove pulled a 3" plastic
ruler from his wallet and laid it next to the track for scale.

He set the SureFire in the track, casting a horizontal beam along its pattern which increased the contrast of the tire's impression. Unzipping his coat, he took out a small digital camera from his shirt pocket and photographed the tire's print. Looking at the camera's display, he studied the result to ensure he'd captured a useable image. He moved over to the older track he had been following and got back down on his knees. Again he leaned over and blew the fresh snow away from the print, exposing the same interlocking Z pattern.

He now believed the vehicle had come up from the highway in a light snow storm and had driven up near the Harris Ranch where Bob had heard the shots. Then it had come back down, turned off at this junction and headed to the other side of the valley.

Cove put his SureFire light back in its belt pouch, blew warm air through his cupped hands and retrieved the night vision goggles from the seat. He turned off his headlights and stepped away from the truck into the darkness. He brought the NVGs to his eyes and picked apart the landscape. A cold breeze snuck into his open coat and caused a shiver. It was five miles across the valley. He could see about five miles up, and another five down the valley. Fifty square miles of sagebrush, intermittent alfalfa fields, and a few scattered ranch houses marked by their yard lights. No vehicle lights. *Where the hell are you guys?*

# *Chapter 3*

He brought the Bic up to his glass pipe, snapped the flame on, and sucked the vapor into his lungs, letting it hang for a moment. He rolled his head on the top of the truck's seat, feeling the flow of the meth shoot through his body. His bottle was topped off, and his bones vibrated. A harsh coppery taste brought him to reality for a moment, and he looked back out where he'd been watching the vehicle lights. He froze not seeing them, and he felt his pores opening. He laid the pipe and the lighter on the dash, retrieved the binoculars, and brought them up to his glaring eyes. *Where'd you bastards go?* The headlights came back on. He realized the vehicle was at the junction and smiled. *Are you gonna come over here and play?* He scratched at something creeping under the skin of his jutting Adam's apple and watched the rig continue up the road towards Harris's ranch. Snowflakes struck his windshield and transformed into tiny stars. He traded the binoculars for his pipe and Bic. *One more good hit.*

\*\*\*\*\*

Cove continued following the two sets of tracks up the valley until he could see the yard light at the Harris ranch. He noted there were lights on inside the house. *Bob's probably got a pot of coffee going,* he thought. Cove pulled his cell out of his pocket and confirmed there were no bars on it. He reached to his radio mic clipped to the dash and looked down at the radio, confirming it was set to transmit on the Custer County sheriff's frequency. He pressed the transmit button, bringing the mic near his mouth. "Sheriff, ...seven-three-one is just about on-scene." He paused and listened.

"Roger that, seven-three-one," a female voice answered. "No update from the RP."

Cove was pleased, but not surprised that Sarah hadn't given up his location or any details of what he was working on. If anyone were listening on a scanner, for all they knew, he could be anywhere in Custer County's five thousand square miles. All any listener would know was somewhere, someplace, a game warden was working on an unknown incident.

"What does she mean by RP?" Julie asked.

"She's talking about Bob Harris, the reporting party."

"Is there a Fish and Game dispatch you use?" she asked.

"No, we work through the sheriff's offices around the state. It works well, especially in these rural counties; it helps coordinate our efforts with their deputies, too. It's usually the deputies I get my back-up from."

Cove's headlights found the end of the vehicle tracks. The rig had pulled off to the left side of the road, stopped and then had turned around. *This must be where Harris heard the shooting from,* Cove thought. He pulled his truck over and studied the tracks.

He turned to Julie. "You can get out, but stay close. Walk where I walk. This fresh snow's a big deal."

Cove shut the truck off, but kept the lights on, illuminating the scene. From where the rig had parked,

Cove could see a single set of footprints disappearing into the sage and returning. He retrieved a green ball cap with a badge embroidered on it from his rear seat and put it on his head. Grabbing a small headlamp from his console, he put it over his hat and turned the light on. He walked over and examined the footprints with his hands wedged into his coat pockets. Julie stood a few feet behind him. Cove's light found a snow-covered lump. He put a leather glove on and brushed the fresh snow off it, exposing a blue aluminum beer can. He turned to Julie. "All these guys like Keystone," Cove said. "It's the poacher's preferred choice. My boss calls it probable cause." He left the can and began walking parallel to the line of footprints leading into the sagebrush with Julie following. As he walked, he compared his stride to the tracks he was following. The person's stride was longer than his. *He's got to be well over six-foot.* The footprints were covered with a slight dusting of snow and had the pointed toe and canted heel of a cowboy boot. Cove leaned down and blew the snow out of the boot prints. There was no visible tread. Pulling out a small tape measure, Cove asked Julie to hold the end of the tape on the heel of a footprint impression. He stretched the tape out to the next heel track. "Thirty-one inches."

Cove stood up and cast his light in the direction they were headed. He could see the all too familiar shape of a dead deer laying in the sagebrush. What snow had fallen on the doe's hair had melted on her warm body, and steam was radiating off the animal's dark back.

"Deer," Cove said. "Shot and left." His light wandered behind the carcass. "Shit, there's another one." He said, looking beyond the doe.

"No!" Julie's voice had risen in pitch. "Why? Why'd he do this?"

Cove didn't answer. He walked over to the doe, looking at what was left of her head. The heavy earthy odor of the deer, combined with the coppery smell of blood, hung in the air. The bullet had entered just below her left eye and had exited from the back of the cranium. Cove shined his headlamp behind the deer and could see a spray of blood and tissue on the snow caused by the exit of the bullet. A large amount of dark shiny blood had drained from the wound into the snow. Both of her ears were down at unnatural angles, looking as if they belonged to a flop-eared goat. *High velocity, for damn sure,* Cove thought.

Cove walked over and looked at the buck. Its brown antlers had four points on each side and spread just past its ears. "A three-year old," Cove said.

He could see where its front legs had thrashed, arcing back and forth through the snow and down into the hard-frozen dirt in a paraplegic attempt to get up before it had bled to death. There was no snow on top of the thrashing, unlike the dust in the shooter's tracks. *Good gawd,* Cove thought. *This poor thing was still alive when the shooter left; he didn't have the decency to put it out of its misery.* Reaching down, he pulled up a front leg and illuminated it with his headlamp. He could see where the animal had abraded its skin while flailing in its panic. *A bad way to die,* he thought. Cove stepped back from the buck, his own blood pulsing through his neck. He reached into his coat, pulled out his digital camera, and took two photos of the buck. Grabbing the two front legs, he rolled it over, exposing a large avulsed exit wound high behind the shoulder, about the size of a baseball. *Not a kid shootin' a twenty-two,* Cove thought shaking his head. He laid his three-inch ruler next to the exit wound and snapped a third photo. Pocketing the camera and ruler, he shined his flashlight directly into the buck's still open eyes. The light reflected back almost as bright as a deer's eyes caught by headlights. *It died well after the doe,"* Cove thought.

He turned to Julie. "We're not gonna find a bullet in either one. Both are pass-throughs." He looked back towards the doe and shined his light on the deer's tracks. He realized Julie hadn't spoken since her outburst at seeing the two dead deer. *I wonder what she's thinking?*

Cove looked at the deer tracks. A few of the buck's larger hoof prints stepped on top of the smaller track and revealed it had been trailing behind the doe. He concluded the two had been headed for Harris's snow-covered alfalfa field and had been frozen by the bright lights. The doe had been shot and dropped dead in her tracks. The buck spooked at the shot, bounced a few feet, stopped and started to walk off when it too was cut down with a shot that severed its spine. Cove canted his head, chewed on his lip while restudying the scene, at first disbelieving the snow's story. *He killed the doe first, then shot the buck, and never walked over to look at the still struggling animal.* This revelation caused Cove to pause. His head again tilted in thought. Poachers revered antlers, and not shooting the buck first was odd. Further, according to the shooter's tracks, all of the focus had been on the doe and none on the struggling buck laying a few feet away. *This guy's different,* he thought, *no interest in the buck.* Cove walked back to the doe and noticed two round imprints in the snow facing her abdomen. Turning his head slightly, he studied these prints, but was challenged to understand what they were. Looking at the nearest footprints, Cove decided the guy had kneeled down besides the carcass. He pulled his camera out and took a photograph of the doe laying in its coagulating blood and made sure to include the two imprints in the photos. Stepping closer he took a photo of what was left of the doe's head. He studied the imprints next to the carcass. *The guy knelt down.* Cove squatted and placed his knees in the impressions. *No doubt about it, he kneeled.* Cove remained in the position feeling the cold conduct into his bones as he attempted to understand why the guy had knelt. Realizing the position was uncomfortable, he pulled his knees closer together. *The guy's bigger than me.*

*Cove's inquiries left two unanswered questions:* Why did the guy kneel down? And why all the focus on the doe?

"I need to collect the beer can," Cove said, as he stood up and started walking back to the road.

"Charley!" Julie snapped.

Cove stopped and pulled his headlamp off to avoid blinding her. He turned around and looked at her, his right ear cocked towards her. His light was shining down between their bodies and reflecting off the snow to their faces. Her face was flushed and she was frowning.

"You didn't answer my question!" Julie demanded. "Why'd he do this? Why?"

"Look, Julie... I didn't give you an answer because I don't know why these bastards do this. Some people like killin'; killing for no reason." He paused, reached up and gave her shoulder a squeeze. "I'll promise you this; sooner or later I'll figure out who did this and I'll ask him, but I'm not sure *he'll* even understand why he did it." He hesitated again, not sure how much he should tell her about the investigation. "I think this is probably the same guy that shot the two other deer—both does, but please keep that between you and me. This is the first scene I've had good snow to show me what happened. People lie to me every day and I get tired of it. I like working in the snow, 'cause it always tells the truth. This is my first good look at his stride. He's tall, and at least tonight, he was all by himself. The beer can could be a break; hopefully, it has prints—but we rarely get fingerprints on poaching cases because the scenes just aren't conducive to it—not like a cop working a burglary. The other thing about this deal is it's not kids drinking and shooting stuff with twenty-twos." He paused, scratching his head. "I've tagged my share of spot lighters, and none were by themselves. Ignoring the buck is also an odd deal; I've never seen that before. This guy's different."

Julie was still frowning. "Are you going to just leave them out here?"

Cove pointed at the left side of his head. "I was born deaf in this ear. So once in a while I might miss what you say, but no, I'm not going to leave them here. I'll give 'em to some family that can use the meat." He walked back to the road with Julie following in his tracks. Pulling the camera from his coat, he photographed the beer can, and gingerly picked it up by its bottom edge. He carried it over and set it on the hood of his truck, looked back at the tracks, and thought about what he was looking at. Based on the way the vehicle had been weaving back and forth, the apparent lack of a passenger, and the position of where the shooter had angled his truck in relation to his target, Cove concluded the shooter had been using the truck's lights and hadn't been using a handheld spotlight– since a person could not shoot a rifle and hold a spotlight at the same time.

"Now you get to meet my partner," Cove said, and dropped the tailgate. "Say hello to Annie." The dog jumped out and ran over to Julie, wiggling with enthusiasm. Julie knelt down and gave the dog a hug, rubbed her sides and tried unsuccessfully to avoid the canine's tongue. *I think she needed that,* Cove thought and he wasn't thinking of his dog.

Julie stood up, smiling. "I saw the kennel and wondered if you had a pooch!"

Cove nodded. "You two can play later, but we've still got a crime-scene to finish." Cove told Annie to heel and the two walked back over to where the beer can had been found. Julie stood by the truck, watching the two.

"Annie! Brass! Get the brass girl, find the brass!" Annie began sniffing around the footprints, worked further out and after a few moments, she stuck her nose into the snow near where the beer can had been. She gave a snort and sat down, staring up at Cove with her ears up and alert, wagging her tail in the snow. He walked over and shined the light where she'd last put her nose. His gloves brushed the snow from the spot, revealing a bottlenecked rifle casing. "Good girl, Annie!" He picked up the brass casing by inserting a pen inside its mouth and angled the base into the light from his headlamp. The headstamp showed it was a .300 WSM, which stood for Winchester Short Magnum. It was a new cartridge introduced by Winchester in the last three or four years and it was the first one Cove had seen. This fact caught his attention like the sudden flash of an unexpected light in a black room. Cove rewarded the dog by letting her get a good sniff of the evidence while he enthusiastically rubbed her back. He then had the dog cast about looking for other evidence. Annie sniffed around the road and into the sagebrush for a few minutes and returned to him and sat down in the snow. He patted her and rubbed her back.

"Shouldn't there be another shell casing?" Julie asked.

"Yeah, Cove replied. "But I can't believe it's here or Annie would have found it. I've got faith in her. The guy's shootin' from the driver's window. The gun's action was inside the cab. When he chambered the second round, the fired casing would have been ejected inside the cab," Cove said, looking at the brass in his hand. "I think this one musta rolled out with the beer can. Either he didn't eject the second brass, or it's inside his rig."

Cove pushed his coat sleeve up and looked at his watch. It was now 5:20 a.m. He looked across the valley. "Let's leave these deer here for now and follow the tracks out. Maybe we can catch this guy yet."

Cove pulled two evidence bags from a cardboard box on his back seat. He put the beer can in one, the shell casing in the other and put them both back in the box. He didn't take the time to label the evidence; it was time to go hunt the shooter. Walking back to the tailgate, Cove waved his arm. "Annie, kennel!" The chocolate lab bounded into the back of the truck and Cove shut the tailgate.

*****

His truck was parked on a knob across the valley from where he had killed the deer. He was thinking about the piano he'd had when he was a kid while his fingers tapped the steering wheel. He watched the headlights move down the valley towards the junction he'd crossed on. He didn't know it was the law, but the little meth-man in his head told him whomever it was wanted to kill him. Reaching down to his ignition, he started the engine, let the clutch out and angled off the hill towards the county road. He turned onto the snow-covered roadbed and accelerated down the valley. After about a mile, he pulled over at a sign with "Morse Creek" routed into its dark wood. He slipped the stainless steel rifle into a padded nylon gun case and took it over to a small culvert crossing under the road. He slipped the cased rifle deep into the culvert's cavity and placed a piece of sagebrush over it. "You bastards ain't gonna catch me with this rifle," he mumbled and reached down, feeling his holstered revolver. Unzipping his pants, he drained the Keystone from his bladder and smelled the cold tangy odors of the sage as he looked at the shadows of the Lemhi Range, looming black and white in the darkness. His brain flashed on the image of the doe's blood oozing into the fresh snow, and it brought the memory of a time when *his* blood colored the snow. It was fifth grade, and his drunken father had just smacked him in the face with a backhand, smashing his nose. He couldn't remember what he had done to deserve "the tune up" as his dad called the beatings, but the memory of watching his own blood flow into the snow had stuck with him.

He drove down the road, his hand gripping the .357, thinking about the assassin tailing him. Running his tongue across his dry teeth, he caught the taste of ammonia and reached over and grabbed a Keystone.

*****

They continued down the other side of the valley, following their suspect's trail. When they got to the Furey Lane Junction, they turned and followed the single set of snowed-over tracks and crossed the bridge over the creek-like Pahsimeroi River. They turned left onto the Lemhi County road, heading down the valley. Cove pulled his cell phone out of his pocket and saw three bars. He pressed the speed dial for the Custer County Sheriff's Office and listened to two rings before the dispatcher picked up. "Hey Sarah, it's Charley. We left the scene and have crossed over to the Lemhi side. I think our guy might still be out here."

"Who's we?" Sarah inquired.

Charley paused... *shit,* he thought shaking his head. *I oughta claim it's just me and Annie...* "I've got a reporter with me, Julie Lake. She's doing a story on poaching. Don't tell Fred."

Sarah chortled. "Sure Charley, I can keep a secret, but it's going to cost you."

"Great," Cove replied with less enthusiasm. "This guy killed two deer by Harris's. You might give Bob a call when the sun's up and let him know I'll get a hold of him later today. And if you're okay with it, I'll just have you flight-follow me for now insteada getting Lemhi County involved, if that's okay?"

"No problem Charley, just keep me posted if your situation changes. I can still get Fred's butt outa bed if you need him. And have a good time with that little reporter friend of yours."

Cove snapped the phone closed and rolled his eyes in the darkened cab. He liked to keep his life private, but in the tiny little burg of Challis, Idaho it was always a challenge. If word got out the game warden was spending long-lonely nights with the new reporter, even though it was related to his job, it would give the town something to talk about.

They continued down the valley, locating where their shooter had pulled off the road and then had driven through the low sagebrush, heading up a nearby hill. Cove studied the tracks for a moment and then turned off, following them to the top of the hill. He got out, pulled out his Surefire light and looked around. There were no footprints, but the vehicle tracks departing the hill had no snow in them. *He's close,* he thought. Cove shut his flashlight off and looked back across the valley where they had come from. He realized the guy had sat up on the hill watching his backtrack and had more than likely seen them drive up the other side of the valley—and perhaps, seen them coming back down. Cove jumped back in the truck. "We're not too far behind this guy. Hang on, this might get rough." He came off the hill bouncing through the brush, and sped down the county road following the fresh tracks.

When Cove got to the Morse Creek sign, he almost missed the footprints leading off the road. He stopped and took a quick look around with his light, seeing the prints from the cowboy boots stop facing the Lemhi Range and a large spot of yellow snow. He jumped back in his truck and gave it the gas while bringing his seatbelt across his torso. "He got out and took a pee."

"Wouldn't there be DNA in that?" Julie asked.

*Maybe she's a CSI TV fan,* Cove wondered. *But it's a good question.* "Urine doesn't have enough DNA in it to make it useable. At least for males. It's a different deal with females, but there's not a game warden alive that'd believe this is a woman doing this stuff," Cove explained. "If he'd stopped to poop, you'd have your story: *'Game Warden Collects Fecal Matter.'* Solid waste is a different deal. It's always got DNA in it, but urine doesn't."

Cove looked down the valley for taillights. Nothing. And then he saw headlights and a yellow flashing light. *Shit,* he thought. "Here comes the snowplow. So much for trackin' our guy."

When the plow got closer, Cove reached down to his radio control and hit a switch, activating his blue high-intensity overhead light. He shut it off after a few flashes and stopped on the road, waiting for the snowplow. The driver pulled next to him and rolled down his window. "You're out here awful damned early," the operator said.

"No kidding," Cove replied. "You see any vehicles that were headed down?"

"Yeah, there was one rig, he seemed to be in a hurry. What he'd do?"

"The usual," Cove said, giving his stock answer. "How long ago?"

"Maybe ten minutes. Maybe less."

Cove tilted his head. "What kind of truck?"

"Oh, sheez... let me think... it mighta been a Dodge." He looked up and then back at Cove. "Yeah, it was a Dodge."

"Could ya tell what color?"

"I think it was gray—but shit, I was watching my blade—you never know if you're coming onto a drunk or not; light colored for sure."

"Did it have some kinda overhead lights on it or something?" Cove asked.

"As a matter of fact, I remember my yellow flasher lighting up a roll bar." Replied the driver. "It had two lights up there. But they were off."

"Round or square?" Cove felt like he was playing some party game with the driver.

"Round ones," declared the driver.

Cove's jaw set and he paused thinking. County snowplow drivers got around *a lot*. After a snowfall they drive county roads for two or three days, they see a lot of country and a lot of vehicles.

"You recognize it?"

"No," the driver paused shaking his head. "I don't think so."

"What's your name?" Cove asked.

"Lance Ludkin."

"Do me a favor. If you see that rig again, write down the plate and leave a message at the sheriff's office in Challis. My name's Charley; Game Warden Charley Cove."

# Chapter 4

Cove stared past his headlights, looking for the red glow of taillights. He was able to go faster on the plowed road, but by the time they hit the T-junction at the highway, he had not seen the taillights. Idling at the highway, he looked at its surface and thought about his quarry that had to be just a few minutes ahead of him. *Did the guy turn left towards Challis or right, headed for Salmon?* He glanced at his dash clock and noted it was 6:12 a.m. *Still another hour before dawn.*

Although the snow had been plowed on the highway, there was enough remaining snow to show that several vehicles that had passed, but nothing revealed the direction his target had headed. If he could find a light colored Dodge pickup with a roll bar and overhead lights in the next few minutes, he could light it up with his emergency lightbar and have the stop hold up in court. But his edge of being able to pull over any vehicle in the Pahsimeroi was gone. Flipping a coin in his head, he turned left onto the highway and headed towards Challis.

Cove thought about radioing Custer County and asking for a unit to stop any Dodge with overhead lights, but didn't want to put this information out over the air. Anyone listening in on a scanner would know exactly what the vehicle he was chasing looked like, and there was a good chance the information would get back to his shooter. He decided to wait the fifteen minutes until he had cell coverage again.

"I'll come back up here later today and pick up the deer," Cove explained to Julie. "We'll keep looking for him on the way back to Challis. At least we've got an idea of what the truck looks like now."

"I take it you'll dust the beer can for fingerprints?" Julie asked.

"Actually," Cove replied nodding his head, "I think the super glue method might work better. I've never done it, but I know Fred Mendiola can do it." Cove looked over at Julie. "He's a deputy. I assume you've met him?"

"Yes." Julie said. "I've tried to interview him on a couple of stories, but I don't think he trusts me."

"Well..." Cove replied. "If I didn't trust you I wouldn't have called you out on this run." Cove thought about what he had just said and wondered if he was being truthful; was it really an attempt to show the public what poachers did to wildlife? "I would appreciate it if you drag your feet on doing anything with this story. I don't want this guy knowing we're onto him."

"Don't worry, Charley, I won't. I will not write anything without discussing it with you first. After seeing what he did to those deer, I would feel horrible if I messed up your chance of putting this creep in prison."

Hearing this, Cove's head tilted down and his voice lowered. "I appreciate you saying that, but this guy isn't going to prison. Not for shooting those two deer. In Idaho it's a misdemeanor. If I could tie him to a third deer it would jack it up to a felony, but he still wouldn't go to prison. As I've said, I suspect this is the same guy that shot the other two deer this month, but I can't prove it."

Cove's mind drifted away from the conversation and he thought about the MO of this shooter—or method of operation—on the other two deer he'd examined. All involved headshots late at night with a high velocity round. All, until tonight, were does. Assuming the same offender killed all of them, tonight's buck was the first behavioral anomaly. The shooter's focus on the doe, not the buck, went to his theory it was the same guy. The fact that this guy hadn't even walked over to the buck bugged him.

Julie's voice brought him back. "I can't believe a person can do this and not go to prison," she said, shaking her head. "I don't see any difference between what this person did and other serious crimes. This is horrible!"

Cove let out a deep breath. "Our justice system focuses on crimes against people. Wildlife plays fourth or fifth fiddle in its band. It pisses me off. As a whole, prosecutors aren't big on wildlife cases, especially our local guy." He glanced over at her. "Excuse me if I sound like a broken record. A few judges are real champions of wildlife, but they're scarce. The one we have here in Custer County is great though. If I catch this shooter it's my job as a game warden to be the advocate for those two deer, to make sure the case gets the attention it deserves. If you could get Mike Pallid, our prosecutor, to tell the truth, I think he'd say he believes poaching is a victimless crime. You know it's not true 'cause of what you saw tonight. Most folks in this community love wildlife, but for some reason there's an overriding belief here that poachin's okay. They don't get it." Cove turned to Julie. "Once in a while there is some justice for these critters and this case isn't a done deal. I'm stoked by what we got tonight–or this morning. The shell casing Annie found is a big thing; it's an odd cartridge and anything out of the ordinary with evidence is significant. A lot of people think you can only match a bullet back to a gun, but I've had more luck with the lab matching fired casings than bullets. I'm hoping Fred can get a print off the beer can, plus we know what his truck looks like and I think we'll find it sooner or later. Maybe the snowplow guy will see it and catch the plate."

Julie didn't reply and Cove thought about the evidence. If he could find a .300 WSM rifle in his suspect's possession, and if the lab was able to match it to the fired casing he found, it would be a court-worthy case–not a slam dunk–but one even prosecutor Mike Pallid would be challenged to find an excuse to dismiss. If Mendiola was able to get a print off the beer can, he'd still have to come up with a suspect to match it with. He knew it was possible to recover a print and have the state forensic lab run it through the FBI's Automatic Fingerprint Identification System database, or AFIS, and come up with a hit if the person had ever been printed. Cove had developed a good working relationship with the forensic firearms examiner at the lab, who'd turned out to champion wildlife cases, but had no such luck with the rest of the underfunded facility. Idaho's forensic lab was run by the state police and had one priority: Crimes against people. Cove understood why, but he hated to see wildlife crimes shoved aside. He'd seen too many bloodied animals that had been killed for no good reason, but most of justice system's cogs he dealt with didn't look upon them as significant crimes. Shooting an animal and driving off was no different than someone dumping a load of garbage.

Passing Morgan Creek, Cove looked at his cell phone and saw it had one bar. He hit his speed dial for the sheriff's office. Dispatcher Sarah Hegel picked up on the first ring. "Sheriff's Office."

"Hey, it's Charley. Have you got somebody that can watch north of town for a vehicle coming in?"

"Yeah, I've got Joey sitting here drinking Pepsi. What ya looking for?"

"It's a light colored Dodge pickup with two lights mounted on a roll bar."

"I'll get him out there."

"Great. Have him stop and hold if he sees it, I'm fifteen out. And don't put it over the air."

"Jesus H. Christ," Sarah said. "I wasn't born yesterday. Knock it off, Charley. By the way, how you gettin' along with your new girlfriend?"

Cove didn't reply and snapped the phone shut wondering what Julie had heard. The "new girlfriend" comment had opened up a can of bad memories, but he knew Sarah well enough to know she hadn't meant any harm.

Within five minutes, Cove's radio brought him back to reality. "Custer, three-two-five, traffic." It was the voice of Deputy Sheriff Joey Gabbro with his call sign of 3-2-5 advising dispatch he was about to pull over a vehicle.

"Three-two-five, Custer." Sarah's voice snapped.

"I'll be out with a seven-Charles, seven-four-eight-nine with one-aboard," Gabbro answered, calling out the vehicle's license plate and number of passengers.

Cove reached down and turned on his blue light. He brought his truck up to seventy miles an hour, five over the posted speed limit, and grabbed his mic, pressing the transmit button. "Three-two-five, seven-three-one, I'm five out," Cove said, thinking about the situation. *If I didn't have this civilian, I'd stomp on it.*

He placed the microphone back in its bracket in time to hear deputy Gabbro respond to his transmission. "Seven-three-one, this is not your attempt-to-locate, disregard."

Cove came off his sudden adrenalin rush, turned his blue off, and brought his truck back to sixty. He glanced at Julie and said, "Damn, I thought we had him."

"Me too," Julie said.

"I'd buy you breakfast," Cove said, "but I don't think it would be a good idea in this little rumor-burg."

"It's a great offer," Julie said, "but I've got to get ready for work anyway. How 'bout I buy you lunch sometime and I can interview you about poachers?"

Her offer perked him up and he agreed to meet with her in the future. Just short of town they passed the deputy's truck; he was parked behind an older Chevy pickup truck with his overhead lights flashing. The officer was sitting in his driver's seat and looked to be writing a ticket.

They turned off the highway onto Main Street, thinking the shooter must have turned towards Salmon and not Challis. The town was awake. The city snowplow had been working, and the orange glow of dawn was starting to show above the Lost River Range. He drove the seven blocks through Challis to Julie's street and pulled in behind her Subaru.

"Thanks for the company," he said. "I'll let you know if I catch this guy."

"I'll ring your neck if you don't," Julie said smiling. "Let me know about the fingerprint thing and anything else you come up with. I'd like to turn this into a story." She got out of the truck and turned back to him. "And thanks for the ride, it was great."

Cove nodded and watched as Julie stepped to the back of the truck. He heard her say goodbye to Annie. He backed out onto the street and Julie waved from her porch, still wearing a smile.

Cove headed for the sheriff's office thinking of her wish to stay in the loop. It hadn't surprised him—she'd seen and smelled the carnage. In a sense, she'd purchased some ownership in the case. The problem Cove now faced was, ethically, he shouldn't be sharing details of a criminal investigation with anyone outside the law enforcement community, especially the press. He was okay with the ride-along, but revealing anything further was questionable at best. Cove believed he could trust her, but he'd been burned before. Either way, he'd have to deal with the issue when it arose.

Cove pulled into the sheriff's office, parked his truck, and walked in. Sarah Hegel was sitting at her dispatch center and she nodded at him as headed for the coffee in the back room. He grabbed a cream colored cup off the shelf. It had his last name painted on it in what looked like bright red nail polish. He grabbed the glass coffee pot off its burner and filled his mug, passing on the sugar and creamer that sat next to the coffee machine. He walked back into the main office and sat down next to Sarah. There was a multi-line phone on her right, with one glowing red light and three flat-screened computer monitors in front of her. She was wearing a headset over one ear with a lip mic bent in front of her mouth and her fingers were inputting something into the computer, all while having a one sided conversation with Deputy Gabbro.

Cove mouthed a "thanks" to Sarah and tasted the coffee. It was classic jailhouse coffee made at God-knows-what-time and had sat cooking away on its burner for half the night, blacker than black. *Bitter and burned,* Cove thought, *just what I need.* It was pushing 7:30 a.m. and he'd been up for four hours.

Sarah clicked off and turned to Cove, smiling. "You're looking a little rough this morning, Charley." She turned back to a computer screen and clicked with her mouse. "I called Harris and told him you'd found two dead deer and you'd get a hold of him later."

"Thanks," Cove said. "I've gotta run back out there and get the carcasses. I'll find Bob and thank him for calling this thing in. I woulda picked them up while I was out there, but I thought I might catch the guy coming back down the valley. He couldn't have been very far ahead of us."

"So how do you know it's a Dodge if you didn't find it?" Sarah asked.

"A snowplow driver coming up the Lemhi side saw him. He was working up and the guy was headed down," Cove explained. "What time's Fred coming on?"

"He went ten-eight when you were getting your coffee, so any minute if he's headed here. You shoulda let me call him out," she hesitated and then met his gaze. "Look, Charley," she said, lowering her voice. "I shouldn't have called her your girlfriend. I wasn't thinking," She lowered her head. "We all miss Liz. I'm so sorry."

"It's okay." Cove said, looking into the steam from his coffee.

The front door rattled open. Deputy Joey Gabbro stomped through it with his black cowboy boots and gray Stetson, interrupting Sarah's heart-to-heart. The guy stood five foot nine in his two-inch heels, young and scrawny with curly brown hair, a goatee, and cheeks always looking like they were three days behind a shave. A black-uniform coat added needed bulk to his torso and set off the nickel-plated semi-auto Colt .45 tilted forward on his duty belt.

"Hey Cove," Gabbro said. "A silver Dodge went by me while I was out on that stop. I'm assuming it was your ATL?"

Cove's head rotated like a tank's turret. "With a roll bar and lights?" he asked, squinting his eyes and disbelieving what he'd just heard.

"Yeah, but I had that stop going. It was that Nelson guy I got on a deuce last fall. I knew he'd lost his license over it. I didn't have any choice." Gabbro said, and shrugged his shoulders.

Cove pulled the skin of his forehead together with his thumb and fingers and looked at the deputy almost sideways. "Tell me you got the plate."

"It was moving too fast," Gabbro replied dismissively.

*You've got to be kidding me,* Cove thought. He could not believe Gabbro had gotten distracted and pulled somebody over that could have been tagged later. If the driver had been an imminent safety issue, Cove could have understood it, but *any* officer worth his salt would have stayed on station, watching for the suspect ATL. Gabbro had always had an attitude about Fish and Game cases being a waste of time. Cove had received information from a confidential source that the deputy had annually filled his ex-wife's deer tag and this morning's performance reinforced the information. Cove met Sarah's stare and she rolled her eyes before glancing back at the computer screens.

The dispatch door opened again and Deputy Fred Mendiola came in wearing a bigger version of the same short black coat Gabbro was wearing. Mendiola was big. Six foot three, two hundred and fifty pounds. He had twenty-four years on the job and had managed to survive a career in a county where backup was frequently forty minutes away. He was a dark-complected Basque with salt and pepper hair and a shaved but shadowed face. As Chief Deputy, Mendiola was second in command, but since the sheriff was taking extended medical leave, he was it. Taking his coat off, the deputy wrapped his big hand around a coffee cup, topped it off, and turned to Cove, "Bring your half-breed-ass into my office and tell me what the hell you're doing up so damned early."

Cove stepped in behind him and shut the door still smoking over Gabbro's failure. He pulled up a chair and set his coffee on the deputy's desk. Mendiola sat on the other side, still wearing his black coat.

"You look like shit, Charley," Mendiola smiled. "I heard you call in 'on scene' on my portable in the wee hours. What the hell was that all about?"

Cove filled him in on the event and included the fact he thought it was the same shooter who had killed the other string of deer that had recently been shot and left.

"How many's that?" Mendiola frowned.

"Four in two weeks counting these, but hell, there must be more."

"Why don't you think it's kids?" Mendiola asked.

"It's not." Cove said. "It's one guy out there all by himself. If it were kids it'd be two or three drinking and screwing around, partying. Hard to party when you're alone. This morning's deal was right below Bob Harris's field where his cow got shot. I think it might be the same dimwit or a big stinking coincidence." Cove took a sip of coffee. "Besides, I found a .300 WSM fired shell casing at this one. A box of 'em must cost fifty or sixty bucks. I don't know any kids shootin' two or three-dollar bullets."

Mendiola's head tilted. "That's interesting, I've only heard of one of them here, and as a matter of fact..." Mendiola swiveled around in his chair and slid open a file cabinet. He reached in and retrieved a large manila envelope, turned back to his desk and pulled out a stack of documents. He went through it, pulled out a sheet of paper, grasped a pair of glasses that were hanging from his shirt pocket and put them on. "Yeah, here it is, the inventory list. One each, Winchester Model 70, .300 WSM with Leupold scope." He looked up at Cove. "It was stolen in a burglary this fall. I think he'd only had it for a coupla months."

"Who's place?" Cove asked.

"Ralph Petersham's, down there by the hot springs. Happened around Thanksgiving. They were out of town for a weekend, came home and discovered somebody had taken his guns. He kept all his firearms under his bed. The guy took all six of 'em and his wife lost some jewelry."

"Got anybody you're liking for it?" Cove inquired.

"Not really," Mendiola answered. "I've got the usual short list of shitheads, but whoever it was didn't leave a business card."

Cove picked up the inventory sheet and looked at it. "My shooter dropped a beer can, too." Cove said. "What do you think the odds are of it still having any prints on it?"

"Slim in this kind of weather, but I can stick it in the glue box and see if we get anything," Mendiola offered.

"You ever try it on shell casings? Cove asked.

"Yeah, years ago." Mendiola answered. "I was never able to make it work. It's my understanding the heat cooks 'em off when they're fired; I read an article that some guy in England's working on an electrical process that might work, so maybe someday," Mendiola explained.

Cove went out to his truck, still thinking about deputy Gabbro letting his guy pass by. He brought the bagged Keystone can back into Mendiola's office and set it on his desk. The big deputy pulled on a pair of blue-nitrile gloves and took the can out of the packaging, picked it up by the bottom edge, and sat it on the table. He opened a closet and brought down a small empty glass aquarium and set it on a gray credenza. The inside of the aquarium was hazed over with what looked like heavy water stains. Mendiola set the can inside the aquarium and took off his gloves.

Mendiola turned back to Cove and lowered his voice. "In the future, you might try and put something like this in a padded box so it doesn't wipe any of the latents off."

Cove felt his face flush. "I never did claim to be a genius."

Fingerprint evidence was common with crimes against people, but not with wildlife crimes. During his career Cove had dealt with numerous types of evidence; but had never had one that involved fingerprints, they weren't commonly left in the sticks.

Mendiola pulled a roll of aluminum foil from the closet, tore a piece off of it the size of a playing card, and formed a crude boat-hull shaped container. He picked up a small bottle of super glue from the aquarium and squirted a teaspoon of clear cyanoacrylate into the aluminum foil and placed it near the beer can. He tore off a second piece of foil, rubbed his thumb on his nose and pressed his thumb on the aluminum scrap. "This'll be our test print. This will confirm the stuff is working. We don't need to examine the can until this test print comes up." He set the small piece of foil in with the can, walked over to the coffee pot, picked up a Styrofoam cup and topped it off with the last of the coffee. He placed the steaming coffee in the aquarium and put a piece of cardboard on top of it for a lid. "The coffee will give it some humidity. I'll keep an eye on it, but it usually takes about four or five hours."

"Who worked Harris's cow?" Cove asked.

"Gabbro," Mendiola said.

Cove felt his skin turn red. "He come up with anything?"

The deputy lowered his voice and looked at his desktop. "You gotta look for something in order to find it." He looked up at Cove. "Do me a favor and ask him though, he needs a little stress." Mendiola nodded. "Sometimes Joey's like a dog in the weeds."

Cove thought about the burglary. "Did Petersham lose any .300 ammo in the theft?"

Mendiola looked back at the inventory sheet. "It ain't listed, but a lot of times, people are so pissed off they don't notice the small stuff for a few days."

Cove sipped his coffee. "I might pay him a visit, but he and I aren't best-buds."

He copied Petersham's phone number off the burglary report and thanked Mendiola. He stepped out of the deputy's office and found Gabbro drinking a diet Coke in the back room. "You dig a bullet out of Harris's cow?"

"Nope. No sense getting dirty without a suspect," Gabbro said, and then added; "Shit, it's just a frigging cow."

*Lazy bastard,* Cove thought, but kept his poker face. "Find any brass?" He asked, knowing what the answer was.

"Nope."

"Shot in the head?" Cove asked.

"That's where all the blood was at."

"Exit wound?" Cove asked.

"I don't know. There's no suspect. If I need it I can go get it. Ain't going nowhere if its still in the skull."

Cove kept his mouth shut, turned, and walked out to his truck. He dropped the tailgate and let Annie out. She ran behind the sheriff's office to her usual and accustomed place. When she came back, she jumped up into the truck bed, hustled a caress from Cove, and took up her padded bed inside her box.

As Cove got into his truck, he thought about the buck laying in the snow and its struggles to get up. He wondered why anyone would let an animal suffer like that and he thought about his case. He had investigative momentum going, a lead to chase, and he was going to keep this thing rolling despite Gabbro's ball dropping.

# *Chapter 5*

He pulled the Dodge into the alley and parked where he could get a good view of Main Street. The spot gave him a panorama of the old wooden building and the sidewalk out front, all while he remained tucked out of sight. It was the place he had first spotted her. The redhead. Laying his meth-skinny skull back on his seat, he looked in the rear view mirror and stared. Trashcans and leafless brush. Nothing moved. No little set of eyes staring at him from the junk. He rolled his head to the right and checked the mirror through the passenger window, then the same on the driver's side. Nothing. He looked back to the building and down the street. The town was just waking up. His toes played his old toy spinet piano his mother had given him. It was red and had 25 keys with a tiny little bench just his size.

A white GMC pickup passed his hidey-hole; the driver failed to catch his stare. A worm twitched under the skin on his shoulder, and he rubbed it back and forth on the seat. Listening to the chime-like tones produced by his spinet's tiny hammers striking its metal rods, he thought about his jewels hidden in the Crown Royal bag and the bastards watching him. He looked through the passenger side window and studied the unpainted dog-eared wooden privacy fence at the edge of the alley. The knotholes stared back. He broke their glare and looked across the street at the building, watching for the redhead as he thought about the warm doe.

*****

Cove retrieved the shell casing from its evidence bag. Angling the base of the casing towards his side window, he could see where the rifle's firing pin had struck the primer. Around this impression, he could see numerous tiny circular marks. They were about the width of a fat horse hair and had been impressed into the soft metal by the gun's bolt face when it had been fired. The marks were mirror images of milling etches that had been created during the rifle's manufacturing. Digging into his seat console, he found his eye loupe and placed it over his eye, squinting to hold it in place. He brought the base of the casing up to the loupe until it was in focus. He studied the impressed rings on the primer that were magnified fourteen times by the lens. There were too many circular marks to count. They were all uniform in width and separation with the exception of the third ring from the outside. A portion of this ring was significantly wider than the others and Cove knew this was as unique as his own thumbprint. He shifted his concentration to the bottom of the firing pin dent. He was able to see a tiny odd-shaped mark that resembled a half-star that had been left by a manufacturing imperfection of the gun's firing pin.

Cove reached up to his truck's visor for a fine-tipped felt pen. He marked the side of the shell casing with the date and his initials and placed it back in the evidence bag. He looked at the paper that he had written Ralph Petersham's phone number on and thought about the relationship he had with him. Cove had seen Petersham around town, but the two had never met—until Cove witnessed him shooting at a coyote from the highway–and had cited him for it. Attempting to shoot the coyote was legal, but not from a public road. Petersham had been hostile over the ticket, entered a not-guilty plea and the case had languished until the prosecutor dismissed it. Cove had asked the prosecutor why he'd dumped it and received a closed mouth stare.

"I didn't have time for it." He'd explained. "He was just shooting at a damned coyote. The case needed to go away. It was a waste of my time."

Pulling his phone from his coat pocket, he thought about having Mendiola make the call, but brought the phone up and punched in the numbers.

"Ralph? It's Charley Cove, you got a minute?"

"What the hell ya want now?"

Cove rolled his eyes. "I'm working a case involving a three-hundred WSM and heard you had one stolen."

There was a long pause on the other end. "You saying I killed something with that rifle and then reported it stolen? You think I'm a goddamned moron?"

Cove's head started to shake back and forth, *not a moron...* "Look Ralph," he slowed his cadence and lowered his voice. "I know your rifle was stolen. I'm not looking at you for this thing, but it's possible the guy that stole your rifle is the guy I'm after. If you can help me on this thing, there's a chance I can get your rifle back." Cove could hear Petersham breathing into the phone and he wondered if he was going to hang up.

Petersham responded, "Well... I suppose. Whaddya wanta know?"

"Have you got any shell casings you fired from that rifle?" Cove asked.

Petersham's split level house sat among a dispersed subdivision of ten-acre lots. Behind his house were two corralled Appaloosa horses, looking bored, standing next to a rickety pole-barn that was sided with used wooden pallets. A stack of faded-green hay bales were stacked in the building. Petersham met him at the door barefoot, his arms folded above his gut. He was in his sixties, had short gray hair cut with a flat top, and was wearing sweat pants and a red sleeveless T-shirt, exposing his pale shoulders and sagging arm muscles.

"This better not be some kinda bullshit game warden thing," Petersham declared.

"Ralph, are you going to let me look at your shells, or not?" Cove asked, meeting his glare.

Petersham stepped aside and motioned Cove in. The living room drapes were closed and a television with a movie frozen on its screen sat in front of a peach colored couch.

"The empty shells are over there," Petersham said, nodding toward a dining table.

Cove walked over and took a seat. The table sat in front of a sliding glass door and looked out into Petersham's corral. His two horses stared back at the house, their breath turning to vapor in the cold air. There was a red and black cardboard box of Federal Premium Vital Shock cartridges sitting on the table. Petersham pulled up a chair opposite of Cove and sat down. "I was saving them to reload. New, they're sixty goddamned bucks a box."

Cove picked up the container, and took out one of the fired bottleneck cases and looked at its base. "Did they steal any loaded ammo from you?"

"Yeah, two boxes. I hunted elk with that gun for three days and then the prick broke in."

"Have any luck?" Cove asked, still staring at the empty brass.

Petersham looked at Cove, hesitated and finally said, "No, too many fuckin' wolves."

*Why?* Cove wondered. *Why'd you have to think about how to answer a simple question? Was it your hatred of wolves or something else?*

He pulled the evidence bag from the inside pocket of his coat, retrieved the marked shell casing and set it on the table. Holding both cases side by side, he compared their bases. Both were stamped F-C for Federal Cartridge and both had a slight offset firing pin strike. Cove looked at Petersham. "Was the stolen ammo Federal too?"

"Yeah, they were both hundred 'n eighty grain soft points."

Pulling out his black eye loupe, Cove placed it over his right eye socket, closed his left eye, and leaned over, focusing the lens on the bases of both casings held side by side.

"What are you doing?" Petersham asked.

Cove didn't answer; he was slowly rotating Petersham's casing while holding the evidence casing stationary. The circular milling marks impressed into the soft metal primer of Petersham's brass case were the same width as the one found at the crime scene. Cove studied the third milling mark of Petersham's case and found it too had a spot wider than the rest of it. He rotated the case until both thick ring portions of the two cases were at the twelve o'clock position. It was like looking at two identical yearbook photos. Cove felt his cheeks fill with blood. He studied the primer strike of the Petersham case and found what he was looking for—the half-star shaped mark.

Cove set the casings down, removed the eye loupe from his face and caught Petersham's stare.

"Well?" he asked.

Cove looked down at the cartridge box and nodded. "Hang onto these if you would. I might need to send them to the lab."

Cove got back in his truck, considering the significance of what he'd just discovered—his shooter was a thief.

*****

He saw the redhead coming down the sidewalk and felt the same buzzing rush he'd felt when he'd put the crosshairs on the doe's head. She turned and walked into the building. *Goddamn!* Sitting there, he let his head roll back and forth on the seat, exalted over seeing her again. Looking in his rear mirror he checked the garbage cans and realized one of the lids was sitting at a different angle. *You're in the can.*

Firing up his truck, he pulled out onto Main Street, exited the twelve-block town and turned left on the highway heading downriver. *Goddamn,* he thought. *I shoulda run over those fuckin' trashcans.*

When he got to Ruby Creek, he turned off the highway onto the dirt road leading to his singlewide trailer and pulled behind it. He studied the snow around the faded building and looked up and down the river that flowed behind his place. His nearest neighbor lived on the highway down towards Morgan Creek, a half mile away. There were no unfamiliar tracks around the trailer. Reaching down to his shifter boot, he removed his Crown Royal bag and looked behind him, making sure they hadn't followed him home. Sitting in his truck, he pulled out the glass pipe and stared into its bowl. He loaded it and sparked the lighter, holding the flame under the orb. The ghost gradually appeared from the vapors and turned into a hazy image of a solitary young figure, perched forward on a red piano bench with fingers moving over an invisible keyboard. He listened for the music, but it never came.

*****

Cove pulled into the Sinclair station next to the pumps, got out and stuck the gas nozzle into his truck. Feeling the pains of hunger, he grabbed his travel mug and walked into the building. A young female clerk was talking on her cell phone. Cove nodded at her and walked past the junk food aisle to the back. He pulled three breakfast burritos out of a glass-door freezer and placed them in the microwave. He topped off his coffee mug, handed the still gabbing clerk a ten, recovered his steaming burritos and walked back out to his truck. Annie greeted him from the bed. He opened up one of the burritos and gave it to her. As he got in his truck, his phone buzzed. Looking down at the display, he saw it was the prosecutor's office.

"How you doing, Mike? " Cove asked, with an even voice.

"I just got a call from Ralph Petersham. He says you're working on his burglary. What are *you* doing on a burglary?"

"I'm not, I'm working on a Fish and Game case, multiple deer shot with his stolen rifle."

"Who's got the rifle?" Pallid asked.

"I don't know yet. Somebody shot two deer in the Pahsimeroi last night and I found a shell casing at the scene. Petersham's got leftover brass he fired with his rifle and they match."

"The lab say it's a hundred percent?"

"I haven't sent them to the lab. I looked at them and they match. The lab will come to the same conclusion."

"How... never mind." Pallid shifted gears. "The sheriff's department know you're working on this?"

Cove flashed back to Gabbro watching the shooter's truck pass by. "Yeah, Mendiola's trying to pull some prints off a beer can for me."

"Well...," Pallid said, with a pause. "Let me know what you come up with. I can keep Ralph informed."

"Will do," Cove said, and closed the phone. *A first name basis.*

Cove headed for the Pahsimeroi on Highway 93. The road wound along the Salmon River, except for a few places where wide river bends led off into jungles of cottonwood, edged by reddish-brown cliffs. It was a crisp, blue-sky morning. The storm had broken and the peaks from the Lost River Range stuck up into the cloudless sky.

Large pancakes of slush ice eased down the river, its banks lined with tall leafless cottonwood trees.

Cove passed Morgan Creek and thought about the run with Julie sitting beside him in his truck. It brought back the memory of Liz. He flipped the truck's visor down and looked up at her picture. Brown hair and a grin as big as life itself. She looked too young and real to be gone. *Two steps forward and three back.*

When Cove got to the junction on the Pahsimeroi where he'd compared the tire tracks, he stopped and looked across the valley. Reaching behind his console, he grabbed a pair of 10x50 Pentax binoculars, turned his window down, felt the winter air and glassed towards the Lemhi Range. He found the hill the shooter had parked on. *The guy was watching us.*

Cove continued up the road and could see the kill site when he was an eighth of a mile away. There were a dozen or more black and white magpies marking the spot. Cove stopped where the shooter had parked and walked over to the deer carcasses. Not much had changed. The birds had fed on the open tissue, but the cold had preserved the carcasses. He pulled his folding knife from his pocket and rolled up his sleeves. It took him twenty minutes to eviscerate both animals. A coyote yapped from a low hill and Cove studied the sagebrush slope, but failed to spot the animal. Stooping down to a gut-pile, he cut the heart free from the lungs and placed the organ under a sagebrush and covered it with snow so the birds wouldn't find it. Glancing back towards the rise, the warden spoke, "A treat for you, my friend." He backed his truck up to the two deer and used an electric winch mounted in its bed to load them. Annie sniffed at them and got back in her kennel, unimpressed. The gut-piles were left for the scavengers.

Cove rubbed snow on his hands and forearms, cleaning the blood off, while looking around the Pahsimeroi. The air was fresh with the smell of sage. He was standing at about 5,000 feet above sea level. The Lemhi Range jutted up to the east with Mogg Mountain breaking through at 10,573 feet. The Lost River Range behind him was capped by Grouse Mountain pushing through 11,000 feet, and between lay the wide-open sage flat, checkered with a few scattered alfalfa fields. Everything was covered with snow and capped with an overpowering blue sky. The spectacle should have cleansed anyone's soul. Firing up the engine, he reached down and turned the truck's heater on high. He held his raw hands up to the warm air, his thoughts stuck on Liz.

Cove found the rancher sitting on a tractor encircled by a hundred coal-black cows. Bob Harris was as aged and weathered as his wooden fenceposts. He'd used the tractor to haul an eleven-hundred-pound round bale of hay and distribute it to his herd in a long winding circle. The gate to the field was open. Cove drove in and pulled next to tractor. He shut his truck down and the rancher turned off the racket of his diesel.

Harris's leather-skinned face was stubbled with a quarter-inch of gray beard growth. He wore an old faded pair of brown heavily-insulated coveralls and a wool baseball-style hat. "You catch those kids this morning? They shouldn't be shooting like that around here."

"No." Cove shook his head. "It ain't kids anyway, just one guy. He may be the yahoo that shot your cow." Cove paused, giving the rancher time to respond, but the grizzled old man just stared, frowning, wearing a quizzical look. "Who drives a silver Dodge with roll bar and two lights mounted on it?" Cove asked.

"I don't know who's driving it, but that deputy does," Harris said.

"What are you talking about?" Cove asked, turning his good ear to the rancher.

"Well... two days after my cow got shot I seen that damned truck parked on the road right where they shot my cow. The sun was just coming over Big Creek. I was headed to feed and thought it was odd–hell, I never see anybody up here that early, so I got the plate and called it in to Deputy Gabbro; he's the one that came out and investigated it."

"Get a look at the guy?" Cove asked.

"Not real good. He acted as if he was taking a pee on the backside of his truck–tried to look away like I wasn't there. Christ, how do you not see somebody out here? I don't think there was anybody with him." Harris said, rubbing his chin. "He was a rough looking, skinny bastard."

"How old?" Cove asked.

"Gawd... maybe forty," Harris replied, shaking his head.

"Tall or short?" Cove continued.

"Oh shit, taller 'n six feet." Harris said, and looked over at the nearest cow. "It was cold that morning and he wasn't wearing a coat. Had a black leather vest that kind of hung on him."

"You still got the plate number?" Cove asked, with a cant of his head.

Harris glanced towards his house. "It might be in my truck," he said, pointing with his chin. "I think I wrote it down on some junk mail so I don't know whether it's still in there, but the deputy's got it."

"Four door? Club cab?" Cove asked.

Harris took the glove off his hand, exposing fingers that had seen too many winters and rubbed his earlobe for a moment. "Naw, I think it was a reg'lar cab."

Cove thanked Harris and drove back down the Pahsimeroi road to the bottom of the valley, and dropped the two deer carcasses off at Armando Barreras's. The Hispanic was a hard working, soft-spoken ranch hand who worked for any cattleman needing cheap labor. He lived with his wife and a handful of kids in an old faded singlewide trailer. The family didn't have much, and as far as Cove could tell, they met his agency's indigent definition of eligibility to receive animals he'd salvaged. Deputy Mendiola had told Cove of persistent rumors of cockfights being held in the Pahsimeroi and he'd speculated Barreras might be involved, but nothing had ever confirmed the whispers. Whether it was true or not, giving the family the deer put the meat to good use and Cove believed another friendly face in this lonely territory was a good thing.

Pulling back onto the county road, Cove checked his cell phone for a signal and punched in Fred Mendiola's speed dial. The deputy picked up and Cove asked him how the beer can was doing in the aquarium.

"It looks like we're getting something, but it needs to cook a bit longer."

"I'll be there in an hour or so," Cove said. "By the way, I went down to Petersham's—he had some brass from his three-hundred. Whoever shot these two deer out here used his rifle."

"Shit on a shingle," Mendiola said. "Now that's interesting."

"Yeah," Cove answered. "And Harris got a plate off a truck matching what the snowplow driver saw. Bob thought it might be the guy that shot his cow and called it in to Gabbro."

"When you get in here," Mendiola said, "let's get with Gabbro and see who it comes back to."

The case's momentum was smoking along. Cove drove the highway, winding back up along the Salmon River to Challis. He covered the four blocks to the courthouse, pulled in behind it and parked in front of the sheriff's office. Looking around the lot, Cove noted Gabbro's patrol truck was gone.

When Cove walked through the door, Mendiola was shaking his head and had a frown on his lips. "No luck on the plate. I called Gabbro, and he said it would be in the case folder, but it ain't there. Said he didn't run the plate, since Harris saw the truck up there a couple a days after the cow got shot. He thinks it's nothing."

"You're shitting me," Cove exclaimed. "Where's he at now?"

"Burning county gas on the highway. I jumped his ass for letting your guy get by him this morning. He headed out with his pants in a wad, saying he was gonna go work traffic. He's probably gonna piss off some taxpayer."

"Let me grab some coffee," Cove said.

He walked in the back room, took his mug off the shelf and topped it off. He went into Mendiola's office, pulled up an old oak chair in front of the deputy's desk and sat down, letting his body slump and his eyes close. He massaged his eye lids and took a drink of coffee.

"Here's your beer can."

Cove sat up. Mendiola was wearing blue nitrile gloves and was holding the Keystone can by its bottom edge, studying it with a magnifying glass.

"I'm guessing it's the guy's left thumb. It's in the right spot," Mendiola explained. "It's just a partial, but it might be enough. Too bad Gabbro misplaced the plate number. We could see if we've booked the guy and take a look at his print card."

Cove stood up, leaned over the desk and took a hard look at the can. There were several milky-colored smudged prints that had appeared when the glue had fumed and cured onto the residual oils that had been left behind. But the print that caught the warden's eye was higher up near the top; it had sharply defined ridges and was black from latent print dust that had been applied over the glue.

Cove took the magnifying glass and looked at it. "That's a loop-type print, isn't it?"

"Yeah, I've already taken a picture of it," Mendiola said. "I'll lift it in a bit and photograph it again when it's on the card. I think those others got rubbed by your evidence bag."

Cove's face flushed. "One of these days, you need to show me how the big guys take care of evidence like this, but I gotta get home and email my time sheet in before somebody in Boise gets his nose outta joint. And take care of the can for me. I'd grab it now, but I'd just screw it up."

Cove pulled behind his house, dropped the tailgate and gave his partner a quick rub down. Walking through his back doorway, he took off the coat he had worn for the last thirteen hours. He dropped his gun belt on the carpet, unlaced his boots, sat down in his easy chair, and used his toes to remove the heavy clunkers from each foot.

*****

Digging out his Crown Royal bag, he got out of his truck, unlocked the trailer's rear door and stepped through with his revolver hanging from his hand. He looked down the hallway to the living room and kitchen, and saw no unfamiliar shadows. Looking through the doorway to his right, into his bedroom, lay a sheetless, blue and white striped mattress on the floor with blankets heaped in the middle. The top drawer of a cheap dresser was halfway open. On its top sat a glass terrarium; his pet lay inside. *Nothing's disturbed.* Flaring his nostrils, he minced the odors, *but you've been here.* He moved down the hallway and checked the bathroom and the spare bedroom. He stopped and stared into the living room with its couch, chrome-legged dining table, two mismatched shoddy chairs and the kitchen at the far end of the singlewide. A television sat on cinderblocks in front of an old stained cream-colored couch. A DVD player lay on the floor next to it. A cardboard box sat beside the player, half-full of DVD cases and a semi-smashed beer can. Clothes were strewn on the floors of each room. Cabinet doors were open, pots and pans were piled around the kitchen and a plate with a half-eaten meal resembling fried eggs sat on the table. He studied his jumbled mess and concluded nothing had been touched. Holstering his weapon, he walked over and looked down at the dried food left on the plate, felt his fingers tremble. *Goddamn, I've been on this fuckin' run for three, four days?* He asked himself. *I gotta eat something.* Scooting the dirty breakfast plate aside, he sat down at the table, touched the mojo hanging from his neck and pulled out his stash of crystal from the Crown bag. Sweeping the mouse turds off the table with his arm, he brought the plastic bag up and looked at what was left of the eight ball. *About half,* he thought. Flicking it with his middle finger, he nodded– knowing it and the other two he had stashed would get him through his run. *'Gotta save some of this sugar for when I hit the wall and crash.*

Cocking his head, he stared up at the ceiling and whispered, "You pricks up there again?" He drew his .357 and continued staring at the ceiling. He focused on the one bullet hole he'd put through the roof and wondered if he'd hit the bastard that night. After a moment, he looked at the left side of the wheel-gun and felt its cold blue steel with his thumb. He ran his eyes along the barrel, *Smith and Wesson, my ol' goddamn tweaker buds.* Easing the hammer part way back, he spun the cylinder around, making a clacking buzz that sounded like a rattlesnake. When it stopped clicking, he turned the gun's muzzle towards his face looking at the copper jacketed hollow points staring back from the revolver's chambers. Slowly rotating the cylinder, he counted the six bullets and mumbled, "five for you and one for me." He turned his focus into the bore of the barrel and wondered if the ghost was hidden in its black void.

Laying the gun on the table, he felt a worm fussing around under his forearm skin, but ignored it and pulled his pipe and lighter from the purple dope bag. He laid them beside the plastic bag containing his candy. Reaching into the baggie, he selected two small gem-like crystals and placed them into the pipe's vent. He brought the pipe up to his face and stared into the bowl through its blackened surface. *How 'bout a concerto?* After the image failed to appear, he picked up the Bic and flipped it on, rotating the bowl over the flame. Holding the glass stem to his lips, he inhaled the milky vapor and felt the heat flow into his chest. He set the pipe down, slumped back into the chair and held the fumes, letting them chew into his lungs. Exhaling, he rolled his eyeballs back and forth and felt the flush of meth suck into his brain's innards. He slumped down in the chair, head back, and let the chemical soak for several minutes while he moved his tongue across his lower lip, tapping here and there as if it were a slick keyboard, listening to the piano's notes. *Gotta find Red's house.*

# *Chapter 6*

Cove's eyes snapped open in the dark room. He knew he'd fallen asleep in his easy chair, but he didn't know what had startled him out of his snooze. Feeling his heart pound, he slowed his breathing, slid his hand to his Glock and realized it wasn't there. His heart missed a beat. The bear roared again. "Shit," Cove said out loud and relaxed. "I gotta change that damn ringtone." Standing up, he took a step and tripped over his gun belt as the grizzly roared for the third time. He got up from the floor, shaking his head. The cell phone was glowing from his coat pocket. Fishing it out, he didn't need to look at the display. He'd set the growling bear ringtone so it would go off when his boss called.

"Where the hell's your time sheet, cowboy?"

"Oh gawd, sorry about that George," Cove said, lowering his voice. "Which excuse you wanna hear this time?"

George Nayman was Cove's boss headquartered in Salmon, some sixty miles downriver from Challis. Cove believed him to be a warden's warden and had nothing but respect for the guy.

"Oh, lets see..." Nayman paused. "How about you were too busy arresting the little shits that've been laying your deer down up there?" Nayman suggested. "That'd be the one I'd prefer tonight. I got a nasty-gram from Boise complaining this was the third pay-period in a row you've been late. I'm thinking you might be going for some kinda record."

"I'll crank up my laptop when we're done chattin', but I *have* been busy." Cove explained in detail what he'd found at the kill scene and what he'd come up with since. The piece of the pie Cove left out was the slice with Julie Lake in it. Nayman was curious about Cove's summary of the MO–a lone shooter focusing on females and with little apparent interest in bucks. Both wardens agreed the killing needed to come to a stop and that it wasn't going to happen until the guy was caught. Neither was optimistic about Mike Pallid putting any effort into prosecuting the guy. Nayman's one bit of advice was to catch the guy on the Lemhi County side of the Pahsimeroi. "Our prosecutor down here'd at least take it to court, and no jury in Idaho likes game shot and left."

Cove hung up and fed Annie while his laptop was booting up. *I oughta go sit on that hill tonight,* Cove thought, *but he's gotta be draggin' too.* He logged into the state employee's web portal and filled out his electronic time sheet. Logging out, he clicked on the Google search page and hesitated. "Nothing like a little web stalking," Cove mumbled to himself and typed in 'journalist Julie Lake' and hit the enter button. The first response received nearly twelve thousand results. Cove framed her name in quotation marks and hit the enter key again, bringing the number of hits down to nearly three thousand pages.

Cove began scrolling down, clicking and looking at Julie's old stories. It was an interesting collage. Lake had written stories about crimes, wolves, eagles, and social inequities. Most had a western slant. All seemed to have a recurring theme: Somebody, or some critter had been victimized and somebody, or some entity, was dropping the ball. It sounded all too familiar. *At least she seems to like critters,* Cove thought. Feeling uncomfortable with his stalking-like surfing, he shut the laptop's lid and took off his thick ballistic vest.

"Jeeze, Annie, I'm starving!" Cove said to his dog and popped two frozen burritos into his microwave, opened up a Corona, tipped it up, tasted the edge of the hops and looked into the bottle's amber liquid.

*****

Julie couldn't sleep. She kept rubbing her teary eyes and temples. It wouldn't quit. She'd laid in bed thinking about the two deer shot and left in the snow—the scene played over and over like an endless tape. The doe's head blown open and the still-staring eyes of the buck, the odor hanging in the air from the wet deer hair and the metallic copper smell coming from the fresh blood. It was a nightmare that wouldn't end. She'd covered accidents, and homicides in Detroit and none of them made any sense. When she was chasing those stories, she'd interviewed the witnesses and the wives and the husbands and girlfriends. She knew the grief in their eyes and heard the despair in their voices. She'd gone home and cried. This wildlife case was hitting her hard too, but for some reason, the senselessness of what she'd seen in the Pahsimeroi was on a different level. What bothered her most was that nobody was wailing. Where was the outrage?

She got up, put a set of fleece sweats on and booted up her computer. Selecting her email, she typed out an outline of a story about poaching and sent it out to an editor she thought would be interested. *Charley,* she thought. *You're going to have to catch this creep before I have a story, but I am going to write it.*

Walking into her kitchen, Julie set her teapot on the stove and selected a caffeine-free teabag. Digging into her nylon briefcase, she found Cove's business card and returned to her computer. One of the things that had bothered her on the drive home from the Pahsimeroi was how Cove dealt with the recurring carnage he must see with his job. She was having a tough time with it herself– why wasn't he? She typed his email address in and started the note by thanking him for letting her shadow him on the ride-along. She explained the trouble she was having dealing with the senseless killing and asked him the nagging question, *"How do you cope with it?"* She went on and explained that the experience had reaffirmed her desire to write a story about poaching–or maybe poachers–and again reiterated her promise not to publish anything without discussing it with him first. *Part of the story,* she thought, *might be about how wardens deal with this stuff.* Hitting the send button, she reflected on Cove. She'd heard passion in his voice when he'd told her about his frustrations with the local prosecutor. Cove's interpretation of the crime scene had fascinated her and it left her with the belief that he knew his job, but anything beyond his profession was a mystery. The guy hadn't talked about his family or mentioned a relationship. She'd caught him looking at her, but he'd been all business and had not even hinted with a flirtation. She smiled, recalling dropping the boyfriend bomb. *Mystery man with a gun and a badge,* she thought, squinting her eyes.

*****

Some days it was an ammonia flavor, and others it was the sweetness of acetone, but right now his mouth tasted like the smoke from a garbage fire. No matter what his mouth tasted like, it was always dry and gritty.

Finishing his Keystone, he crunched the can down with his bony hands, lobbed it at the television and just missed the porn star laying naked and exhausted on her partner. He picked up the remote and turned off the DVD player, saving the next scene. The last performance had urged him to get on with it. Grabbing the Crown Royal bag, he studied his singlewide to make sure everything was in its place. He picked his revolver up from the table and used it to slide the half-eaten breakfast plate back to where it belonged. Grabbing his truck keys, he walked outside into the night.

He stood behind his trailer, gun in hand, giving his eyes a chance to adjust. He heard an owl hooting in the cottonwoods along the creek. *Goddamn, you really a bird?* After a few minutes of smelling the sage oil, the Milky Way slowly became a bright smudge of a million twinkling stars across the sky and the snow covered sagebrush hills sat where they belonged. He stared up into the dark cliffs across the river and made sure he didn't see anything that wasn't supposed to be there. No tiny glow of a lit cigarette watched him. Everything looked to be as it should and he hadn't heard the footsteps on his roof.

Firing up his Dodge, he slipped his stash bag up under the shifter boot, drove out his snowy driveway and turned onto the highway.

*****

Cove opened his eyes and glanced at the glow of his alarm clock. It was 6:50 a.m. He lay in bed and thought about the case. It'd passed the first twenty-four-hour period and his efforts had gained him fruit. He had a good description of the shooter's truck and he believed sooner or later he'd either see the Dodge or get a tip about it. Harris had given him a rough description of the guy associated with the truck, plus he knew the guy was a thief.

Homicide investigators talk about what they call the first forty-eight rule. Statistically, the closure rate of murders not solved within the first forty-eight hours of an investigation are cut in half. Cove believed wildlife criminal investigations had a similar clock ticking in the background.

Cove knew he had to keep the momentum up. He rolled over and looked at his brown dog. "Annie, time to get rolling." He got up, showered, fried four eggs, and made a pot of fresh ground coffee.

With a mug in one hand, Cove dug his camera from his coat hanging on the wall. After downloading the images to his computer, he created a computerized folder named 'Pah-3' and placed the crime scene photos inside it. He placed the new e-folder beside two others he'd named 'Pah-1' and 'Pah-2' that contained images and notes from the other killings matching the MO of the most recent Pahsimeroi incident.

He opened up Microsoft's Word program and wrote bullet point notes of his interviews with the snow plow driver and Bob Harris, focusing on the descriptions of the Dodge and the driver. He added his observations he'd made at the crime scene, including his analysis of the wounds of both deer and the shooter's footprints and tire prints. He included the thirty-one inch stride length Julie had helped him measure and saved the notes into the 'Pah-3' folder. From his bedroom, Cove found a binder labeled *Tire and Footprint Forensics,* which he'd been issued at a class he'd attended when he was working on his criminology minor at college. Cove opened the binder, walked back to his table and laid it next to his computer. Thumbing through it, he came to the part on stride length and found the equation he was looking for. For males, the decimal .415 divided into stride length would give you the approximate height of a person, depending on their individuality and how aggressively they were walking. Cove hadn't considered his shooter might be a female; the profile just didn't compute. Opening the calculator app on his computer, he did the math. *Seventy-four point six inches.* His shooter was roughly six foot two.

Cove clicked through the photographs in the Pah-1 and Pah-2 folders and studied them while his brain worked in the background. All were Mule Deer does, all shot in the head, and the exit wounds had the same blown-out appearance consistent with a high-powered rifle. The major difference between the older cases and the most recent was the lack of snow. He looked hard for knee prints, but couldn't discern any. The soil had been frozen at the scenes and the ground had been too hard to produce any imprints. Seeing nothing in the images he hadn't noticed before, he closed the folders and looked up at his window that had a thermometer mounted on its exterior surface. It was twenty-two degrees outside and he could see nothing but a deep-blue sky above a snow-clad sagebrush ridge.

Picking up his cell phone, Cove scrolled down and found the number for the state crime lab. He dialed the number. He got the receptionist, identified himself and asked to talk to the latent fingerprint examiner. After less than a minute, a male voice identified himself. Cove explained the case to him and asked whether he would be able to enter one latent print into the AFIS database for a search.

"Look," the examiner said. "There is no way we have time for a case of that nature right now. As usual, things are crazy. My boss mandates we prioritize significant crimes. If you had a victim, perhaps I could find the time, but I don't right now. I'm sorry." The analyst paused for a moment and Cove let him hang, finally the guy replied, "Send it down and I'll get to it when I can, but it'll be several weeks." With the guy still on the line, Cove's phone beeped and he glanced at the display, not recognizing the incoming number. Biting his lip, Cove thanked the examiner and closed the phone, missing the other call. Sipping his coffee, Cove opened his phone back up and studied the number he'd missed. *Somebody local.* Hitting the send button, his phone redialed the missed number. Cove looked at his computer's screen while he listened to the phone ringing. While he waited, he opened up his email and saw the note from Julie Lake. Giving up on the call, he closed the phone and opened up Julie's email. After he read the note, he sat back in his chair, folded his arms and pondered her question. *How do I deal with it?* In the course of his eight years as a warden, Cove had seen fifty or sixty similar killings. Leaning over the keyboard he started to type. *"You've got me cornered on that one. I think my skin just gets thicker, but they all bug me."* Cove hit the enter key and thought about the reporter.

Within a few seconds, a fresh email appeared in his inbox. *"How about we meet for coffee?"* Cove considered the offer and thought about the ticking clock. In reality, he had been pursuing this same shooter for two, going on three weeks and he rationalized another hour wouldn't make any difference. Instead of replying to her email offer, he picked up his phone, found Julie's number and hit the send button. They agreed to meet at the small coffee shop on Main in ten minutes.

Cove drove down Main, thinking about the conversation he'd had with the forensic guy at the lab and cursed himself for not including the case's link to the burglary. He parked his patrol truck in front of the coffee shop, walked in, and took a seat at a table with his back to the wall where he could look out at the street. Within a few moments, Julie appeared in the window and stopped at his truck to greet Annie. She was wearing jeans, the blue down coat she'd had on during the call out, and a white wool hat pulled overhead. Walking into the cafe, she took the off the hat and shook out her long, slightly curly hair. She gave Cove a smile, and sat down.

The waitress walked over and addressed both he and Julie by their first names before taking their orders. Julie leaned in. Cove caught her scent as she lowered her voice and asked him whether he'd made any progress on the case.

Cove paused and nodded. "Fred got a partial print off the beer can." He did not fill Julie in on the Petersham connection. "I just got off the phone with the lab, and they're too busy with so called 'real crime' to mess with it," he said, as he took a sip of coffee that produced a sharp bite. He set it down and reached for the cream container.

"That could be an angle for my story," Julie said, shaking her head, "but I'll have to think about it."

Cove brought his cup just short of his chin and paused, looked into Julie's twinkling green eyes and lowered his voice. "Between you and me," he said, rotating his head, "Our shooter drove by Gabbro while he had the other rig stopped yesterday morning. We must have just missed him. It's a silver Dodge." Cove felt guilty about telling her of the subpar performance of another officer, but letting it out gave him some relief.

"You're kidding," Julie replied, squinting her eyes.

"I wish I were, I'm pissed. I think we'd have the guy's rifle by now."

The two drank their coffee and Julie admitted she'd had a hard time getting to sleep, thinking of the two deer. Cove listened to her and studied her face as she talked. He had no wise words for her, but stayed tuned into what she was saying. She asked whether he'd slept okay and he almost told her about waking up to a growling bear.

Cove's phone rang. Looking at the number, he recognized it was the same one he'd missed earlier. He looked back at Julie. "Excuse me," he said, and held the phone up to his right ear.

It was Armando Barreras. He'd found a deer that had been shot and left above his trailer.

Cove felt the heat rise in his neck. "Any idea on how long it's been dead?" He asked.

"I think it must have been shot last night. It's still warm. Can I have it?"

"No... well not yet, just don't touch it. I'll be up there in forty minutes and meet you at your house." Cove snapped the phone shut and looked back at Julie.

"Another deer in the Pahsimeroi. I should have gone out last night, but I was pooped. Assuming this is the same guy, he's drinking a different brand of coffee than I am. This is two nights in a row." Cove stood up, finished his mug and looked at Julie. "I could use some company..."

Julie smiled. "I would love to go, Charley, but I'm working on a deadline. I should be on my computer right now."

Cove put the mug down. "I'd like to hear what you're working on sometime. I'll get the coffee if you get the tip." He paid the waitress at the cash register and walked out the door, thinking about Barreras's phone call.

Julie finished her coffee and watched through the shop's window as Cove got in his truck and drove off. She reached in her pants pocket and pulled out a handful of change for the tip. Half of the coins were copper pennies and their smell hit her, reminding her of the odor of blood.

# *Chapter 7*

Driving down Main, Cove pulled his cell out of his coat pocket and speed dialed Mendiola. "I'm headed up the Pahsimeroi. Sounds like the shooter dumped another one last night. Do me a favor if you would," Cove said. "Call up the fingerprint guy at the state lab and tell him you've got a serial shooter running around *your* county and sniping deer and cattle–hell, killin' a cow's a felony–and burglarizing residences. Tell him you need some help with a latent and the situation is escalating. Make it sound like crime's oughta control up here; hell, it *is* outta control," Cove declared. "I talked to him this morning and he acted like it was a litter case."

"No problem," Mendiola said. "I'll email him the JPEG of the print first to suck him in. Hard to turn down something when you've already got it. Oh, and I'll just happen to leave out the fact that all we've got linking your shooter to Harris's cow but speculation."

Cove ignored Mendiola's dig. He brought up the missing license plate number Gabbro had lost and urged the chief deputy to hound his guy about it. "Maybe he can find it. If I run into Harris up there, I'm going to ask him whether he's still got the license number and he's going to ask me why I'm asking *him*."

Cove turned onto the highway heading to the Pahsimeroi. The weather was holding clear, but the wind had come up by the time he turned up the valley. He found Armando Barreras near his singlewide, wearing a pair of worn buckskin colored insulated coveralls and looking under the hood of his blue and white 1980 Ford pickup. As Cove pulled into the driveway, he rolled down his window. Barreras slammed the hood down and walked over to Cove. The Hispanic was skinny, in his thirties, and had a slender black mustache.

"How 'bout I follow you up?" Cove asked, and nodded towards his truck. "If your ol' Ford's running we can load the deer up and you can have it."

"Oh, man." Barreras said with a Hispanic accent. "Three deer would go a long way with my family this winter."

It dawned on Cove that the guy he was talking to was over six-foot. Looking down at the guy's feet, he confirmed Barreras was wearing cowboy boots, which wasn't a surprise, but it got him wondering. Cove looked back up into his eyes. "What were you doing when you found this deer?"

Barreras frowned and hesitated. "I was up there dumpin' the bones from them other deer."

"Do me a favor," Cove said, "Park twenty or thirty yards short of where this is. I'll wanna look at the tracks."

Cove followed the ranch hand's old Ford up the road, mentally comparing him to the profile of his shooter. *Could he be associated with the silver Dodge? He needs meat for his family, so if he's part of this, why would he leave 'em?*

After about three miles, Barreras's truck pulled over. The plows had worked up and down the road, but there was still a strip of untrodden snow along the shoulder.

Cove could see a half dozen magpies interested in something about sixty yards off into the sage.

"How'd you find it?" Cove asked, glancing over at the tires on the Ford.

"I seen them magpies. Walked out there to see what they was excited about and found it. Figured you'd wanna know."

Cove nodded and walked along the road, found where a vehicle had pulled off and tracked along the untrodden snow at the edge of the sage. The tracks had the same interlocking Z elements he had photographed at the junction. He glanced over at the ranch hand's tires and confirmed they had a different tread. The tracks of two people had walked out into the sage and back, all on the same path. Cove studied the trail. *Barreras walked over the shooter's tracks or he shot the deer and walked over his own tracks to make this story up. Maybe he walked over his own tracks to make it look like two guys, or maybe he was here with the shooter last night.*

Retrieving a can of gray spray paint from his truck, Cove gave the tire track impression a light coating of paint delivered from a low angle with Barreras watching. Pulling his camera out of his coat, Cove took a photograph of the imprint and noticed the curious look on the ranch hand's face. "The paint makes for a much better photograph; it's hard to get good pictures of tracks in the snow without it." Cove laid his three-inch ruler down on the track and took a second photo.

Turning to the ranch hand, Cove said, "Let's walk beside these tracks, not on top of 'em," and nodded forward with his head. Cove led, with Barreras following.

At the end of the trail lay a dead doe; head blown apart like the other four. Cove looked beyond the deer and could see a spray of blood spatter caused by the bullet's exit. *High velocity, no doubt about it.* Staring at the boot prints, Cove glanced over at Barreras's fresh tracks. *They look the same.* Again, Cove studied the footprints on the trodden path. Pulling his tape measure out of his pants pocket, Cove took several measurements of the prints. One imprint was twelve and a half inches and the other one was thirteen and a half. *Two different guys. Barreras's story is good—maybe.* With the ranch hand watching, Cove leaned over and measured the tracks Barreras had just made. He discovered they were the shorter of the two tracks.

"What ya measuring *my* tracks for?" Barreras asked suspiciously.

"Armando," Cove said, looking at him. "What size boots you wear?"

"Elevens," he answered with a nervous edge. "Why?"

"Cause this guy's got a bigger foot than yours and I'm trying to figure out what size boot he wears," Cove answered, nodding. "Guessing he wears twelves, maybe thirteens then, eh?"

Barreras's eyes opened a bit. "Oh... sure."

Cove stared at the tracks around the doe and found what he was looking for—knee prints near the doe's abdomen. Folding his arms on his chest, Cove stared at the imprints and canted his head. *What in the hell's this guy up to?* Pulling his camera out, Cove stepped back, took a photo of the deer with the tracks around it, then moved in closer and photographed the knee prints. He took a close-up of the head wound. *That'll make a good shot for a jury.* Cove squatted down and looked at where the shooter had knelt. He could vaguely see the imprint of the weave of cloth in the snow and thought about doing a plaster cast of the imprints, but dismissed the idea, since he couldn't fathom doing any kind of cloth comparison with a casting in the future. "Hold the end of this tape to the heel on that track if you would," Cove said, pointing to a boot print as he pulled the tape out to the next heel mark. "Thirty-one inches." *Same guy for sure.*

"You're Indian, ain'tcha?" Barreras asked.

He looked at the ranch hand and nodded. "Yep, mixed blood. My father was full."

Cove pulled out a black-handled folding Kershaw knife that he kept clipped inside his pants pocket. He flicked open the three-inch blade with a one-handed snap, and pushed it into the deer's thigh muscle. He hesitated and looked at the Hispanic. "Most of the time I think my Indian blood helps me with this job, but sometimes I think it makes it harder." Cove pulled the knife out of the deer, wiped it with a snowball, folded the blade back into its handle and clipped it in his pants pocket. "Our people believe that all things are connected—you, me, this deer, ... the coyotes, the sagebrush, these mountains," he said, nodding towards the Lemhi Range. "And we all deserve the same respect—we're all equal." Cove reached into his shirt pocket, pulled out a pen-sized aluminum-cased thermometer, removed its cover, and slipped the glass rod into the incision he'd just made. "So when someone does something like this, it really bothers me. It doesn't make any sense." Cove shook his head. "But what really grinds on me is that the court system doesn't see it the same way my Salish blood does–everything ain't equal." Cove caught the ranch hand staring at him. "A lott'a times, wildlife cases get pled down or dumped, they call it *judicial economy* ...and it pisses me off. The people that first inhabited this valley would have considered this a grave crime."

Barreras nodded, his mouth slightly ajar, and didn't speak for a moment, but after a bit he gestured with his hand towards the thermometer. "What's that for?"

"Body temperature. It'll tell me how long it's been dead, or at least give me an idea," Cove explained while studying the deer. *Full grown doe, maybe a hundred and fifty pounds. The air temperature's got to be about freezing.*

"How long you been doing this?" Barreras asked.

Cove gave him an odd look. "Figuring out how long stuff's been dead?"

"No," Barreras said. "A warden. How long you been a game warden?"

"Oh," he said, with his eyes twinkling, "eight years."

Cove pulled his coat sleeve back and checked his watch. *Eleven-fifteen.* Removing his wallet from his rear pants pocket, he fished out a card with a graph on it. Pulling the thermometer out, Cove wiped it on the deer's course hair, and read the instrument's scale. *Seventy-eight degrees.* Cove paused and let his brain calculate. *It's lost twenty-two degrees since it was shot.* Turning back to Barreras he asked, "You hear any rigs last night?"

"No, nothing," Barreras answered.

Cove looked at the graph on the card. *Eight hours. It's been dead for about eight hours.* Cove looked at his fingertips and counted backwards, flicking a finger out for each hour. "It must have been about two or three this morning. He's sure a night owl," Cove said, more to himself than to Barreras.

Grabbing a hind leg, Cove rolled the deer onto its back and took his gloves off. "Hold this leg and I'll clean it for you," he said, and leaned down to the deer's pelvis. When he was finished, Cove clipped the knife back inside his pocket. The two slid the animal to Barreras's truck and loaded it.

Cove chewed his lip and thought for a moment, studying the Lost River Range, weighing whether to ask– wondering if he could trust Barreras with information he didn't want out. "You recall seeing a silver Dodge up here with a rollbar? Got two lights bolted to the bar?"

Barreras paused, licked his lips, and brought his palm up to his lips. He spoke with his hand covering his mouth. "I mighta seen that rig up here once or twice, but I don't pay much attention."

Cove caught the body language and threw him another question.

"Any idea who it belongs too?" He leaned in, studying the ranch hand's face.

Barreras looked at his boots. "No idea."

Cove's hair came up on the back of his neck. *Why did he cover his mouth? Why'd he look down?*

He knew Hispanics had a cultural practice of trying to please people in authority and they'd sometimes lie with the sole motivation of appeasement, but that cultural anomaly didn't explain the deception he'd just witnessed. *What are you holding back, Armando?* Thinking about his next question, he canted his good ear towards him. "When was the last time you saw it?" Cove asked, watching his face.

Barreras looked at the deer in the bed of his truck and hesitated. "I dunno... maybe last week?"

"If you see it again, try and get the plate for me, but keep this between you and me, if you would."

Cove thanked Barreras and stood watching the ranch hand drive down the valley, debating if he'd just screwed up, and wondering if the guy was going to tip his cards to the shooter.

Turning to the back of his truck, he dropped the tailgate. "Okay, Annie: Brass! Find the brass!" He swung his hand like a softball pitcher, directing the chocolate labrador to where the shooter had stepped out of his truck. Glancing at his hands, he realized his fingers were still covered in the doe's blood. He squatted down and watched Annie work, tail wagging and focused. He took a handful of snow and began rubbing the blood off his hands. The snow was abrasive and ice cold. Except for a trace of blood at the edges of his fingernails, his hands were clean. His dog found nothing.

*****

He finished the porn video and threw another empty Keystone can at the television, but this time it clanged off the screen. Laying his head back on the couch, he closed his eyes and brought his hands down to his lap, letting his fingers play on the keyboard that wasn't there. His meth-soaked brain brought forth his little red piano and its twenty-five white and black keys. His fingers played out the first song his mother had taught him and his voice quietly sang out, "Twinkle, twinkle, little star, how I wonder what you are? Up above the world so high, like a diamond in the sky..." The recollection of those days brought a smile to his face that hung until he betrayed himself with the memory of his father hollering he was a "no-good-little-shit-homo" and had stomped the red toy into an unrecognizable pile of rubble.

Grabbing his .357, he pointed it towards the empty TV screen and pulled the double-action trigger back, raising the gun's hammer up as he added pressure. He closed his eyes and continued the pull until the explosion rang his ears and jolted him back. The bullet had ripped a hole through the thin trailer wall just above the television.

Looking at the new opening, he could see a pupil staring at him. He glared back at it, sitting on the couch, staring for maybe five minutes–or maybe five hours–he wasn't sure. Finally, he jumped up, charged out the back door with his revolver and studied where the bastard must have stood. Nothing, not even a track. He opened up his truck door and fished his Crown Royal bag out of the shifter boot. He reached in farther, finding his Ziploc bag of marijuana roaches and took both inside.

He sat down at the kitchen table and slid the dirty plate out of the way. He stuck a pre-rolled joint between his lips, found his Bic inside the purple bag and lit the marijuana cigarette. He sucked the smoke into his lungs, needing to get his head straight. After holding the harsh toke, he exhaled, coughing and squinting his eyes. He laid the still smoking roach on the plate and drew his revolver. He pushed the thumb piece forward, flopped the cylinder out and removed the shell casing he'd fired. Leaning back, he reached into his jeans and found a loaded round. He dropped it in the empty chamber and flicked the six-round cylinder back into the gun's frame.

The marijuana didn't do its trick; he wanted his piano back. He pulled his pipe and meth out of the Crown bag and loaded the glass bowl. He rolled the pipe back and forth over the flame and watched as the crystals turned into vapor. From within the cloud, his ghost appeared, sitting on the bench playing the keys of the red piano. And the redhead sat beside him.

*****

Cove drove up the Pahsimeroi road to the Furey Lane junction, pulled over and looked across the valley at the hillside where he believed the shooter had watched from. Reaching up to the truck's visor, he flipped it down, exposing a nylon organizer. He removed a pen-sized Gerber diamond knife sharpener. To the left of the organizer was the photograph of Liz. Her image met his gaze. He narrowed his dark-brown eyes, took a deep breath, and felt his stomach contract. After a moment, he flipped up the visor. Shifting in his seat, he reached down and pulled the folding knife out of his pants pocket. He flicked it open one-handed and tested the edge on the flat of his thumbnail. *Not sharp enough,* he thought. Sliding the blade across the sharpener's surface, Cove focused on two things—the repetitive back and forth movement, while maintaining a constant ten-degree blade angle on the diamond surface and the cognitive problem stewing in his brain. The blade made a metallic swishing noise as he moved it across the fine abrasive surface. Back and forth, each stroke causing the blade to mimic its previous tone. One side of the blade and then the other. By the time the knife's edge passed Cove's thumbnail test, he was convinced that Barreras had held something back and he believed he knew what might make the guy come clean.

Cove continued up the road towards Bob Harris's ranch, passing the place where the doe and buck had been killed. The birds had moved on from the kill scene. He caught Harris pulling out of his driveway in a dirty brown ten-year-old flatbed Ford one-ton pickup. Rolling down his driver's window, Cove pulled next to the rancher's truck and was greeted with a weathered smile.

"We had another doe killed down by Armando's last night," Cove said.

"Damn," Harris replied, turning his gray whiskered face back towards his windshield. "If this bastard had a job, he'd be too damned tired to be up all night running around shooting stuff. I thought about that the other night when I called the sheriff."

"I gotta agree," Cove said, looking at the fingertips on his hand. He paused for a moment, realizing that all five of his fingernails had blood under their edges. His mind played the slide show of the dead deer. Finally he looked up at Harris. "Hey, you and Armando get along okay?"

"He's a damned good worker. He does some irrigating for me in the summer when I'm moving cows in the hills and what not." Looking towards the nearby fence, he continued, "He and one of his Mexican friends built that pole fence for me—worked their butts off," Harris said and then stared at Cove. "Why you asking? You don't goddamn think it's him, do ya?"

"No. I think it's the guy driving the silver Dodge you saw." Cove paused. "By the way, Gabbro can't find that plate you called in. You wouldn't still have the envelope you wrote it on would you?"

Harris looked back down at his seat, glanced across his dashboard, and turned back to Cove. "I mighta thrown it out. I think it was on some damn junk mail."

Cove nodded and rubbed his whiskers. "Where's that dead cow? Gabbro says the bullet might still be in it. Mind if I try to dig it out?"

"Have at it." Harris pointed down the road. "It's down there in the corner of that field. The birds and coyotes have pretty well cleaned it up, I suppose."

Cove thanked the rancher and drove to the end of the field where the remains of the cow lay. Putting on a pair of leather gloves, Cove dropped the tailgate and told Annie she could get out. He pulled a leather-sheathed single-bit axe from behind the dog's box and climbed over the wooden poles of the fence. He brushed the snow off what remained of the cow. White bones jutted from the black skin. A front leg had been pulled off and lay next to the rib cage, a coyote's canine had bitten through the shoulder blade. Removing the axe's sheath, Cove severed the spinal column behind the skull with two swings and set the axe down. Kneeling in the snow, he rolled the heavy head over and examined it. The eyes had weathered into the skull and scavengers had chewed off the nose cartilage. Looking up into the sinuses, Cove could see where the shooter's bullet had shattered the honeycombed sinus structure. Studying the rear of the animal's head, he could not find any indication of an exit wound. Picking the axe back up, Cove chopped across the two eye orbits and then back from each orbit along the sides of the skull until the top of the skull came loose, exposing what remained of the brain. The bullet had entered the right nostril and had burst into the animal's cranium, turning the brain tissue into what resembled pink frozen cottage cheese. Cove flicked his knife open and probed the white mush until he found what he was looking for. He fished it out with his gloved fingers. Climbing over the fence, he looked back at the cow and couldn't help but notice his own knee prints in the snow. *He's not digging for bullets.*

He put the axe in the truck bed, told Annie to kennel-up, closed the tailgate, and found a yellow rag in the pocket of his side door. Cove wiped the bullet off with the rag, dumped water over it from a plastic bottle, wiped it off again and set it on the dash. He got back in his seat, started the engine and turned the truck's heater on high. Reaching over to his glove box, Cove retrieved a slender black plastic box, opened the lid, and pulled out a set of digital calipers.

He picked the recovered slug off the dash and examined it. It was a rifle bullet that had morphed from a long, slender projectile into a smashed, disfigured shape, much like a mushroom complete with cap and stem. It was made of soft gray lead, covered with a thin copper jacket. Picking up the calipers, Cove measured the diameter of the bullet's intact base. "Thirty-caliber," Cove said to himself with a slight nod. Looking closely at the bullet's cylinder-shaped rear, Cove counted four narrow grooves twisting slightly to the right. The markings had been impressed by the barrel's rifling. It was just what he was expecting to see. Cove had worked a case the previous winter involving a thirty-caliber rifle bullet with four land impressions. He had learned that all recently manufactured thirty-caliber Winchesters, including those chambered in .300 WSM, had a rifling configuration of four lands with a right hand twist. Most Ruger and Remington rifle barrels were manufactured with six rifling lands, but a few had five. It was the barrel's lands that had left the grooves in the bullet and had spun it like a quarterback throwing a football, giving the projectile its accuracy.

*Too coincidental,* Cove thought. Looking out the windshield, he chewed his lip and felt the weight of the slug. He thought about another similar bullet that he'd dug out of a bloated cow elk in early November. The elk had been shot and left during the bull season. For now, this bullet would go in an evidence bag, but in the long run it'd end up in a plastic jar with others of the same ilk in his office.

Cove turned his rig around and drove down the valley, heading for the house trailer belonging to Armando Barreras. When he arrived, Barreras's blue and white Ford was backed up to a shed. The ranch hand was standing behind the tailgate, still wearing his insulated coveralls. Reaching into his shirt pocket, Cove pushed the "record" button on his audio recorder. He parked next to the Ford, got out and greeted the man. Barreras had a half sheet of plywood on the tailgate he was using as a cutting board to butcher the deer. Most of the skinned carcass was still in the bed of the truck. There were two piles of cut meat on the plywood.

"Not going to let it hang, eh?" Cove asked.

"Too cold, it'd freeze," Barreras said.

"Armando," Cove said, nodding his head slowly and elevating his eyebrows. "You and I need to have a heart-to-heart."

The Hispanic turned to Cove with a long slender boning knife in one hand and a chunk of cut venison in the other and stared back wearing a frown. "What are you talking about?"

"You work for Bob Harris once in a while, right?" Cove stated.

"Yeah, I do," Barreras answered. "Why you asking?"

"He treats you with respect and pays you a fair wage, right?"

Barreras nodded. "Mr. Harris helped me get my wife up from Mexico. He's a good man."

"You heard he had a cow shot a few weeks ago, eh?"

"Yeah," Barreras said, and shrugged his shoulders. "Everybody heard about it." His eyes squinted, emphasizing his frown. "What's that got to do with me?"

Cove nodded at the deer. "I've got reason to believe this deer you're going to feed your family–plus those other two I gave you–and Bob's cow–were all shot by the same guy, the one driving that silver Dodge I asked about," he paused and looked into the ranch hand's eyes. Cove pulled the bullet out of his pocket and displayed it as if he were revealing the Holy Grail.

The evidentiary value of the bullet without the shooter's rifle wasn't much, but Cove felt he needed some kind of physical prop.

"Armando, everything I've ever heard about you is that you're a hardworking, honest man." He winced recalling the cockfighting rumors. "They say the same thing about Bob Harris in this valley, but Bob can't handle losing many cows. He's land rich and cash poor. The bank'll be breathing down his neck if this continues. And here's the deal." Cove paused and let the phrase sink in, his lips tight but wide, showing neither a frown nor a smile. "You know more about the silver Dodge than you're tellin' me." He paused and spoke with emphasis. "*I know it. I can feel it in my bones.*" Cove's head twisted and his eyes narrowed, staring dead into the Hispanic's eyes. "Armando," Cove said in a slow staccato voice, steadily tapping out each word. "Who's the guy that drives the Dodge?"

It was now or never. Cove was on edge. Either the ranch hand was going to look down and deny it, or give it up.

Barreras turned back, and stared at the half butchered deer. He laid the knife on the cutting board. His head sagged. Cove caught the body language and held his breath. He knew this was it. After a moment, Barreras looked back at Cove and let out a sigh. "The guy's loco," he said glancing over at his singlewide.

"This conversation is just between you and me," Cove said, lowering his voice and wearing a dead serious expression. "Your name doesn't go in a report. I don't tell my boss. Nobody is gonna know who told me. I won't put you or your family at risk. I swear on my father's grave. I promise, but I need to stop this killin'. Who is it, Armando?"

After a lull, Barreras answered. "His name is Leo, that's all I know."

Cove's blood surged and he leaned in with his good ear. "How do you know that?"

"He got stuck one night on the other side of the valley. I saw his rig the next morning and pulled him out of a hole."

"Why do you think he's crazy?" Cove asked, while studying Barreras's body language.

"He kept looking around like he was afraid of something and muttering about worms," Barreras said, shaking his head. "It was out there in the sage above Morse Creek." Barreras glanced across the valley. "He was looking around like something was sneaking up on him. Nothing but scrub sagebrush for a mile and he's all paranoid."

Cove soaked the details for a moment. "You know where he lives?"

"He mentioned something about a creek, but didn't say which one." Barreras glanced back at the pile of meat, but returned his gaze to Cove. "I'm sorry I didn't tell you this, Mr. Cove, but I was afraid he might do something."

"It's Charley, and don't worry about it, Armando." Cove nodded towards the house trailer. "I understand. He'll never find out. What's he look like?

"Tall and skinny, with a busted nose."

"Age? Hair color?" Cove continued his questions.

"I dunno—kinda like a old dirty cow dog. If he bathed and had a big plate of fajitas, he'd look different. Forty maybe, it's hard to say, but long, scraggly, light colored hair. He got a big tooth hanging around his neck he kept touching," Barreras said, his Hispanic accent getting stronger. "His eyes don't look right, cheeks are sunken in, kinda like a witch or zombie," Barreras said, frowning.

# *Chapter 8*

Charley Cove was juiced. He felt like a locomotive with a boiler full of steam. *I oughta call Julie,* he thought, but before he could act, his phone let out its familiar bear growl ringtone.

"George, I was just thinking about calling you," Cove said, feeling the guilt of the lie.

"Got some good news about your shooter, I hope," Nayman said.

"He killed another doe late last night, but I got a first name–it's Leo."

"How'd you figure that out?" Nayman asked.

"A little bird told me. Said the guy looks like a zombie. You might ask around the Lemhi sheriff's office if they've had any of their's escape lately," Cove said, smiling. "But seriously, the guy sounds scraggly; you might ask whether it rings any bells with the deputies. He's well over six foot and skinny. Wears cowboy boots," Cove said.

"He leave any evidence at this latest scene?" Nayman asked.

"Not much. The same tire tread track, but Pallid's going to argue there are a million tires with that pattern."

"What's your next step?" Nayman asked.

"As soon as I get home, I'm going to call up Motor Vehicles and have them run the vehicle description with a first name of Leonard in Lemhi and Custer Counties and have 'em fill in the rest with wild-cards. It's gotta be a short list. Tonight I'm gonna spend the night on the hill out here. The guy just doesn't quit," Cove answered.

"I suspect you're going to be sleeping in your bed tonight, not out chasing some zombie. The reason I'm calling is I got a call from Boise, and you're officially grounded. Nothing over forty hours. Period. Thirty would be better. They're bitching me out over the fact one of my guys—that being you—is running with two hundred and thirty-eight hours of comp-time. Thirty-eight over policy," Nayman said.

Cove paused, feeling like a balloon with a pinhole. He pulled off the road and put the transmission in park.

"I'll tell you what," Nayman said. "I've got this trainee I need to spend some time working shiners with. We'll go sit on your hill tonight. You go home, do all the computer sleuthing this afternoon and we'll go do the real game warden stuff."

"Shit," Cove said, rubbing his forehead. "Well... but promise you'll get me outta bed if you see a light moving up the valley after midnight. Two rigs'll give us a better chance of pinching him in."

"Yeah, no problem," Nayman answered. "The Easter Bunny flies around in a red sled, too. Go home. Turn your phone off. It ain't gonna ring."

*Son of a bitch. Forty hours.* Cove put the phone back into his coat pocket and focused on what he needed to do. He pulled onto the road, dug the phone back out and punched in Mendiola's speed dial.

"Our shooter's name is Leo," Cove said. "Got any Leos on your short list of burglars?"

"Not off hand," Mendiola answered. "How'd you find that out?"

"Don't ask," Cove answered. "My source says he's tall and skinny and was acting goofy, like he's paranoid."

"Maybe a tweaker," Mendiola said.

"Got any doper sources you could bounce it off of?" Cove asked.

"Yeah, but the word will get out. Drug informants are always playing it both ways. It's up to you."

"Let me cogitate on it," Cove said. "I'll see you in thirty; I'm just about to the river."

Cove drove down the valley, turned onto the highway and headed for Challis, driving up the river canyon. When he entered cell coverage, his phone beeped. He flipped it open, saw the text icon and selected it. "*Mr. Game Warden: Any luck yet catching our deer killer? -JL*" Cove flipped the phone closed.

When he pulled into the Custer County Sheriff's office, he noticed Mendiola's truck was gone, but saw deputy Gabbro's truck parked in the lot. Cove walked into the office and went for his coffee cup in the back room. He found Gabbro sitting in uniform, working away at a computer and wearing a three-day beard.

The room was about sixteen by sixteen. The place smelled of old paint and cleaned up vomit—the nasal flavors of a jailhouse. It was called the booking room or coffee room, depending on what its function was at the time. There was an open door, exposing a small restroom on one side, a closed heavy steel door that accessed the jail, and a nearby holding cell with dirty white bars. The only thing inside the cell was a stained mattress on a steel framed single bunk. A refrigerator was next to a wall, covered with a collection of coffee mugs. Below the mugs was a small white painted table with a double potted coffee brewer and the desktop computer where Gabbro was working. Next to it was a short, varnished counter with a contraption that looked like an antique computer– in fact it was an Intoxilyzer 5000, used to determining the blood alcohol content of an arrestee's breath. It had a dirty keyboard and a mouthpiece ready for the next drunk. A fingerprint cardholder and a black inkpad were attached to the counter's edge.

"How you doing, Joey?" Cove asked.

"Okay, ...just writing up an accident report."

"Where'd Fred go?" Cove inquired, filling up his mug.

Gabbro looked at the warden. "He said something about some follow up he had to do. I don't know what he's working on."

Cove took a sip of coffee and sat down. "You haven't seen that silver Dodge around, have you?"

Gabbro licked his lips. "Nope," he said, and nodded his head up and down while looking at the computer monitor.

Cove stared at the deputy, not believing what he'd just seen; the guy had given him a negative answer combined with positive body language. He replayed it in his brain; listening to Gabbro's voice and watching the deputy's head nod up and down. Sipping his coffee, Cove sat shaken, believing he had just been drawn into a cardless poker game.

The deputy stood up without looking at Cove and walked over to the refrigerator. "I could use a Pepsi." He opened the door and pulled out a can, popped the top, and dropped some change in a coffee can. Sitting back down in his chair, Gabbro looked back at Cove, took a swallow, and set the can beside the keyboard. "You gettin' anywhere on your case?"

"Yeah, the shooter's first name's Leo. Ring any bells?" Cove asked, studying the deputy's face.

Cove thought he caught a flush.

Gabbro hesitated, looked down and turned back to the computer screen. "No, not offhand."

Cove stared at the deputy. *What's going on?* He wondered. After a moment, Cove spoke, playing his next card. "I dug a bullet out of Harris's beef cow today."

Gabbro swiveled back with his face flushed. "That's *my* case. What didja do that for?"

"Well, I was out there and Harris showed me where it was. Figured what the hell, save you a trip, and I dug it out." Cove hesitated, and then looked the deputy in the eye and quoted him. "As you said, it's *'just a cow,'* no big deal."

Gabbro frowned and studied Cove for a moment. "Well, give it to me. I'll put it in my case folder."

*Yeah, like the license plate number,* Cove thought. He shook his head. "How 'bout I hold on to it. It'll make a better chain-of-custody if we ever go to trial." He finished his coffee, stepped into the bathroom, rinsed his mug out, replaced it on the rack, and walked out to his truck. He sat in the driver's seat, feeling the stubble on his chin, and thought about Gabbro.

Pulling out his cell phone, he scrolled through the directory, found Julie's number and pressed the send button.

"Charley! You catch the creep yet?"

"Nope, not yet," Cove answered. He wondered how much he should tell her and felt like a rope in a tug-of-war. "You can't tell anyone, but I got a first name."

"How'd you find that out?"

"Confidential source," Cove answered.

"Quit worrying about me blabbing your secrets, Charley," Julie answered. "How about I buy you a beer tonight?"

*****

He drove his Dodge into the alley and stopped, facing the building across the street, still hidden. *Red's gotta be in there.* Rolling down his window, he flared his nostrils and sniffed, brought his hand up to his neck and massaged his lucky mojo charm. Swiveling around, he looked out his rear window and stared at the two garbage cans, memorizing the angle of the lids. After he was satisfied, he looked through the passenger window at the knotholes on the fence, studying each for staring eyeballs.

Turning the ignition key back on, he looked at the clock on the dashboard. *4:46. Two-bits says she punches the clock out at 5:00.* Looking up, he watched the traffic move back and forth on Main. He stared at each driver. None caught his gaze. Flicking his attention back to the building, he studied the door and felt a worm twitch inside his right eyeball. He reached up and rubbed it with his knuckle. He cupped his hand over his mouth, filled it with his breath and brought it to his nose. He smelled the acidic smell of cat-piss from his last pipe. An older blue Econoline van passed by his hole. *A van, that'd be perfect.*

Looking back at the building, he saw the door open. *Holy mother of Jesus!* Red stepped out of the building and he caught a glimpse of her smile and felt the heat. He watched as she turned up the street, her jean-covered legs moving with a steadfast stride, one hand clutching a dark-blue computer bag. Opening his mouth, he let his tongue slip between his teeth and he moved it back and forth across his lower lip. He watched her turn off Main Street, and she disappeared around the corner. *Shit-fuck!* He glanced behind him, turned back around and stared up and down what little of the street he could see. Reaching down, he started the truck, pulled out without looking left and made a quick right hand turn onto Main. He caught the yelp of a horn coming from his left side and glanced in time to see a wine-colored SUV stopped in the street a few feet away with a female driver glaring and holding her hands up. *Goddamn bitch.* He eased up Main, slowly turned onto the side street and pulled off to the side. He stared down the street until he spied her moving on the sidewalk. *Jesus! She moves like a ballerina. Goddamn!* Rolling down his window he put his nose in the air. *I'll bet ya smell sweet!*

He sat in his Dodge and watched her cross a second side street. She walked to the front door of a house, pulled keys from the computer bag, unlocked the door, and disappeared inside. *Goddamn!*

*****

Cove had just gotten off the phone with the Department of Motor Vehicles in Boise when his phone rang. Picking it up, he looked at the display and saw it was Mendiola.

"Tell me the lab's got a hit on our print?" Cove asked.

"No, but get your ass moving. Somebody about hit your guy on main. I'm just coming up Valley Avenue. The wit said she last seen him turning onto Third from Main."

Cove grabbed his gun belt, wrapped it around his waist and buckled it. "Annie, you gotta stay here," he said, as he ran out the door past his hanging coat. Slamming the truck's tailgate, he jumped in and fired up the engine. Pulling onto the road, he snapped his seat belt across him and turned on his headlights. The sun was already below the hills behind him, and the light was at the in-between phase of day and night. He came down the Garden Creek road in a rush and was shortly on Main. He turned right on Third and noted Julie's house was lit up. Continuing the hunt, his head swiveled right and left as he passed each side road. Seeing Mendiola's rig coming up Valley, he flashed his lights. He turned off on Fourth, and got back on Main and headed down through the town towards the highway. He saw several pickups moving, but no silver Dodge. *Where are you?* Just before the highway, he pulled off behind the Y-Inn where he could watch both Main and Highway 93.

Cove looked up Main and picked up the lights of what appeared to be a Dodge truck headed his way. Grabbing his binoculars off the dash, he studied the truck and confirmed the Dodge grill. *Have I got enough for a stop that'll hold up in court? If he doesn't have the rifle, we could be screwed. It'd put the hink on him and he'll get rid of it. Maybe I oughta just get his plate?* Watching the vehicle come down the half-dark street, Cove picked up his microphone and pushed the transmit button. "Three-two-one, seven-three-one. I'm down here at the bottom and have a *possible* coming down Main." Cove laid the mic in his lap.

"Roger that," Mendiola's voice said through the radio. "I'm coming down Valley and I'll bump over."

"If this is him, why don't you do the stop on the fail-to-yield you got called in. I'll pull in behind you as secondary." Cove radioed.

If Mendiola hit his blue lights and made the stop, the guy shouldn't be concerned it was about the shootings—only about the near miss—and it should hold up in court if it turned out the .300 WSM rifle was sitting on the seat.

"Roger that," Mendiola answered.

Cove stared at the vehicle, looking for the roll bar and lights as the truck approached in the fading light. The color started to look right and then he realized he was studying a tan Dodge without a rollbar.

"Three-two-one, seven-three-one, this isn't it." Cove put the microphone back into its dash bracket, rolled his neck back and heard it pop.

He watched the Dodge drive by as Mendiola pulled his truck beside the warden's and rolled his passenger window down, the two trucks facing the same direction, neck to neck.

"So who called it in?" Cove asked, looking from his truck window.

"Some lady. Said she almost hit a guy who pulled out of that little spot back behind the post office. Said he wasn't looking where he was going–thought he was drunk. 'Said it was a silver Dodge pickup with a roll bar," Mendiola explained. "Sarah picked up on it and asked her whether it had overhead lights. That's when she hollered at me to roll."

"No plate, right?" Cove asked.

"No, she didn't get one, but Sarah's got her number if you wanna talk to her."

"Turned off on Third, eh?" Cove asked, tilting his head.

"That's what she said. Described the vehicle as moving real slow. I think it's why she musta thought he was drunk. Coulda been jabbering on his cell phone, I suppose, but she didn't mention it to Sarah."

After twenty minutes of small talk while watching for the vehicle, Mendiola turned to Cove. "Let's go get a burger."

Cove looked at his watch. "Sounds good, but I can't. I gotta meet somebody in a bit." Cove said, and looked back up the street.

"You gotta date with your little reporter, Charley?" Mendiola said with a grin.

"It ain't a date."

*****

Leo pulled in behind his singlewide and looked at the tracks in the snow, illuminated by his headlights. Stepping out of the Dodge, he clicked the door shut, stood and listened. He touched the mojo hanging from his neck and looked up into the night watching for stars, but none peeked from the dark overcast sky. The owl hooted from the cottonwoods, and a cold breeze came down the canyon. Satisfied, he opened the rear trailer door and stepped into its black interior, tipped his head back and flared his nostrils, easing the air of the trailer into his nose. Sensing. Flicking the hall light on, he moved to his right and stepped into his bedroom, turned the light on and stared at his captive. "I'll bet you're hungry," he whispered, "I'll see if 'n I've got some grub." Moving down the hall, he looked into both the bathroom and the spare bedroom, studying the lay of each item. He turned on the living room light and looked at the couch, the dining table, and the kitchen area. When he got to the table, he stopped and listened for footsteps on the roof. Nothing. He caught the glare of the bullet hole above the TV staring at him and studied it for a moment. Picking up a Burger King sack off the floor, he ripped a piece of paper off and stuffed it into the hole. In the kitchen, he opened up the cupboard under the sink and pulled out a galvanized metal box like mouse trap. Shaking it, he held it up to his ear and listened with wide eyes and flushed face. "Anybody home in there?" Satisfied with what he'd heard, he turned and walked to the far end of the trailer to his bedroom. Leaning down to the terrarium, he was greeted by the metallic clicking noise that imitated the spinning cylinder of a revolver. He smiled, looking at the head that stared back with its flicking tongue. "Dinner time, big guy." Leo eased the trap's metal lid up and looked in. A small gray mouse was huddled in the corner. A second, half-eaten rodent lay near it. Easing his hand into the box, he froze until the mouse relaxed and then grabbed it by its tail and pulled it out of the trap. It hung squeaking, frantically trying to gain traction in the air with its legs. Lifting the terrarium lid, Leo stared at the rattler; his face now focused and suddenly sober. The snake's tongue flickered forth tasting the odors; its tail silenced. The mouse fell onto the graveled floor of the terrarium and ran a few inches before the snake's snap-like strike grabbed it by its head. It held it for no more than a second and then dropped it. The mouse ran around the cage, seized, and fell on its side and began to convulse, kicking its legs. The snake gave a half yawn and then opened its mouth and unhinged its jaws, readying for its meal. Leo stood watching the show with his eyes fixed, fingering his mojo, and thinking about Red.

*****

Cove fed Annie, got out of his uniform and found a pair of clean blue Levis, a blue cotton chambray long sleeved shirt. *How long since I wore civvies?* Putting on a gray nylon covered fleece coat, Cove paused for a moment and then turned around and walked back into his bedroom. Kneeling down in front of a vertical gun safe, he dialed the combination and opened the door. He removed an AirLite five-shot Smith and Wesson .38 snubbed-nose revolver and a speed loader holding five extra Hydra-Shock hollow-points. He put them in his coat pocket.

"Annie, you stay put. I'll be back in an hour or so." Cove walked outside, past his patrol truck, got in his Tundra and drove down Main Street. He passed the post office and glanced back into the alley where Mendiola had said the Dodge had come from. Driving around the block, Cove entered the alley, and drove up to where he could look out on Main Street. He turned his lights off and sat thinking. *What in the hell was he doing back here?* Without answering the niggling question, he pulled out onto Main, drove down to the Borah Bar and parked, recalling the last time he'd been inside; he'd come to backup Mendiola on a squabble between a handful of cowboys feeling their vinegar.

Walking into the darkened room, Cove paused and looked around. The place smelled of beer and people. Shania Twain's low pitched voice sang from the jukebox. A brunette built like a two-door Buick leaned over the wooden bar, wiping down the varnished surface, seemingly oblivious to his entry. She wore a low-cut orange T-shirt, exposing her breasts along with a spiderweb tattoo cradled in her cleavage. She looked up at Cove and flashed an inviting smile, still polishing the bar. Two males, both wearing camouflage baseball hats, sat on stools in front of the bar, holding brown Budweiser bottles. Cove caught their eyes. The one on the left rotated back to the bar and the younger one–who looked familiar–glanced over and gave him a neutral nod. Julie was sitting at a small side table to his left; she saw him and smiled.

"Hey, warden." A slurred voice came from his right. "You find the asshole stole my rifle?"

Cove turned and looked into the dark corner, It was Ralph Petersham. Cove stepped over to him. "Not yet," he said lowering his voice and wondering what the guy had told the rest of Challis. "I'll give you a call if do, though."

"Sit down, buy ya a drink," Petersham gestured to the empty chair beside him, raised a shot glass containing a tea colored liquid, downed it, and chased it with a Budweiser.

Cove marveled at his flip-flop of friendliness. "Thanks for the offer, Ralph," he said, and glanced over at Julie. "I'll take a rain-check; I'm meeting somebody."

Petersham gave Julie a dirty-old-man leer, looked back at the warden, rolled his head, and waved him off.

Cove walked over to Julie and sat facing her with his back to the wall. Her blue coat hung on the chair; her white wool hat sat on the table next to a burning candle. She was wearing a green turtle-necked sweater and blue jeans. Her cheeks were flushed from the cold, setting off her long coppery red hair and beaming white smile.

"Your face tells me you walked here," Cove said.

"It's a nice night. Besides, why drive four blocks after sitting in front of a computer all day?"

The bartender appeared and met Cove's eyes; he looked at Julie and asked what she was going to have.

"A glass of Keystone, please," Julie answered.

Cove's eyebrows lowered and he looked at the bartender. "Corona, with a lime please."

When the bartender left, Julie leaned in and lowered her voice. "I think she was checking you out, Charley!"

Cove rolled his eyes. "Yeah, her and her twin sisters."

Julie grinned and flashed her eyes towards Petersham. "What was that all about with the guy in the corner?"

"He had his home broken into," Cove answered, and paused, looking into her eyes. "Just between you and me."

"Charley," Julie injected. "I don't gab about business; yours or mine. Anything you tell me about a creep you're chasing goes nowhere, and while I'm at it, the same goes for you on stories I'm working on."

"I'm sorry, it's just..." Charley said, looking down and then back up. "I matched the shell casing we found the other night to a casing that this guy had fired from his rifle before his house got broken into. It happened in November; a bunch of guns were taken. The shooter is using his stolen rifle."

Julie looked at Cove and narrowed her eyes. "When did you find that out? What else are you holding back, Mr. Warden? If you're going to be my secret source, you're going to have to be more forthcoming than this," she said turning her smile back on.

The bartender set a bottle of Corona, a blue can of Keystone, and an empty glass on the table. Cove pushed the lime down into his beer and took a swallow.

Julie popped the Keystone open, tilted the glass and poured the beer into it. "Don't say it, Charley," she said with her green eyes smiling at him. "I'm not a poacher just cause I like this stuff, most beer's too bitter."

Cove raised his beer and took a sip through upturned lips.

"So," Julie said, "Tell me how you figured out this creep's first name?"

"I gave somebody in the Pahsimeroi the vehicle description and asked whether he recognized it—it was obvious he did, but it was like pulling teeth. Motor

Vehicles in Boise is running the information through their database. I have to believe they'll hit on him, and then I'll have his full name and last known address. There can't be more than a couple of Leonards in these two backwood counties driving silver Dodges. I might have to get a driver's license photo of everybody and show them to my source, or maybe I'll do a drive-by in my personal truck and get a look at the rigs. See if I can find one with a rollbar and spotlights."

"And then you'll go arrest him?"

"No, I don't have enough yet. I need his rifle; a confession would be apple pie. I'd like to get a warrant to search his place and truck."

"Anyway," Cove said. "It sounds like he drove by your house this evening. Right about five."

Julie looked at Cove and put her glass down. "Serious? My house?"

"Yeah," Cove nodded. "It sounds like it was his truck, anyway. He came out of that little alley by the post office, about hit some lady, and then turned down Third. Mendiola called me up and we chased around town looking for the guy, but never found him."

Julie rolled her eyes. "No way!"

The bartender set another round on their table, and nodded over at Petersham. "Compliments of Ralph," she said, and left for the jukebox.

Cove looked over and nodded at him.

From the jukebox, Merle Haggard began singing, "Twinkle twinkle lucky star, can you send me luck where you are? Can you make a rainbow shine that far? Twinkle twinkle lucky star..."

The two sat wordlessly, sipping their beers and listening to the old country singer croon his words. Finally Julie looked at Cove with downturned lips. "I asked my editor about you, Charley; she told me what happened to your friend."

Cove rotated his Corona, rubbed the condensation off the clear glass with his thumb and looked into the golden liquid. Lines of tiny star like bubbles were forming and moving up through the brew, becoming larger as they rose. Leaning the bottle away from him, he watched them ascend, listened to the jukebox, and finally took a swallow.

# *Chapter 9*

George Nayman had a roll of black electrician's tape and was covering the tiny glowing lights on the truck's dashboard.

The top of Nayman's head looked as if it had been buffed and waxed; a side-strip of short-gray bristles gave off his age. He'd been around for sixty years and had worn a gun belt for the last half. A wooly mustache mimicked the stubble on the sides of his head. He was a slender six-foot, but was starting to show a paunch.

Rookie game warden Dax Sparks was sitting to Nayman's right and held a pair of night vision goggles to his eyes, staring out through the truck's windshield. Sparks was a blond baby-faced twenty-four-year old officer who looked as though he was eighteen. Behind his back, he was called "the kid" or "junior" by the other wardens. He was five-foot nine inches and built like a boxer. Physically, the two wardens were as similar as chalk and cheese.

"I call this Cove's Hill," Nayman said. "It's the best spot in the lower end of the Pahsimeroi to watch for shiners." Nayman ripped a piece of black tape off the roll and stuck it on a green light on the two-way radio. He looked around the truck's interior and was satisfied with his handiwork. "Dark as a dungeon in here now."

The rig was now blacked out in classic game warden shiner-hunting mode. The only light in the Pahsimeroi was now coming from outside the vehicle and most of it starlight. The two sat quietly while their eyes adjusted and a far off yard light began to appear in the darkness. Their truck was parked on a hill on the west side. With the night vision goggles, they could see beyond the nearby Custer County road and across the county line marked by the Pahsimeroi River. Beyond that they could see the Lemhi County Road, the two roads paralleled the river up the valley.

The gray haired warden took a deep breath and let it out. "I don't know how many nights Charley's spent up here since Liz was killed, but I know it's been a lot more than he's showing on his time sheet, 'cause truck mileage don't fib." Nayman glanced at the rookie. "Whenever you can, try to put your personal life ahead of this job, 'cause it'll do its damnedest to chew into it. How my wife's put up with it, I'll never know." George picked up a set of 10x50 binoculars from the dash and glassed out into the blackness, looking for truck lights. "Trying to get Charley to take time off is like trying to get a duck to quit quacking."

Sparks continued to study the valley through the NVGs and finally replied, "Were they living together?"

"I dunno about that, but they were as tight as two coats of paint," Nayman answered. "I suspect they'd got hitched."

The weighty conversation ceased. Nayman turned on the FM radio. Its display night blinded them and he covered it with two strips of tape. Adjusting the dial, he found a basketball game, but kept the volume down. "You a sports fan, Dax?" Nayman asked.

"Not really," the rookie replied, "but it's not bothering me," Sparks lied. He actually hated basketball and couldn't understand why anybody would listen to two unrecognized teams playing at some far off venue, but he was the low man on the totem and knew when to keep his lips tight.

Forty minutes into the surveillance, Sparks heard Nayman's first growl-like snore. He could see the old warden had made a pillow out of an extra coat and had his head leaning on the window with his mouth open. Sparks reached over and slowly turned the radio's knob until he found what he was searching for—George Noory's talk show about the paranormal. Sparks had hit the jackpot; Noory's subject was cattle mutilations. The rookie was skeptical, but since he had no personal knowledge about the mutilation rumors, he found the discussion riveting. And it was much easier to listen to than an obscure basketball game.

Every few minutes the rookie would turn the NVGs on and check the valley. Without the goggles he could see the far off yard lights marking three scattered ranches perched in the blackness. And that was it. With the goggles up to his face, there wasn't anything he couldn't see. The optics didn't magnify, but the view was eerily astounding, especially the stars. The cloud cover had cleared, revealing a sight that would have made any astronomer envious. With the goggles, it was unfathomable how many stars were framed between the two mountain ranges.

From the truck's speakers, the talk show host was interviewing a Montana sheriff who claimed he'd dealt with twenty-one mutilations in six years. The rookie wasn't entirely swallowing the lawman's story, but he found it more entertaining than basketball. Besides, maybe he and the old warden would catch a mutilator and solve the mystery. Sparks was examining the side canyons and ridges of the Lemhi Range across the valley when the NVGs caught a green glow brightening up the view to the left. Turning, he picked up the headlights of a vehicle moving along the far side of the valley and he quit breathing. *Damn!* Sparks thought, *my first shiner!* He cracked his window and turned the engine off.

Nayman was still snoring away. The moving headlights were a good ten miles away and Sparks decided to make sure it was something worth waking the old guy up for. He planned on letting it get past the first ranch light, but before the rig got that far, it stopped. "George, we've got a rig coming up the Lemhi road. I think it just stopped," he said, and glanced at his watch. "It's two-seventeen."

Nayman stopped snoring and sat up. He took the binoculars off the dash, brought them up to his eyes, and caught the vehicle lights with the glasses. "Probably just a drunk cowboy coming back from the bars," he said, and rolled his window down. "Even from this far in this cold air, I think we could hear a rifle shot." Both of their heads were focused on the rig. Nayman was watching through the big binoculars and Sparks with the NVGs. Neither warden spoke. After a few minutes, the lights resumed their movement up the valley. The two watched intently. "Was he weaving like this when you first saw him?" Nayman asked.

Sparks watched for a moment and replied. "No, but he sure is now."

Two additional lights came on from high on the vehicle. "Son of a bitch," Nayman said in a lowered voice. "It's Cove's shooter, sure as shit." he paused, "and Charley's gonna be pissed if I don't call him out."

The two wardens sat and watched with the cold air lapping in from the open window, along with the occasional distant bark and yapping of two coyotes. "Let's just sit up here for a while and give him some rope," Nayman said. "Maybe he'll cross over at the junction."

After twenty minutes of eyestrain, the vehicle had not stopped and it had passed the Furey Lane junction. "The prick's going to stay on the other side, at least for now," Nayman said softly. "Hand me the NVGs. Let's go set up at the junction; otherwise we're gonna lose him behind those hills."

Nayman took the goggles. He snapped them onto the device's head harness and put the unit on top of his head. He tightened the tension knob and pulled on the NVGs, checking to see if they were secured. Starting up the engine, the radio came back on with a young female voice hawking a miracle diet-pill. Sparks reached over and turned it off.

Nayman smiled and glanced towards the rookie. "Tired of cattle mutilations, Dax?"

"I was just listening," Sparks replied. "Have you had any mutilations around here?"

"Sure," Nayman said smiling. "I'll tell you about 'em sometime, right after I give you the secret handshake."

Nayman drove off the hill wearing the NVGs. The sagebrush made a screeching noise on the truck's undercarriage, and they bounced over a badger hole. The rookie buckled his seatbelt. He couldn't see anything but stars. Widening his eyes, he attempted to discern where they were headed. Sensing Sparks' discomfort, Nayman turned toward him with a smile turned green by the NVGs. "You're just gonna have to trust me."

Sparks felt the truck rise onto the county road and turn right onto its surface. For a second, he felt better–until the patrol truck sped up. Sparks estimated their rig was doing forty, but it was just a guess–he couldn't see the road or the brush flying by.

Reaching over, Nayman flipped a dashboard toggle switch that cut power to the truck's brake lights. "Dax, make damn sure you remind me to turn the cutouts back on." He began slowing down at the unseen junction. "Let's just sit here for a while and see whether he crosses over."

Nayman stopped the vehicle, rolled his window halfway down and turned the engine off. "Now, here's the deal on working shiners." Nayman looked towards Sparks. "They're almost always drinking, they're usually young and full of shit-fire, so they can get mouthy and bold if you let 'em. You gotta make the contact in a manner where they know you're not gonna put up with any bullshit. Your voice's gotta set the tone. If we light this shithead up, we'll treat it as a high-risk stop. I'll do the talking. You get the AR15 outa the rack, chamber a round and cover us from the crook of your door. It's a damn good way to get a complaint letter, but I'd rather deal with that than a funeral."

"What's the judge going to do with this guy?" Sparks asked.

"Well, that's part of the deal here. If we pulled him over right now, and he's got a loaded rifle on his seat–and I'm sure he does–we can pinch him for hunting with artificial light 'cause of his overheads and the way he's weaving around, but it's only a hundred and fifty-dollar fine. Cove's got five deer and a cow he thinks this guy's killed. He and I both know there has to be at least twice that many–who-knows how many he's killed? People just haven't found 'em or called. We'll seize his rifle and any ammo he's got. Hopefully, the lab can match the brass Charley's got to his rifle, which would tie two deer to this guy, that'd bring it up another three-hundred bucks."

"That's it?" Sparks asked. "No jail?"

"He'd probably get a couple three days on the deer, and that's great, since jail's the great equalizer when it comes to justice, but the biggie is this: Charley pulled a bullet out of the cow and he thinks this guy shot it. Rustling a cow in Idaho's a big deal, unlike shootin' the King's deer, cattle killing's a felony," Nayman explained while staring through the NVGs. "If the lab can match the bullet to this rifle–that we ain't seized yet–even Charley's prosecutor might get off his ass and do his job. Ranchers pay a lot of taxes. They have influence in these counties."

"We're about ready to lose this guy behind some hills," Nayman said. "I think the best thing is to just sit here and see what happens. He's either gonna come back down the same road, or he'll cross over up above and come down our road. If he does, we'll figure it out with the goggles and move to the other side. Either way, I'd like to do the stop in Lemhi County and use our prosecutor. Custer County's prosecutor ain't worth much."

\*\*\*\*\*

With one hand holding a Keystone, he rolled the truck's wheel back and forth, easing from one side of the road to the other, staring at the sagebrush illuminated by his headlights. Nothing but twinkling crystals of snow sparkled back at him. Finally, he'd had enough not finding any deer. The night was driving him crazy. He stopped in the middle of the road, turned off his lights and killed the engine. He pushed his window's switch and rolled it all the way down, finished the beer, and chucked the can out the window. Canting his head outside, he listened. Sticking his hand under his black leather vest, he felt the handle of his revolver parked in its cross-draw holster, just forward of his left hip. The only thing he could smell was the oily odor of the sage. After a bit, he could finally see a few yards into the brush. He didn't like being in the darkness—it reminded him of those long nights waiting for his old man to come home from the bars—but he knew there was safety in its blackness. Reaching down to the shifter boot, he stuck his hand under it, removed his Crown Royal bag and set it on his lap. He needed his edge.

\*\*\*\*\*

"That's curious," Nayman said. "He just shut his lights off. You can't see it without these NVGs." He paused, staring with the goggles. "I could see the green glow

coming from beyond the hill, but not now. He's shut
down."

Sparks pulled his cell phone out and checked the
display. "I've got coverage if you think we should get
Charley out here."

Nayman started to take the goggles off, but stopped
and continued staring where their target had disappeared.
"I know what you're thinking, and agree. If Charley didn't
have so damn much comp-time built up, I'd have him over
on the other side of the valley blacked out and paralleling
this prick, but I told him I wasn't calling him out. It is
what it is."

*****

Leo flicked on his flashlight and laid it besides his rifle.
He fished out the meth and pipe out of the Crown bag.
Holding the bagged crystals over the light, he grasped two
rocks with trembling fingers, and as carefully as he could,
dropped them into the pipe's vent hole. Placing the Ziploc
back into the Crown bag, he found his lighter and snapped
it on. He held the pipe up and looked into the bowl. His
hands were shaking so bad he wasn't able to focus, and he
let the flame die. *I need to eat something.*

A coyote howled from the darkness, and Leo listened,
wondering if its mate would answer. There was no reply,
but he sat listening. Finally, he lit the Bic and held the
glass bowl over the flame as steadily as he could, staring
into the hazing chamber. When the vapors got too intense
for his finger covering the vent hole, he brought the stem
to his lips and inhaled, rotating the bowl slowly over the

flame and sucking in the foggy juice. Finally, he turned the lighter off and sat back in the seat, letting his head roll, keeping the vapors in. His only thought rolling through his brain: *Un-fucking believable.* After he could hold it no more, he exhaled and felt the worms begin their crawl.

\*\*\*\*\*

"You think he's got a deer down or something?" The rookie asked.

"No, we woulda heard a shot," Nayman answered. "I don't know what the shit he's up to." He shook his head. "This guy's a loner. Maybe he's got a date with a magazine or hell, maybe he's out mutilating a cow in the sagebrush," Nayman turned his head towards Sparks and chuckled. "The best thing we can do is have patience. More times than naught, I've screwed up working shiners by getting too eager. Patience can be your best friend. Let's just give him some time."

The two continued staring into the night.

\*\*\*\*\*

Leo's neurons were jumping across his brain's synapses, firing like spark plugs in a goosed-up V8 engine. Rolling his head out the window, he sniffed, tasting the dead air. At first he thought it was the parasites screwing into his brain, so he took another sample of the night. His eyes flared. *The fucker's are here. Goddamn!* His hand went to the revolver and squeezed, his fingers turning white. "You bastards wanna hear the lion roar?" he asked out loud. Letting go of the revolver, he reached down and started the engine. He flipped on both sets of lights and turned around, feeling the tooth swing on his neck like a pendulum.

*****

"He's turned the lights back on," Nayman declared. "Can you see the glow yet, Dax?"

"No, nothing." Sparks replied.

After a few minutes of staring through the goggles, Nayman spoke. "If we were to drive up there and start following him, we might be screwed into a head-on stop if he turns around. Nothing worse than a headlight-to-headlight stop. You can't see nothing," Nayman said, and paused, watching the green glow coming from behind the hill. "He mighta turned around; it's getting brighter."

Suddenly, all four lights appeared on the other side of the valley, clearly moving faster than when he'd gone up. Sparks was staring through the binoculars. "I don't think he's weaving anymore."

"Son of a bitch," Nayman said. "If we'd been jabbering on the radio I'd say he was listening to a scanner. Let's let him get a ways below us. We'll pull in behind him blacked out and try to figure what he's up to. I sure as shit don't think he's shot anything."

When the vehicle was even with them across the valley, Nayman fired up the truck's engine, rolled up his window, and sped across Furey Lane, trying to get over to the Lemhi road without wrecking in the dark.

"I think next time we should try and find two sets of NVGs," Sparks said, holding onto the handle above the truck's door.

*****

After five miles, Leo still had not seen anything on his backtrack. No new vehicle tracks and no lights, but he trusted his wired senses. "Ya ain't fooling me, asshole," he said to himself. His mouth had the hard-plastic acid taste from the meth. He grabbed another Keystone, popped it open and took a large mouthful, swished it around and spat it out the widow. Slowing down, he chugged down three mouthfuls and glanced behind him.

At the Morse Creek sign, he stopped and put the rifle into the soft case. He got out, slid it into the dry culvert and covered it with sagebrush. Undoing his fly, he took a long pee and stared up into the stars. When he was done, he buttoned up his pants and headed to the truck. Reaching the door, he froze.

*****

"He's stopping," Nayman said, letting off on the accelerator. "Brake lights are on."

"Wonder if he's gonna shoot?" Sparks said, staring at the taillights a half-mile ahead and rolling down his window.

"We'll creep up a bit," Nayman said, "but stick your head out and listen."

\*\*\*\*\*

Flaring his nostrils, he inhaled and smelled nothing but the sage. He stuck his finger in his mouth and held it up. *The wind's coming up from below.* Reaching for the door handle, Leo stopped and cocked his head—and heard the engine. *Goddamn!*

\*\*\*\*\*

"He's moving again," Nayman said, leaning his boot into the accelerator. "I never saw any muzzle flash."

Sparks pulled his head in and rolled the window back up.

"Shit!" Nayman exclaimed. "He's hauling ass. I think he's running."

"No way he saw us," Sparks said, shaking his head.

They continued driving blacked out, with Nayman wearing the night vision goggles, but they could see the taillights pulling ahead. "He's gaining on us," Sparks said.

"We're going to have to try and light him up," Nayman said. "We can't drive fast enough wearing these goggles," Nayman hit the brakes and ripped the goggles off his head. He flicked the rig's lights on and floored the truck. With the headlights brightening but shortening their view, the two wardens lost sight of the two tiny red taillights they were chasing.

"I'll leave the blue emergency lights off until we get on him. He might think we're just a pissed-off rancher."

"Here's where he stopped—he got out." Sparks said, spotting the footprints.

"We'll come back later, lets see if we can catch him."

\*\*\*\*\*

Leo saw the headlights reflected in his rearview mirror. Holding his breath, he reached down and felt his .357. Finally he exhaled and accelerated, and leaning out his window and hollering, "C'mon motherfuckers, Uncle Leo'll feed ya some shit-burnin' lead."

\*\*\*\*\*

Every few minutes, Nayman would let off on the gas and kill the lights just long enough to confirm the taillights were still up ahead. "Keep an eye out for tire tracks heading off into the sage," Nayman instructed the rookie. "He might turn off his lights and try to ditch us. I'm not gonna push this chase with this snow on the road. Running in four-wheel at this speed's hard on the drive train, and no shiner's worth wrecking over." Nayman glanced at the rookie. "Don't forget that."

\*\*\*\*\*

Leo saw the red glow of the stop sign at the T-intersection and slowed, but blew on through, accelerating onto the semi-slick pavement, causing the vehicle's bed to skid to the right. The rear of his truck sideswiped a highway sign. Leo frantically spun the wheel back towards the river but he managed to get the rig under control. "Goddamn! Come on up to my trailer and I'll show you how to party!"

***** 

When Nayman got to the junction, he slowed to a crawl. He looked both ways and saw the skid marks heading to the left. He accelerated, following them towards Challis. "Did ya see that sign he 'bout took out?"

"Yeah, looks like he almost went in the river."

"Grab the mic," Nayman said. "See if Custer County's got a deputy on duty who can sit on the highway."

***** 

Leo turned off the highway onto the road that led to his trailer and turned off his headlights. He wheeled in behind his singlewide, ran inside and turned on the TV. He flipped on the kitchen and front porch lights, grabbed a box of revolver cartridges from the top of the refrigerator and dumped them in his coat pocket. Exiting through the rear door, he pulled a fresh Keystone out of the truck and took a deep breath. He snapped the beer open and took a drink while walking over to the corner of the trailer. Taking a second swallow, he peered around the dark edge of the building and spoke into the night. "Let's git it done," he said, staring at the road. He pulled the revolver out of its holster, standing in the cold darkness, watching and waiting.

# *Chapter 10*

Charley Cove's beating heart felt like the rumble of distant thunder. He was pissed. He sat on the edge of his bed in the morning's twilight, wearing a T-shirt and boxer shorts. He held the phone to his ear while massaging his forehead. Glancing at the alarm clock, he saw that it was three minutes past seven.

"Son of a bitch, George!" Cove barked. "Two goddamned rigs and we woulda boxed him in."

Nayman ignored the ass chewing. "There's silver paint on the sign post he clipped. We backtracked up the Lemhi side, found a beer can where he turned around and stopped to take a pee at Morse Creek."

"What kind of beer?" Cove asked, knowing the answer, but was focused on the image of the yellow snow he'd seen the night before.

"Keystone," Nayman answered.

"What'd he do at Morse Creek besides pee?" Cove asked.

"Nothing," Nayman said. "Just walked off the road and peed."

*Why's he walking off the road in the middle of the night to pee?* Cove wondered. "And you chased him all the way into town?"

"More or less. We never saw him after we turned onto the highway," Nayman said. "When we hit Challis, we turned around and backtracked. Went all the way back up to where he'd turned around. I dunno where we lost him."

"You sure he headed this way and not towards Salmon?" Cove asked.

"Shit, Charley," Nayman said. "Now, I know what it feels like when you've got a guy in the box. He turned left and so did we. Never saw him after that."

"This is three nights in a row," Cove said. "We both need to be out there tonight. You guys can't do this with one rig."

"Look, Charley," Nayman said. "I told Boise you're down to forty hours a week, so forget it. You can chase leads on this thing during the day, and Dax and I'll work the night patrol. Quit your whining. Eight hours a day max, and I'd prefer six. The season's closed on this discussion."

"How about you and the kid taking two rigs up there?" Cove asked.

"We can't do that until he's through his training, you know that. As I said, the season's closed on the subject."

Cove laid the phone back on the nightstand and turned to Annie. She was lying on her dog-bed, thumping her tail and staring back with her ears cocked. "Lets run to town and get some breakfast." He picked up the cell phone, punched in Mendiola's speed dial number and offered to buy him breakfast.

When he pulled into the restaurant's parking lot, the deputy's SUV was parked in front. Cove walked in and found him near the far wall of the room, sitting in a booth facing the door and sipping coffee. As Cove started to sit down, Mendiola grinned at him. "Well?"

"Shut up, Fred," Cove chided. "Don't even start. She's got a boyfriend. Nothing's going on. She's a friend. We had a beer together and that's it."

Mendiola maintained his grin, but didn't take it any farther. "Who was your boss chasing last night? Sarah told me he was asking for a deputy. Doesn't he understand we don't have the manpower to cover a graveyard shift right now?"

"He knows. He was chasing my shooter in the Pahsimeroi. The guy got away." Cove felt hot and slid out of his uniform coat.

"That's what I figured—he told dispatch not to call you out," Mendiola said. "The guy shoot anything?"

"Nayman doesn't think so. Sounds like he got hinked up and rabbited."

"Speaking of which," Mendiola said, turning his smile back on, "I was going to call you last night, but figured you were busy."

Cove frowned, but didn't respond to the bait.

"I got a call from a detective with Pocatello PD," Mendiola explained. "It was after you and I chased our tails around looking for the Dodge. Anyway, they had a guy sell a rifle and two shotguns at a pawnshop. The rifle's Petersham's."

Cove turned his head and stared at Mendiola. "Serious? His .300 WSM?"

"That was my first thought, too," Mendiola said. "But no, it's his .30-'06."

"They get a name?" Cove asked.

"Yeah, Gene Holihan. Ring a bell?" Mendiola asked, with a half smile.

Cove frowned and lowered his eyebrows. "I thought he was dead."

"Yeah, a hundred percent DOA," Mendiola declared. "Gabbro said he was half-in and half-out of the windshield."

The waitress set a mug down on the table and topped it with black coffee. "Morning, Charley, didn't see you sneak in."

"That's the way I am until I get my coffee."

Cove's cell rang. He looked at it and saw it was from dispatch. He looked up at the waitress. "Huevos rancheros, over easy, and whole-wheat toast, please." He flipped the phone open and brought it to his good ear.

"Morning, Sarah, what's up?"

"I just got a call from a guy that wants to tell you about a truck he saw."

"What truck?" Cove said, squinting his eyes.

"He didn't say. Left his name and number."

Cove pulled a small notebook from his shirt pocket and a pen. "Who was it?"

"Lance Ludkin. Said he talked to you the other morning. His cell's 208-303-0725."

"Thanks. Maybe I'll have a plate for you to run in a bit." Cove closed the phone and looked at Mendiola. "The plow driver who saw the Dodge the other morning's got something for me. Cross your fingers." Cove punched the phone number in. On the third ring, the guy answered.

"Lance, Charley Cove."

"I saw that Dodge again last night. You still looking for it?"

"Sure am. Where'd you see it?" Cove asked.

"On the highway the other side of the Pahsimeroi. We were headed to Challis for dinner last night."

"North or south of the Pahsimeroi?" Cove asked.

"Your side,–we'd passed Morgan Creek. Let me think." There was a pause. Cove looked at Mendiola and nodded. "I think we'd gone by Ruby Creek."

"What time was it?" Cove asked.

"About five thirty, I think, 'cause we were running late. It was just getting dark."

"You see the plate?" Cove asked.

"He had his headlights on and I didn't realize it was him until he'd passed us, but it was him. Same roll bar and overhead lights."

"When you say he passed you, which way was he headed?" Cove asked.

"Downriver towards Salmon. We were headed to Challis and he was headed the other way."

Cove rubbed his bad ear. "I really appreciate the call. Holler if you see him again. You get stuck some night in the Pahsimeroi, give me a buzz." He closed the phone, put it in his coat pocket and looked at Mendiola. "Saw him somewhere this side of Ruby Creek. He was headed towards Salmon. Didn't get a plate. We must have just missed him in town last night. Said it was about five-thirty."

"I'll bet he was driving around drunk," Mendiola said, nodding his head. "It woulda been a fruitful stop."

Cove sipped his coffee, looked into the dark liquid and set the mug down. He took a cream container from a bowl and opened it. He dumped it into the coffee and stirred it with a spoon. "He was in town sometime after five last night, almost got in a wreck and then headed north on the highway. Then George and the kid see him in the Pahsimeroi after two last night."

"Busy boy," Mendiola said. "Maybe he's living in Salmon?"

Cove shook his head. "No, George said he was headed back this way. Besides, if that's the case, he drove sixty miles to Challis, turned around and drove back. Woulda got there around six-thirty, then headed towards the Pahsimeroi after midnight. That's a lotta energy for anybody, and besides, they always rabbit for their den. They must think it's like home base in baseball."

Mendiola nodded. "Maybe he *is* a tweaker. Those guys think coffee's for sissies." The deputy took another sip. "Probably is."

Cove put his notebook back in his shirt pocket. "You didn't finish telling me about the dead guy selling stolen guns."

"Oh, yeah, anyway the pawnbroker wanted to see some ID. It's some deal they have with pawn shops, so the guy rolls out Gene Holihan's driver's license, and the pawnbroker Xeroxed the damn thing. They're gonna fax it up."

Cove squinted his eyes, processing what he'd just absorbed. "Weird deal. My source that gave up his first name said he looked like a zombie or witch and now he shows up as a dead guy from Mackay." Cove shook his head and took another sip "It's too early in the morning for something like this."

"I was awake thinking about it half the night." Mendiola said. "Called Sarah before you called and she pulled Holihan's accident report. No wallet's listed in the personal effects."

"So somebody snatched it?" Cove asked.

"That's my guess," Mendiola said. "There woulda been a bunch of people there. Fire for the extraction, the EMTs of course, and the coroner, plus my two guys. He coulda lost it before the wreck, too."

"You'd think the wallet woulda been in his pocket or at least in the cab if his butt didn't make it through the windshield," Cove said.

"I've vetted all the EMTs and Fire guys, I can't think of any of 'em I don't trust," Mendiola said. "I need to find out who towed the wreck in."

The waitress appeared with two plates, set them down and grinned at Cove. "I heard you were out late last night, Charley."

"No, Sally, I wasn't," Cove said. "I was home before ten. That ain't late."

Her eyes were twinkling. "Whatever," she said, and walked off.

Before Mendiola could add anything to her banter, Cove spoke. "What'd the guy look like?"

"I don't know yet," Mendiola said. "They're gonna do a second interview and write it up."

"Any video?" Cove asked.

Mendiola shook his head. "I asked."

The two worked on their meals.

"You gonna sit on your hill tonight?" Mendiola inquired.

"No, I'll be sitting on my butt. I made the mistake of being honest on my time sheet and ended up way over my comp-time limit. Boise jumped George on it and he got his ass chewed cause of me. I'm not his golden boy right now," Cove said, and sipped his coffee. "He and the rookie are going to keep working it, though, but I'm concerned they hinked him up this morning. If he's got half a brain he'll go shine somewhere else and we'll be back to square one."

"George's got a trainee, eh?" Mendiola asked.

"Yeah, Dax Sparks, he's been through the academy. He's green as grass but eager. Likable kid." Cove said.

The bell on the restaurant door jangled and Cove glanced over at an old couple walking in. He turned back to Mendiola. "Any guess when the lab'll get back to you on the print?" Cove asked.

"They got a hit yesterday," Mendiola said from behind his coffee mug.

"You're shittin' me!" Cove said in a half-whisper and leaned in towards the deputy.

Mendiola lowered his coffee mug and smiled. "Yeah, I'm screwing with you. I wouldn't expect anything for a few days. The guy said he's working a murder-suicide with lots of evidence."

Cove's cell rang. He looked at the display and saw it was Julie. He pushed a button on the side, silencing it. "I gotta get moving, Nayman said our guy took a sign out last night this side of the Pahsimeroi and left some paint on it. I want to go take a look at it." Cove stood up and finished his coffee. "You get the tip and I'll get your breakfast."

Cove stopped before pulling onto Main and returned Julie's call.

"Good morning, Mr. Warden!" she said. "You know anything about electricity?"

Cove squinted his eyes down. "Some, what's going on?"

"My range isn't working."

"I'd guess it's a breaker," Cove responded. "I'm just down the block. If you're home, I can take a quick look at it."

"If you don't mind, Charley. I'd really appreciate it. I couldn't make my coffee this morning."

Cove pulled in behind Julie's Subaru and she met him at the door wearing blue jeans, hiking boots, a white turtleneck and a smile. "Thanks for coming. I didn't know who to call."

The comment made Cove wonder why she hadn't called her boyfriend, but wasn't about to ask.

The house was a small, older home, built during one of the town's mining booms. The interior had the same scent Cove had first caught in his truck. It had a small living room and an adjoining combination dining area and kitchen. Several watercolors hung on the walls. A dark leather couch faced an entertainment center full of books, a television and a stereo. A cherry wood coffee table sat in front of the couch. The place was neat and looked homey.

"Where's your breaker box?" Cove asked.

"I should have checked; it's back here in the laundry room. Don't look at my mess, please."

Cove followed her through the kitchen and into a small but organized utility room. The breaker box was on the wall and Cove found a tripped double-breaker. He flipped it on, flipped it off, and back on, confirming to himself that it had indeed tripped.

"There you go," Cove said. "That should do it, but let's turn the range back on and make sure it doesn't pop again."

"I'll put some water on," Julie said, "as long as you've got a few minutes for coffee?"

Cove agreed. He sat down and began filling her in on the efforts of Nayman and Sparks. He was beyond the guilt of revealing investigative details and trusted she wasn't talking about the case around town.

Julie dumped coffee beans into a grinder for a few seconds and poured them into a French press. The room was hit with the chocolate-like aroma of fresh coffee. "Hasn't this creep got anything better to do?" Julie asked. "There's no way he's doing this every night after work; he needs to get a life."

Cove thought about her conclusion. "I know. He *has* to be sleeping during the day. I got a call from the snowplow driver this morning, too. He saw the guy on the highway last night. Fred and I must have just missed him."

The teapot came to a boil. Julie dumped the hot liquid into the press, waited a bit, pushed the plunger down and poured two cups of dark coffee. "Cream or sugar?" she asked, and handed him a cup.

"Black, thanks."

Taking a sip of coffee, Cove's attention was caught by a photograph attached to the refrigerator of a guy about his age, smiling back and wearing a coat and tie.

Julie caught his stare. "That's my brother, Benjamin."

"Where's he live? Cove asked.

"Oshkosh. He's a prosecutor back there," she said smiling.

Cove's head dipped. "Well, I guess you caught me with my boot in my mouth the other night when I was bad mouthing prosecutors."

"You were on a roll, so I decided to keep quiet," Julie said. "I called him and told him about our night up the Pahsimeroi, by the way. We're pretty close. I hope that's okay." She sipped her coffee. "I figured it was since he doesn't live here. He tells me about his cases and I tell him about the stories I'm working on. He's told me about the ineptitude of a particular judge he has to work with. I didn't tell him of your dislike of our local prosecutor though. I knew that conversation was personal." she leaned in, "But I hope the rest was okay?"

Cove nodded. "I wish he'd move here and run against Pallid."

"Are you upset I told him about the dead deer?" she asked.

"No, I'm okay with it. I just don't want any details getting back to 'the creep,' as you call him."

The two finished their coffee and both felt the need to get moving. Cove stepped out on the front porch, reached down to his coat zipper and stopped dead. He stared at the footprint in the snow to the left of the porch—the track of a large cowboy boot. Cove's eye followed the prints along the edge of the house and past the garage where they disappeared around the corner. Turning around, Cove looked at where the tracks had come from. The person had angled in from the sidewalk to the other corner of the house, had walked to the first window and stopped. He shuffled around and then continued past the porch. Pulling a thin tape measure from his pocket, Cove stepped down to the closest track, kneeled in the snow, and measured its length. It was thirteen and a half inches long. "Son of a bitch," Cove whispered.

"What's going on?" Julie asked, stepping out the door.

"Any idea who's tracks these are?" Cove asked, looking up at her.

Julie stepped down and eyed the footprints. She swiveled around looking where they'd come from and turned back to Charley, frowning. "Meter reader?" Julie said, questioning herself.

"That's a good theory," Cove said, and stood up, feeling his stubble. "I'm not sure we even have meter readers anymore." Stretching the tape between two sets of imprints, heel to heel, he measured the stride and felt his veins constricting. "Let's follow them around the corner and see what he was doing."

The two followed tracks to the side of the house where the electric service meter was attached. Whomever the tracks belonged to had shown no interest in it. The trail led into the small backyard that butted the alley. The so-called meter reader had stopped and stood facing the back window. Cove presumed it was Julie's bedroom.

She turned to him, frowning. "I've got a peeping tom?"

Catching her stare, he looked down and restudied the tracks, his eyes moving back and forth while he scratched the back of his head. He was wondering what he should tell her.

"Can you tell when they were made?" Julie asked.

"They're fresh," Cove said raising his eyebrows. "I'd guess sometime last night or early this morning." He thought about the timeline of the Nayman-Sparks patrol, pursuit and the sighting near Ruby Creek. "Maybe while we were drinking those two beers. Did you leave a light on while you were gone?"

"Yes, my bedroom light," Julie answered. "Right in there," she said, nodding at the window. "I always leave it on when I'm gone."

Cove wondered if the guy had been in her back yard when he'd dropped Julie off after the bar. He studied the rear porch. It had been swept clean after the last snowfall, but there was a spot of compressed snow on it. *Looks like he stepped up and checked the knob?* Cove glanced at Julie. "Do you keep your doors locked?"

"Yes. You don't think I'm in danger, do you?" Julie asked, catching his eye.

Cove looked at her, paused and glanced back down at the tracks. "No, this is Challis." Taking a look at the alley, he confirmed there were no fresh vehicle tracks since the last snow. The boot prints continued down the lane towards Main.

Looking back at Julie, he folded his arms across his chest and frowned, still looking into her green eyes. "Look, I don't mean to scare you," he said with his voice lowered. "But to be honest, I don't know what this guy's up to." Pausing for a moment he asked, "Do you keep a gun in the house?"

Julie's eyes widened, but her answer was interrupted by Cove's cell phone.

"Charley," Mendiola said. "Where ya at? I'm gonna interview the coroner about the Holihan thing and was hoping you'd tag along."

Cove looked at Julie. She was frowning at him with her arms folded. "I'm just up the block from your office. Give me five and I'll meet you at your office." Cove closed the cell phone, still thinking of the question he'd asked Julie.

"No, I don't have a gun," she said. "Benjamin loaned me one when I lived in Detroit," she rolled her eyes. "I didn't think I'd need one after I left the city."

"Did he teach you how to shoot?" Cove asked, turning his good ear towards her

"My dad did; he taught both of us."

Nodding, Cove said, "Let me loan you one. I can drop it off this evening, if it's okay."

"Gad! I hate this!" Julie barked. "But yeah, if you don't mind, it might make me feel safer."

Cove got in his truck, backed out of the driveway and studied the snow conditions along the street. Most of the packed snow on the pavement had melted. There was no chance of finding the tire tracks to confirm his theory, but if he was right, the guy had been in town at dusk, driven in front of Julie's house, then headed north on the highway and up the Pahsimeroi after 2:00 a.m., coming back into town during the wee hours to skulk around Julie's. He had to be living near town.

When Cove pulled in behind the courthouse, he could see Deputy Gabbro smoking a cigarette and leaning on the sheriff's building with one black cowboy boot braced against its metal-sheathed wall. Cove pulled in and parked. He got out, walked towards the door and nodded at the deputy. "Joey, how's your day going?"

Gabbro pulled his cell out and brought it to his ear. Cove had not heard the phone ring or vibrate and sensed he was using it as a prop.

Before he got through the door, Mendiola met him. "Your truck or mine?" the deputy asked.

"Let's take mine. Annie'll feel left out," Cove said.

Gabbro snapped his phone shut. "Where you guys headed?"

Mendiola looked at Cove, "See a man about a zombie."

When they were seated in Cove's truck, Mendiola told him the coroner was waiting for them at his house north of town. Cove wasn't gung-ho about telling Mendiola he'd just come from Julie's house, but knew this wasn't the time for secrets.

"After we had breakfast, Julie Lake needed some help with her breaker box. That's where I was when you called."

"Yeah?" Mendiola smiled.

"I found tracks around her house. They're from last night. Somebody was creeping around her neighborhood. I'm almost certain the tracks were left by my shooter."

Mendiola looked at him. "There's plenty of big cowboys around here. Hell, maybe it was me," he said, clapping his boots together on the floor of the truck.

Cove looked down at the deputy's big lace-up boots. "Yeah? So where were you last night?"

"Home with momma. She'd ring my neck if she caught me looking sideways at that little gal."

"And while you're confessing, tell me why you kneel down at a deer you've just shot?" Cove asked him.

"What the hell you talking about?"

Cove explained the knee prints and included the fact the shooter had shown no interest in the buck, and had failed to finish it off.

"You've seen this at all of these kill scenes?" Mendiola asked.

"No, there wasn't any snow at the first two. If there were knee prints in the dirt there, I missed 'em, but he knelt next to the last two does and not the buck. Go figure."

"Shit, I don't know," Mendiola said. "Maybe this asshole's religious and gets down and prays. "Hell, I'd have a come-to-Jesus moment, too, if I knew you were on my trail." The deputy scratched his chin for a moment. "Maybe he starts to gut 'em and gets scared off?"

Cove looked over at Mendiola and was quiet for a bit. "I don't think so," he said shaking his head. "At both scenes, the knee marks are back by the deer's belly, ninety degrees to the spine, he's facing the stomach. I've never seen anyone gut a deer from there. I've had this sense that if I could figure out why he's doing this, I'd get him."

Mendiola took a deep breath. "The first year I worked for the county we had a little baby killed by her mother with a perforated serving spoon. I'll never forget the autopsy photos of the kid's head. The examiner had peeled the skin back and there was a contusion that perfectly matched the spoon. It even showed the holes from the spoon. Her mother had smacked her to shut her up. I tried to understand why she did it. The memory of that little girl and those photos still bug me." Mendiola looked at over at the warden and lowered his voice. "Charley, sometimes we don't really need to know why they do this shit to bring 'em to justice. It can be a dark place to go that you really never come back from."

Mendiola pointed towards a house they were approaching. "This's Dave's."

Cove turned off the Challis Creek Road and entered the driveway of a single-level, cedar-sided home with an attached garage.

Coroner David Erdos met them on his front deck and Cove introduced himself. Dave was gray haired and wrinkled, with a pair of reading glasses set low on his nose. He wore blue jeans and a long-sleeved brown shirt. He'd run for coroner after the incumbent died and was elected without a challenge. The job was part time and paid a pittance.

"I heard you retired from LAPD," Cove said.

"That's right, moved up here to get outta the toilet."

Erdos led them to a heavy oak table with six matching tall-backed chairs. "Have a seat." A thick manila folder lay on the table. On its tab "G. Holihan" was written in capital letters.

Erdos looked at Mendiola and frowned. "You didn't tell me you were bringing the Game Department. Said you wanted information about the Holihan death. What's up?" Erdos pushed his glasses up his nose, glanced at Cove and then looked back at Mendiola.

"We're working on something that might be tied to Holihan's wreck—maybe his death, maybe both." Mendiola explained.

"Okay," Erdos said, his voice raising in pitch.

"You got called out on it, right?" Mendiola asked.

"Yeah, unattended death. That's what coroners do," Erdos said, and gave Cove a glance that could have been interpreted as a scowl.

"Who all was there?" Mendiola queried.

Erdos looked at Mendiola, nodded towards Cove, "Excuse me, but why's the game department working on a death investigation?" He turned to Cove, opened his palms, and added, "No offense, but death investigations are private matters, and I'm an elected official." Erdos laid his palm on the file, looked back at Mendiola and raised his eyebrows.

Cove twisted his head and spoke. "Dave," Cove waited until Erdos looked at him. "The reason I'm here is because Mendiola asked me to be here." Pausing, Cove leaned in. "Whenever the sheriff of this county asks for help, I give it, and as you know, for now, he's the sheriff." Cove's voice lowered. "Secondly, I'm working a wildlife crime that's linked to a theft he's working," Cove canted his head towards Mendiola. "Both violations seem to have ties to Gene Holihan, or his death. I'd think that someone with your background would be cooperative with law enforcement. So pardon me if I look confused."

Erdos opened his mouth, "Ah..."

"You and I have never met." Cove pressed on. "So if you've got an issue with me or my department, this would be a good time to lay it on the table."

Erdos paused and glanced down at the folder. "I got no problems with you or the Fish and Game."

Cove caught Erdos's eyes looking at the floor and wondered why the guy had to choose his words. *Is it my Indian blood?*

"It's just that I get asked all kinds of questions in this two-bit town. Somebody dies here, this goddamn place's got more rumors than sagebrush."

Erdos's eyes shifted back and Cove met his gaze, but didn't bother to respond. He believed he'd just been lied to, but had no theory as to why.

Mendiola jumped in. "Cove's here at my request. He's got full peace officer authority in this state. And I'd appreciate it if you'd cut the bullshit and help us with our investigation." Mendiola paused and leaned in, red faced, his voice coming from the bottom of his lungs. "Now, one more time, Dave. Who was at the wreck when you got there?"

Erdos face had darkened; he opened the file and looked down at it, shuffling through the papers. "I don't know if Gabbro included a list in his report," Erdos said in a softer voice. "I think he was first on the scene. I suppose the EMTs and the fire guys showed up next. I was the last one, of course. Not much reason for a coroner to run blue lights and siren. Deputy Jenks was there too."

"It was on Willow Creek Summit, right?" Cove asked.

"Yeah," Erdos replied. "A couple miles down. He musta been going pretty damn fast coming down the hill."

"How'd you confirm the identity?" Cove asked.

"Well," Erdos nodded. "when I got there, somebody—I think it was an EMT—told me it was Gene. I recall asking her how she knew, and she said it was his truck and it looked like him—she wasn't talking about his face, that's for damn sure. When we got the body back here, his wife wanted to see it. She was sobbing like a banshee; I ended up having her sister talk her out of it. Eventually, I got his dentist involved and we confirmed with his dental records. Even his teeth were messed up, but they were all there. Never really was a question about who he was."

Cove spoke. "Was there any way to compare his face to his driver's license?"

"No. There's no shittin' way. His face was smashed," Erdos answered and turned to Mendiola. "Is somebody saying it wasn't him? Are you questioning my ID?"

"No, nothing like that," Mendiola explained. "This has nothing to do with you. Did you try and compare his driver's license with his face?"

Erdos pushed his glasses back up his nose. "I don't think I ever saw his license." The coroner squinted his eyes, wrinkling his forehead. "In fact, I had to have dispatch run him to make sure he had one. Looking for ID is about the first thing I do when I move a body; I never did find his driver's license."

Mendiola waved his hand towards the file. "Let me take a peek at the photos."

Erdos opened up the file, removed several 8 X 10 color glossies and handed them across the table. Mendiola flipped through the shots, showing Holihan's bloody head on the truck's hood. He pulled one out of the pile that had been taken from the passenger's door, looking into the interior. Cove stood up and examined the photograph over Mendiola's shoulder. It was a mess. The laminated windshield had shattered, but held together. The exception was where Holihan's head and shoulders had burst through it. Most of his torso that wasn't on the vehicle's hood was wedged between the windshield and the steering wheel.

Mendiola pointed his finger at the victim's right rear jean pocket. A worn rectangular outline showed where he'd normally carried a wallet, but the pocket was tight to the pants and obviously empty.

Mendiola looked up at Erdos. "Who took these photographs?"

"I did," Erdos said, and looked at Cove. "What's Holihan's death got to do with your case?"

Cove ignored the question. "Did you open the passenger door to take this photo?"

"It was open when I got there," Erdos said.

"Did it come open during the crash or did someone open it?" Mendiola asked.

"It was open when I got there, and the fire guys didn't get the jaws out until I asked for help removing the body." Erdos scratched his head. "I don't think car doors open during crashes anymore. It might be somebody checking to see if he were still alive, but shit, he was deader than a wedge. Anybody could see that. His skin was the color of concrete."

Mendiola looked up from the photo. "Could the fire guys have used a bar to open the door, or was it still working?

"You'd have to ask somebody else—Gabbro or Jenks maybe."

Cove sat down and looked through the rest of the photos.

"Dave," Cove said looking up. "Did he have a wallet on him?"

"No, that's one thing I always try to find on a body to use for the ID. I'd remember if there'd been a wallet. Hell,

I remember thinking it was odd at the time. Everybody's got a wallet, except some of these kids now days." Erdos shuffled through the file.

"Could it have still been inside the vehicle when you cleared?" Cove asked.

Erdos looked up at Cove and shrugged his shoulders. "It'd rolled more than once after it hit the cow. The interior was a mishmash. If it'd been on the seat before the crash, it coulda been anywhere in there," he said while pulling a document from the pile. "Here's the inventory–yeah, no wallet. The side windows blew out too. It could still be laying up there under the snow, too. There was crap everywhere."

"You know who towed it?" Mendiola asked.

"No, the truck was still there when I left with the body. Ask Gabbro–he probably stayed until the wrecker hooked it up," Erdos replied.

Cove looked at Mendiola and shrugged. The deputy turned back to the coroner and said, "That's all I can think of right now, Dave. The reason we're quizzing you on this is Holihan's driver's license was recently used as an ID to sell some stuff taken in a burglary."

"Really?" Erdos asked, narrowing his eyes. "That's a queer deal. It can't be him." He shook his head. "Maybe he lost it before the wreck. You check his credit cards? Somebody using them, too?" Erdos asked.

"Shit," Mendiola said, rolling his eyes at the ceiling. "I guess I'm gonna have to talk to his widow."

# *Chapter 11*

*Right or left handed?* Charley Cove was studying two side-by-side photos on his computer. One was the nighttime photo of the first knee prints next to the doe he'd found with Julie. The second image was of the deer Barreras had found. Leaning in, Cove rested his chin on his knuckles and stared at the photographs. Both deer were lying with their heads on the left side of the screen, legs towards the camera. Both sets of knee prints were positioned facing the deer's abdomen, almost touching the inside of the rear leg. He moved the two images so they were above and below each other and adjusted the window size so the outline of both deer were the same size. The knee prints were identical in width and placement. Cove let his imagination conjure someone kneeling in this position, and again, he wondered which of his shooter's hands was dominant. He felt this was the key to understanding the knee prints. He mentally leaned forward and rested both hands on the deer. His left hand was on the deer's rib cage, and his right hand rested on the rump. Thinking about the fingerprint on the beer can, he recalled Mendiola saying he'd thought it was a left thumbprint. He thought about it and decided to eliminate that tidbit as a valid hand dominance indicator, since he'd assumed the guy was drinking and driving while holding the beer. Cove thought about how the truck had been angled for the shot and tried to consider what it would feel like to try and shoot a rifle left-handed from the driver's window, or even if a lefty could shoot from the driver's side. His thoughts were interrupted when his computer alerted him to a fresh email.

Clicking on his inbox, Cove saw what he had been waiting for. It was from Martha Alberts with the Department of Transportation. Cove was anticipating this was going to be the golden egg.

*Officer Cove: Sorry, but the database search came up empty. We have no records in either Lemhi or Custer Counties with the name of Leonard (or Leo) with a silver Dodge. Please let me know if I can be of any further assistance. -Martha*

Cove leaned back in his office chair, placed both hands on the back of his head, stared at the email and pursed his lips. He leaned forward, hit the reply button and wrote:

*Martha: Thanks for the run. How about we try two other searches—one with all silver Dodge pickups, Lemhi and Custer, and middle initial L. And the second run, just the silver Dodges in the two counties. As I stated on the phone, an Excel file would be great. Thanks, -Charley Cove.*

Cove hit the send button. He wondered how many vehicles he'd have on the list and picked up his cell phone. He knew Nayman was as reliable as birth and death but needed to confirm his boss was still planning a night patrol. What he didn't want to hear from him was the question of whether or not he'd managed to reduce his comp time.

"Hey, George," Cove said. "You and Dax still planning on working the Pahsimeroi tonight for me?"

"Yeah, I think we'll grab a bite and should be on the road around eleven," Nayman said. "We should be set up by midnight. When we were chasing him last night, he reminded me of those shitheads at Leadore last fall. We got two or three calls on them—all were after two in the morning. What we finally figured out was that they'd go have dinner, hit the bars until they closed and then head out. If they knocked anything down, they'd mark the spot with a beer can, gut it, and come back in the morning to load and tag it. Once we figured the pattern, we nailed 'em. You sure this guy's not a bar fly?"

"The deputies know I'm looking for the truck. Fred woulda called by now if they'd seen it."

Cove filled his boss in on the email he'd gotten from Motor Vehicles and his evolving theory that Leonard might be the shooter's middle name. He also confided he was feeling as if he were grasping at straws with the case.

With this, Nayman's voice switched over to a fatherly tone. "We'll catch a break and at least figure out who he is and where he lives. You're close, Charley." Nayman paused, and his inflection shifted back to being a supervisor. "This might be a good time for you to burn some comp time. Take a break. Go see your mom or something."

Cove was tempted to give his boss a sarcastic answer but promised he'd take some time off. He felt his stomach constrict from the lie. Hanging up, he turned back to his computer.

Looking at the two pictures, he closed them out and brought up the 'Pah-4' folder he'd created after the last doe killing. He opened up the audio recording he'd made of the Armando Barreras interview. Cove would not disclose the ranch hand's name, but had kept the recording in lieu of taking notes. Clicking on the software's play button, he sat back in his chair, folded his arms and closed his eyes. He replayed Armando's body language in his mind as he listened to the ranch hand's accent. The warden caught it the on the first playback: *"He had a big tooth on a necklace he kept touching."*

Cove flipped his phone open and scrolled through his incoming calls, found Barreras's number and pushed the send button.

He was surprised he was home. "It's Charley Cove, how's the deer meat, Armando?"

"Good. My family thanks you."

"You don't have company right now, do you?" Cove asked. "I want to ask you something about the guy with the Dodge."

"Just my wife and kids, but I told you everything I know about him, Charley."

"Yeah, I know and I appreciate it," Cove said. "But you mentioned he had a tooth hanging from his neck and he kept rubbing it. You recall which hand he did that with?"

There was a pause and after a moment Barreras answered. "I think it was his right. Yeah, it was his right hand."

"What kind of tooth is it?" Cove asked.

"I don't know," Barreras answered.

Cove thought about the zombie comment. "Animal or human?"

"It's big," Barreras explained. "Like a dog's tooth, but bigger. It ain't human, I know that."

Cove thanked him, reiterated his promise to keep his name out of it, hung up, and moved to his easy chair. He leaned back with his feet up and questioned the value of what he'd just learned; *the guy's right handed; that sure narrows it down.* The knowledge wasn't going to help him catch the guy, nor was it going to help prosecute him.

A bell-like chime stepped into Cove's consciousness, and he realized he'd fallen asleep. Recognizing the noise as an email alert, he lay there with his eyes closed, reclining on the chair, letting his thoughts come back. He thought about Liz, recalling the last day he spent on the range with her. Her shooting had been off and he sensed she was jerking the trigger. To demonstrate, he had her hold the gun on target while he stood behind her with his arms around her, his hands over hers. She aimed and he pulled the trigger. The first few shots had the proper effect, but their team effort rapidly degenerated into horseplay and a quick trip to the barn.

He thought about Julie and the boot tracks. *If this is my shooter, what in the hell is he doing peeping on her? Why'd he drive by her house? Why's he kneeling at the kills?*

He got out of the easy chair and looked at his computer. The note was from Julie Lake.

*Hey Mr. Warden: If you are serious about loaning me a gun, I'll take you up on your offer and feed you a bowl of stew tonight if you have time. Six-ish okay? -Julie*

The offer was too good to pass up and Cove sent her a quick reply. His thoughts shifted to the loaner gun. Opening up his gun safe, he pulled out the Glock 19 he had given Liz before she'd been called up. The firearm felt empty. Hitting the magazine release, he caught the mag with his left hand and locked the slide back. Liz had unloaded the weapon before she had put it away. Knowing she'd been the last person to touch the gun, Cove reconsidered loaning it to Julie and thought about his lightweight .38 but knew the little gun's heavy recoil was a poor choice for a small shooter. "Don't be jealous, she's just a friend," he whispered.

Cove loaded the Glock magazine with seventeen 9mm hollow points, inserted it into the weapon's grip with a click, and racked the slide, chambering the top round into its barrel.

His cell rang. The display showed it was Mendiola.

"Erdos sure had a corncob up his ass. What ya do to piss him off, Charley?" Mendiola asked. "Your grandmother scalp one of his ancestors?"

"That's the first time I've met him," Cove said. "Maybe he watched too many westerns when he was a kid."

"I met with Holihan's wife," Mendiola said. "Gawd, I hate dealing with widows. She was fine at first, but after a while she started sobbin'. If I had any brains, I woulda had Sarah handle it. I think women are better at those things."

Cove sat in his desk chair and ran his hand through his hair. "What'd she say about his credit cards?"

"I told her somebody'd used his driver's license. That's when she broke down wailing. She talks like he's still alive." Mendiola said. "Anyway, nobody's used 'em. I had to tell her we never found his wallet."

"And he didn't lose it before the wreck?" Cove asked.

"This was the first time she was aware it was missing," Mendiola explained. "I hope she doesn't want us to dig him up, make sure he's still in the casket."

"Whatcha you mean by *us*, Kemo Sabe?" Cove asked. "Digging up corpses ain't in my job description. Speaking of which, you offered to put the word out about Leo with your dope snitches. Shouldn't hink him up anymore than he already is from George's chase. I'm starting to pull my hair out."

"I'll do it tonight. There's some other drug shit going on here I need to bounce around anyway," Mendiola said. "I asked Gabbro about the passenger door on Holihan's vehicle. He said it was open when he got there. And Dave Erdos's right. Vehicle doors don't pop open in wrecks anymore. Somebody opened that door, and it wasn't the fire guys with their jaws."

"Who called it in?" Cove asked.

"I dunno, I'll have Sarah dig through the logs tonight, maybe have her listen to the nine-one-one call... hang on for a sec," Mendiola said.

Cove waited, and the deputy kicked back in. "Where you at?" the deputy asked. "Somebody's reporting an elk in a fence south of town. Can you handle it?"

Cove told Mendiola he'd deal with the elk and wrote down the milepost on a sticky note. Looking at his watch, he realized he wouldn't have time to respond to the call, return home, change his clothes and make it to Julie's in time. He loaded Annie into the patrol truck and put Liz's Glock in the console.

It took twenty minutes to get to where the elk was caught in the wire. She'd attempted to jump the barbed wire fence along the highway right-of-way, and a hind leg had hooked between the first and second strands of wire and slammed her to the ground. She was laying on the highway side of the fence. Cove parked fifty yards short, crossed over the fence, not wanting to be on the busy side of it. When he approached her, she put her head up, and let out a terrified mewing call and struggled to get up. Cove made sure there was no incoming traffic on the road, placed his fence cutters on the second wire next to her hoof and popped the strand. The elk exploded like a sprinter coming out of the blocks, crossed the highway to the other fence, followed it for a few seconds and then cleared it, heading for the Lost River Range. Cove watched her disappear over a hill. He turned and saw Annie standing in the back of the truck with her tail wagging. He looked down at the strand of wire he'd just cut. Brown elk hair clung to three of the barbs. *What a nasty invention.*

He pulled his truck in behind Julie's Subaru, thinking everybody on the block was going to know the warden was inside. *At least it's dark,* Cove thought. Stepping out of his patrol truck, he could see Julie's silhouette watching him through the door's window; she opened it and stuck her head out. "Don't bother coming in if you don't bring your girlfriend!"

Cove stopped and twisted his head.

"Annie," she answered laughing, and looked at the falling flakes. "I'm so happy to see it's snowing again. I'm not used to these dry winters."

"Me, too," Cove said. "The locals talk of cold winters without snow on the ground–classic high desert."

He brought his dog in and told her to lay down, but the drill was broken when Julie greeted her with a good ear rubbing. The aroma of stew and homemade bread hit Cove's senses and his mouth watered. He laid the Glock on the table and sat down. He watched Julie and Annie interact in a mishmash of petting and tail wagging. When Julie broke off the game, she saw the gun and sobered up, staring at Cove. "You think it's him, the creep, don't you?"

"Well..."

"Charley, I looked at the tracks after you left. It doesn't take a game warden to figure out who it was. Don't treat me like a kid. Those are the same tracks."

Cove frowned. "Half this town wears cowboy boots, and every guy that's over six-foot is gonna have a big foot." He nodded and glanced at the gun. "But yeah, it looks like his boot print."

She shook her head and crossed her arms. "There were plenty of weirdos in Detroit. I thought I was leaving them behind. Would you like something to drink?"

"Just water, thanks," Cove replied. "There was an elk caught in a fence up towards the summit. I wasn't planning on coming here in uniform, but I didn't have time to change."

"Is it going to be okay?" She asked.

"It'll be just fine. I should take some wire out there before they put the cows on the range this spring and fix the fence."

Julie set two glasses of ice water with lemon slices on the table, sat down and looked at the black pistol. "What do I need to know about this gun?"

Cove picked the Glock up. "What'd your brother loan you?"

"Nine millimeter Beretta."

Cove nodded. "This one's simpler." He hit the magazine release button and set the loaded mag on the table. He rolled the gun to the left, pulled the slide back and captured the ejected round with his palm. He set the gun down and loaded the loose cartridge back in the magazine.

"It's safe," he said, showing her the empty chamber. "It's a 9mm too, so it'll have about the same recoil." Holding the pistol straight up, he pointed at the trigger and continued, "This little lever here on the trigger is the safety. Your finger engages it when you pull. And the gun will go off when you squeeze, so there's no traditional safety." Cove pushed the slide lock down with his thumb and the slide slammed forward with a metallic clang. He handed the empty weapon to Julie. "Point it at the wall and dry fire it—feel the trigger."

Julie brought the gun up with a two-handed grip, closed her left eye, and the Glock made an audible click. "That's easy enough," she said. "How many bullets does it hold?"

"There'll be sixteen in the magazine and one in the chamber." He took the gun and seated the fully loaded magazine. He racked the slide and set the gun back down. "I could have brought another mag but you're not going to run out of bullets. This is just to let you sleep. Keep your doors locked and you'll be fine." Cove picked up his glass and took a drink.

"Why don't you just give me Annie instead?" Julie said smiling. "I'm sure she'd protect me. I'd let you come visit her once a month."

"Real funny."

Julie stood up and filled two bowls with stew, set them on the table and sat back down. Cove took a sip of the stew, "Jeez, I didn't realize how hungry I was."

"I'll send some home with you," she said. "How long have you lived here?"

"Eight years. It's a good place to be a game warden."

"Are you from Idaho originally?" She asked.

"No, I grew up on the Flathead Reservation in Montana."

"You're Flathead then?"

Cove shook his head with a tight-lipped smile, his brown eyes twinkling. "Salish." His head tilted. "Or half. A tourist thought we were Flatheads; it was Meriwether Lewis. He and his guys were lost and had lamed most of their horses. My father's people must have liked him—they traded them fresh mounts." Cove took a sip of water and lost his smile. "Salish means 'The People' in my father's language. My mother is white."

Julie frowned, catching something. "Are they still around?"

"My mother lives in Polson. That's where I was raised. My father died when I was in high school."

"I'm sorry," her voice trailed off.

Cove shrugged. "He went duck hunting and never came home. Fell through the river ice," Cove said, glancing at Annie. "We think he was trying to save our dog. She made it and he didn't."

"My God." Julie reached in and touched Cove's forearm.

Cove nodded. "It's been almost twenty years. I don't remember why I didn't go with him. That's what really bugs me."

The two stared into each other's eyes and neither spoke. Finally Cove broke the silence. "I'm sorry I didn't respond to you last night when you reached out over Liz's death. Words don't work." He hesitated. "Have you ever lost anyone close to you?"

Julie shook her head. "No, an uncle, but I didn't know him well."

Cove's eyes narrowed and his hand came up to his neck, his fingers massaging his throat. "When she died, I felt like I'd lost my entire life, and in a sense I did. Even my job felt empty." He hesitated. "You don't get over loss like that, you just get used to it." He looked at his glass, took a breath and let it out. "It took me several years to get used to losing my father—I'll never accept it. I'm just *accustomed* to knowing he's gone—it's now the norm. It'll hit me on his birthday, sometimes I feel it when I'm talking to my mother, if that makes any sense?" He looked down at his palms. "I'm not there with Liz yet. Sometimes I think grief is like gravel in a bird's gizzard—it just grinds on itself until it's dust, but it changes you; it bestows a different recognition for life and people."

Julie took a drink of water, thinking about what he'd just said. Cove took a mouthful of stew.

Julie put her glass down. "What was it like growing up there?"

Cove swallowed his food. "You mean on the rez?" He asked, rolling his good ear towards her.

Julie felt a blush of embarrassment. "Yes."

"Sometimes I think it was pretty normal, but I was teased a lot 'cause of my mixed-blood parents. Some of the kids called me breed, half breed, or blanket ass, derogatory stuff. You know how some kids can have a mean streak... My lighter skin and mixed blood gave them something to pick on–probably made them feel better about themselves. A lot of white kids just put me in the Indian box, and some of the Indian kids didn't accept me 'cause of my white mother. I felt it when I was trying to date a white girl in high school. Her father didn't like Indians and warned me to stay away from her. Mendiola calls me half breed sometimes, I'm okay with it because we respect each other and he's doing it with a light heart. He's earned it."

Julie was frowning but leaned in attentively.

He looked at her, put his elbows on the table and interlocked his fingers. "The other thing about growing up on the rez is family. Salish people are close. I spent a lot of time with my uncles and aunts and their kids from my father's side. My cousins–they're like brothers and sisters to me–even my second cousins are that way. Their parents mean practically as much to me as my own. It's that way with all Indians, I think. It goes back to the day when my father's people lived in the Bitterroot in family bands. The adults were every kid's parent. All the elders were looked up to. It wasn't that long ago; my great grandfather's father was born in a brush wikiup and hunted buffalo from horseback. So don't feel sorry for me 'cause I don't have any brother's and sisters. I have lots of them, and we're close. I have lots of family, and we stay in touch. I can't say that about my mother's side of the family. She grew up in southern Idaho and we'd see 'em every few years, but we're not real close."

*****

Leo inhaled the vapors, slumped back on the truck's seat and let his skull roll on the headrest, feeling his blood slosh around like motor oil in a milk jug. Exhaling, he widened his eyes and looked out the open window. He felt the cold air bite into his flesh, his senses magnifying a hundred times over. The white hillside and dark cliffs jumped out as if they were lit by two full moons. It'd been dead quiet, but now he could hear the slush chewing in the river's current, sloshing like the liquid garbage in his brain. Inhaling the raw air brought the taste of his neighbor's horses to his tongue, and they were a half-mile away. *Goddamn!* The shit had really brought him back to life.

He fired up the Dodge, put his meth kit away, and pulled out onto the road, heading for town–his fingers tapping the piano keys on the steering wheel.

*****

"How about your family?" Cove asked, taking another slice of bread.

"Both my parents are healthy, still back in Ripon, not too far from Benjamin," she said, glancing at his picture.

"He and dad used to hunt deer when I was growing up, but I think dad's getting too old and Ben's too busy. A lot of people in that part of Wisconsin go out during deer season. I didn't even know people hunted with a spotlight until I moved here."

"Nobody really *hunts* with a spotlight," Cove said in a lowered voice. "Poachers use spotlights; hunters don't."

\*\*\*\*\*

Turning up Main, Leo glanced down at the duffel on the passenger floor. *Ready to roll.* He pulled around into his little alley hidey-hole, shut his engine off and watched Main. This time he didn't look at the trashcans watching him from the rear. He didn't look through the knotholes in the fence. He stared out onto Main Street, focused on the task at hand. Focused on Red. There were no pedestrians on the sidewalks and no cars had driven by. Challis was dead. The only thing moving were the worms under his skin. He started the engine and eased towards Main with the lights off. When he was sure there was nothing moving, he pulled out, turned right and then left on Third. He eased down the street, looking towards Red's house. When he was halfway there, he saw the pickup truck in the driveway. Coming closer, he made out the emblem on its door. *Goddamn fuckin' Indian game warden!* His hand moved to the revolver holstered on his belt and he felt the worms squirming in his veins.

\*\*\*\*\*

Cove heard a truck drive by, but failed to catch a hint of headlights through the edge of the closed mini blinds covering the window. He set his glass down, pulled the blinds back and peered out, catching the brake lights as the truck turned the corner. The right one was broken allowing white light to escape. "That guy needs to turn his headlights on," he said, raising his eyebrows. "It's blacker than the ace of spades out there."

"Would you care for another bowl, Charley?"

"I'd take a half, please," Cove said, buttering another slice of bread. "What stories are you covering?"

"I'm chasing one about selenium pollution down by the Utah border. It's getting in the creeks, causing deformities in juvenile cutthroat and brown trout."

"Good grief, sounds interesting. Holler if you need the name of a fish biologist down there," Cove said. "I worked a deal upriver here my rookie year. A miner dumped a bunch of acid in the river. I found out about it when a mother called me. Said her kids had been swimming and got burned by it. They were okay, but it killed fish for a ways down below Clayton. I think the whole town knew who did it but nobody would talk."

Cove turned his good ear towards the back of the house. "Did somebody just drive down your alley?"

# *Chapter 12*

"Tell me about the mutilations," Dax Sparks said, lowering his coffee cup.

George Nayman glanced at the couple sitting at the nearby table, lowered his bushy gray eyebrows and looked back at the young warden. "Maybe when we get out on the hill," he whispered. "We don't want to cause a panic with these civilians. Besides, we need to be on Cove's hill in forty-five or so and that subject'll take a day or two."

Nayman had ordered chicken fried steak, mashed potatoes and green beans that looked as though they were fresh from a tin can. He'd ordered a side dish of gravy and covered the entire meal with it, including his green beans. Sparks had ordered a jalapeño burger with sweet potato fries and a salad.

Nayman nodded at Dax's burger. "That pepper 'd burn a hole in my gut." Spearing a fork full of gravy-covered beans, he pointed with them at the kid's plate. "Damn funny lookin' french fries. They any good?"

Sparks slid his plate towards Nayman. "Have one," he said, smiling. "Old dogs need to try something new once in a while."

Nayman took an orange fry, dipped it in gravy, and put it in his mouth. "Ain't you the banty rooster tonight cowboy? I might quote those wise words in this week's Field Training Report," he said, with a semi-grin. "Do a little science project. See if anybody in Boise's got a sense of humor—it'd be a first."

Sparks looked down and pushed his plate back towards his boss. "Maybe you'd better have some more."

\*\*\*\*\*

Leo could smell his flesh decomposing. He'd had plans for the night, and they hadn't included the warden. Turning up the Pahsimeroi's east side, he had one hand on the wheel, the other wrapped around a Keystone. He was listening to Hank Williams, Jr. howling out *Hotel Whiskey*.

He didn't care to shine this early in the night. He preferred the first quarter of the new day, after midnight, but seeing the Indian's truck at Red's place was too much. He'd smoked a joint when he'd hit the highway, but it hadn't rolled his edge; he had to find a doe.

Stopping at Morse Creek, he shut the truck off and waited for his eyes to adjust while rubbing his mojo tooth and thinking about Red. He could hear nothing from the sage. He tested the breeze with his nose and sensed nothing. Fresh snowflakes swirled in through the window and melted on his hand, causing the worms to twitch. He needed a transfusion.

Looking behind him, he could see nothing but his tailgate. Ahead there was one yard light glowing three or four miles up the valley. Reaching down to the shifter boot, he fished-out his Crown Royal bag. Flicking on his flashlight, he selected a large meth rock with his shaking fingers and dropped it into the pipe. "Don't disappoint me, big man," he said, looking inside its guts. Holding the pipe up to his eyes, he snapped on the lighter and placed the flame under the bowl. He rotated it back and forth by the stem, studying the birth of mist inside. The apparition started to appear. It was a little boy sitting on a bench, inside the foggy bowl, hands in his lap with no piano to play and no Red to charm. "Goddamn!" He dropped the lighter and jammed his burning thumb into his mouth. He felt the lump of a fresh blister with his tongue. When the pain subsided, he shined the light on the floor and retrieved the Bic. He examined the pipe's bowl and managed to reload it with another chunk of candy. This time, he brought the glass stem to his lips and fired it up, waiting for the burnt garbage flavor to tell him it was time to inhale, without watching the bowl. When it came, he drew it in and held it, feeling the shit's acid cooking the innards of his lungs. When the worms told him it was time, he exhaled the vapors and dropped his chin to his chest and sat in the darkness.

*****

Julie Lake watched Charley through the window of her front door. He'd thanked her for the meal and was standing on the walkway in a freshening snowfall, eyeing his dog sniffing around the yard. When the dog looked back at him, he walked to his truck and signaled for her to load in the cab. The two disappeared around the corner into the night and Julie closed the curtain over the window, feeling the emptiness of the house. She'd sensed he was adrift and unanchored. Picking up the Glock, she took it into her darkened bedroom. She laid it on the nightstand and started back toward the living room. She glanced back and was startled to see tiny green eyes staring at her like a three-eyed ghost, but realized they were the tritium lights glowing from the weapon's night-sights. Her teapot began to squeal. She walked over and grasped its wooden handle, poured the hot water into her waiting cup and felt the steam vaporing into the room. The fragrance of the hot brew reminded her of the woods behind the house where she grew up. She set the mug on a cork coaster on her cherry-wood coffee table, sat down and picked up her book, *The Summons,* by John Grisham. Opening it to her bookmark, she stopped and laid it back down. She got up and checked the locks on both doors and turned and looked around. The only sound was a ticking clock.

\*\*\*\*\*

Charley Cove stopped his truck at the mouth of the alley behind Julie's house. Shining his SureFire light from the open window, he looked at the tire tracks. Snow had covered their pattern, but he could see the faint outline of the tread. He got out, kneeled down and blew the fresh snow from track, recalling how his father had shown him the trick on a lion's track beside the Flathead River. The interlocking Z-pattern jumped at him.

Crossing over Main Street, he found the entrance to the shooter's hide and noted the fresh but snow-covered tire tracks going around the corner. Feeling his hackles come up, he unbuckled his seat belt and followed the tracks. He turned in expecting to find the Dodge, but the street was empty. Sitting in the alley, he shut off the engine and watched Main Street. There was no way he was going to go home and crawl in bed. Thinking tactically, he realized if the shooter came back to this hideout, he'd come from behind and it'd be a bad place to be sitting. He pulled out onto Main and drove down to the motel at the junction of the highway. He backed his truck into a shadow where he could watch both routes. *What the hell does this guy want with Julie?*

*****

Leo stuck his head out the window and sensed the valley. The sagebrush radiated the oily fetor of Vick's Vapor Rub. A rabbit scream pierced the darkness from down in the river bottoms. Nothing else was moving. He could sense no foe, but a shudder still ran down his spine. Rubbing his mojo, he felt it vibrating, tempering him. He got out and retrieved the cased rifle from the culvert. He set it on the seat next to his blue Keystone box, turned the overhead lights on and headed up the road, staring at the twinkling crystals reflecting from the snow covered sage.

*****

It was Dax Spark's turn to drive. Conversation had been scarce on the drive up from Salmon. As the two wardens turned up the Pahsimeroi, George Nayman spoke. "Lets catch this asshole tonight. Maybe then we can work while the sun's up, like humans."

Nayman showed Sparks the two-rut road leading to Cove's hill. The young warden found its summit and turned the truck's lights off. Light leaked into the truck's interior from curled electrician tape on the instrument panel.

Nayman reached over and tapped on the seat console. "The tape's in here somewhere."

Sparks rummaged around, located the black electrician's tape and recovered the lights. Nayman dug behind the seat, came up with his extra coat and rolled it into a pillow.

"Cattle mutilations," Sparks looked over at the old warden. "Don't be going to sleep until you tell me about 'em."

Nayman's mouth was open, and his eyes were closed. He didn't respond to the request. Sparks shook his head, leaned over, and turned the AM radio on, hoping to find Noory talking about Bigfoot or alien abductions. After a while, he gave up searching for the talk show and turned it off. He picked up the night vision goggles and looked into the green optics while listening to Nayman snoring.

*****

Leo's mouth felt and tasted like a rag moistened with paint thinner. He reached over the rifle, grabbed a beer, and popped it open. Taking a swig, he swished it around, gargled, and spat it out the window beside the truck.

He'd angled to one side of the road and then turned the truck back towards the other side, shining the overheads out into the snowy brush. He slowly worked up the valley, looking for the reflection of eyes. A white jackrabbit burst from the sage and crossed into the road. Leo gunned the engine and jagged the wheel, nailing it.

He drove another three hundred yards and turned around. He drove back and found the rabbit dead in the road. *Dumb-fuckin' rabbit.* He stopped, got out and threw the warm, limp animal in the back of his truck.

*****

Julie felt the tug of sleep coming on and readied herself for bed. She moved her book to the nightstand and changed into her sweats. Attaching a book light to Grisham, she turned off the room's light and crawled in, feeling the weight of the blankets. She opened the novel and continued reading in the darkened house. Grisham was describing how his character, Ray Atlee, had found a closet full of one hundred-dollar bills in his dead father's house in Mississippi. The big mystery was where the money had come from and what Atlee was going to do with the money. Feeling her body slumping after a few minutes of reading, Julie placed her bookmark between the pages. She turned off the little lamp, reached over and gripped the Glock by its polymer handle. Its fully loaded heft felt good, but reminded her of the creep as she slipped the weapon under her pillow.

A winter breeze kicked up, sending a chill through the leaky house. A branch made a scraping sound on the roof.

*****

Leo saw the eyes. Three sets on the right side of the road, just yards into the sagebrush. Turning the wheel, he exposed the deer to the full power of his overheads with

Ted Nugent shrieking out *Cat Scratch Fever*. Two does and a half-grown fawn. He had to position the Dodge at nearly ninety degrees to get a shooting lane from his window. By the time he was situated, two of the deer had bounded into the cover of the night, but one doe had angled into the light and was now nervously walking about fifty yards from the truck. She glanced back, trying to locate her companions, but her night vision was lost. Leo gave a quiet whistle and the doe stopped and stared into the lights. It was the last image that passed through her optic nerves before the one hundred and eighty grain chunk of lead and copper opened her skull.

Leo turned the engine off, bringing silence to the valley. Stepping out from the truck, he left his door open and all four lights on. Walking into the sage, his shadow led the way, each step making a crunch in the snow. He found the doe laying on her side. Her head was a blend of pulped blood, bone, and brains. He perched over her like a priest standing before an altar and breathed in, tasting the metallic odors steaming from the scarlet mess that had been her head.

The Pahsimeroi was speechless. The player sat down on the heels of his boots and let his knees rest in the snow, the lights from the truck illuminating the stage, backlighting his silhouette. Closing his eyes, he moved his fingers slowly across the coarse warm hair of the animal's flank, feeling her keyboard-like ribs and the soft hair on her underbelly. If one had been watching from a distant seat, he might have believed a pianist was about to play something remarkable.

He moved his hand between the doe's still-quivering hind legs and his fingers found the inside of her moist warmth. A meth-charged slug of blood crashed through his veins. The worms chewed into his libido and he felt a stiffening flame in his crotch. His head sagged to his chest. A coyote in the bottoms cocked its ears and heard a low-pitched moan.

*****

Julie Lake flashed awake. *What was that?* She lay in the dark listening, wondering what had stirred her from her sleep and tried to control her breathing. Nothing moved in her house. She stuck her hand under the pillow, grasped the Glock, and held the gun flat on her stomach, feeling its cold weight. She felt her chest rising and falling. *Was it a dream?* No memory of a sleep story came forth.

Outside the wind stirred. She heard the tree limb scraping on the roof. She tried to convince herself that's what must have snapped her out of her sleep. She turned on the nightstand light, looked at her clock, and saw that it was just past midnight. She got up, carrying the Glock and walked through the house, checking the doors. Both were locked, but she was wide awake. She went back to bed, slipped the gun under the pillow and reached for her book. She returned to Grisham's story, hoping the tale would put her back to sleep. She left the light on.

*****

Leo grabbed a fresh beer and continued up the valley. Some of his hunger had been slaked, at least for now. Turning off his overhead lights, he thought about the night he'd sat on the hill and watched the lights go up the road on the far side of the valley. *Goddamn rancher gave me up.* He looked across the valley at the lone yard light set in the flats and played the keyboard on his steering wheel. *Time to send a message.*

He crossed over the Pahsimeroi River on the Hatch Road and turned down the Custer County road towards Harris's ranch house. He stopped on the road a mile from the rancher's house, shut the overheads down, turned the engine off and watched the barnyard. Nothing moved. No lights came on in the house. He rolled his window down, stuck his head out the window, and tasted the breeze. Satisfied, he tore a flap off the Keystone, dug a felt-tip pen out of his glove box and wrote his message. He started the Dodge's engine and drove past the house with his headlights off. When he got to the end of the pole fence where he'd shot the cow, he stopped the truck and shut the engine down. Getting out, he studied the house. *You turn a light on and I'll put a bullet through your window.* He retrieved the jackrabbit from the bed of his truck along with a three-foot length of orange bailing twine and walked over to the fence. He tied a knot around the rabbit's neck and hung it from the top fence rail. Pulling his pocketknife out of his pants, he opened the blade and used it to twist a hole through the cardboard note. Looping the tag of twine through the cardboard, he tied it off with a half hitch.

180

*****

Dax Sparks was making a second attempt at finding the late night paranormal talk show on the AM radio band. He'd tried the FM band and decided they were too far out in the boonies to hear much. Nayman's snoring was driving the young warden nuts, but he wasn't about to wake him up. Giving up on the radio, he dug his iPod out of his shirt pocket and was putting in his earbuds when he caught a new light up the valley. He brought the NVGs up to his eyes and confirmed that it was a vehicle moving down their side of the valley.

"Hey, George!" Sparks paused until he saw his boss's eyes open. "Somebody's coming down the road."

Nayman's head raised off the rolled up coat. "What time is it?" He grumbled.

Sparks pressed the illumination button on his Casio G-Shock. "Just shy of one."

Nayman picked up the binoculars from the dash and watched the vehicle intently. "No overheads."

"I don't think he's doing the weave, either," Sparks noted.

"Might 'a been a card game up the valley." Nayman put the binoculars back on the dash and leaned back into his pillow. "Keep your eyes peeled."

Sparks put his earbuds in and found AC/DC's album, *If You Want Blood*, on his iPod. He tuned out Nayman's snore level with the volume and kept tracking the vehicle with the NVGs. It slowed at the Furey Lane junction and turned towards the Lemhi road, its taillights getting smaller as it crossed the bridge over the Pahsimeroi River.

Listening to his music, Sparks glanced over at the gray haired warden. Nayman's mouth was open and his head was back on his make-shift pillow. He refocused on the truck and watched it turn down the far side of the valley. After about a mile, Sparks saw the brake lights come on. He rolled his window down, turned off the engine, and pulled the earbuds out. The brake lights went off, but the vehicle failed to move. Sparks grabbed the binoculars and found the truck, now magnified ten times. He caught movement in the headlights. The brake lights briefly came back on, and it began moving again.

"What'd he do?" Nayman asked quietly.

"Just stopped for a minute. Didn't hear a shot. I think he got out."

Nayman popped his door open. "Probably an old fart like me," he said, and stepped out into the sage.

# *Chapter 13*

Cove woke up in a quagmire, feeling grit in his eyes and the beginnings of a headache; he was tired. He'd sat in the shadow of the motel, watching for the shooter's Dodge. He finally threw in the towel just past two o'clock and headed home for bed. The only interesting thing he'd observed was a coyote walking in the middle of Main Street, headed uptown.

He got up just past seven and put the coffee on. He was about to call his boss when his phone growled. "Morning, George, you guys do any good last night?"

"Not really," Nayman said. "Nobody came up, one rig went down. All's we could see was headlights and taillights, no overheads showing."

Cove chewed on this for a moment. "Wonder if he's hinked up?"

"Shit, who knows," Nayman said. "I think I'll drag Dax down to the jail here this afternoon and bounce the vehicle description off the deputies."

Cove thought about the blacked out truck he'd seen drive by Julie's house. "That truck have a broken taillight?"

"Not that I recall. Let me ask junior here."

Cove heard the two talking.

Dax came on the line. "One of 'em had some white showing."

"Which side?"

Without hesitating, Sparks answered. "The right one."

Nayman's voice came back on. "Why'n the hell you asking about taillights?"

Cove bit his lip. "Mighta busted it when he took out the sign." Nayman didn't respond, and Cove wondered if his boss had caught his bullshit; the old warden had nearly thirty years on the job and was a legend for sniffing out stories that were short on truth.

"Maybe it was him," Cove said. "Maybe he's changing his pattern. I'll make a run out there and see if there's some pieces of taillight laying by that sign. I've been wanting to take a paint sample off the post, too."

Cove thanked Nayman and Sparks, said goodbye, hung up and poured a cup of coffee. He opened up his laptop and cranked out a quick email.

*Julie: Thanks for dinner last night. It was great. Let me read your fish pollution story when it's done. Did you shoot anybody last night? -Charley*

Cove's email alert chimed. He saw that it was from the Department of Motor Vehicles and opened it.

*Charley: Attached list of all Silver Dodge pickups registered in Lemhi and Custer Counties. There are none in our database with a middle initial of L. Please let me know if I can be of further assistance. -Martha Alberts*

Cove opened the attached Excel file and found seventeen names and addresses. Eleven in Lemhi County and six in Custer County. No Leos and no Leonards. Chewing his lip, he looked through the list and recognized six of them. Staring at each one, he slowly checked them off in his mind. None of the ones he knew fit the physical profile of his shooter. That left twelve unknowns. He clicked on the print icon and listened to his printer spit out the single sheet. He got up to take a quick look at it, set the copy on his desk and sat back down.

Sipping coffee, Cove's eyes focused on an evidence envelope sitting on a pile of papers. It was the bullet he'd recovered from Harris's cow. From his bedroom, he retrieved a two-page list and a plastic peanut butter jar containing three inches of spent bullets. He flipped to the second page and looked down the list of dates and drainages. The document was a list of bullets Cove had dug out of shot-and-left animals. The list was organized by date, drainage, and species along with an assigned evidence number. He found the case he was looking for. A dismayed hunter had found a dead elk south of Challis near Willow Creek Summit. He thought it had been shot and left and had called it in. At the time, the elk season was only open to bulls. Using the caller's description, Cove had found the bloated animal and believed it had been shot from the highway, about three hundred yards away. The blood trail showed it had run for nearly thirty yards before it fell on the open hillside. He'd found an entrance wound entering the chest cavity behind the right front leg and no exit wound. He'd opened the sternum, removed the heart and lungs and found massive trauma to all three organs. After much searching, he'd recovered the spent bullet inside the skin on the far side of the chest cavity after it'd blown through a rib. Cove had not been able to find any witnesses to the shooting and no footprints at the scene, other than those from his caller.

On such dead-end cases, Cove would fill in the details on the sheet and mark the base of the bullet with a reference number using an electric engraving tool. He poured the bullets out of the jar onto the current edition of the Chronicle and fingered through the projectiles until he'd found the one he was looking for. It was a classic mushroomed copper-jacketed lead bullet with the number forty-eight engraved on its base. He opened the desk drawer, found an eye loupe and removed the Harris bullet from the evidence envelope.

Both bullets were .30 caliber. Neither had a crimp ring. Both had the impressions from a barrel having four lands and grooves. Both bullets appeared to have been manufactured by bonding the lead core to the jacket, using a process similar to soldering. Cove placed the loupe in his eye orbit and squinted, holding it in place. He picked up the two bullets and examined them side-by-side, studying the transition between their cylinder-shaped sides and their flat ends. He noted that both had the same tight bevel at the transition between side and base. He concluded that they were, more than likely, the same brand of bullet. Still wearing the loupe over his eye, Cove moved the projectiles butt to butt and rotated them so the rifling impressions of both bullets lined up. His eyes went back and forth, comparing the width of the impressions. They appeared to be identical. *Same class characteristics,* he mused.

Cove removed the eye loupe and thought back on what Petersham had told him about his elk hunt. He recalled Petersham saying he'd hunted with the rifle for three days and remembered how Petersham had paused before he said he hadn't gotten an elk, as if he'd had to think up his answer. *If I ever find your rifle, Ralph* Cove promised himself, *I'm sending it to the lab with both of these bullets.*

Finishing up a bowl of cereal, his cell rang and he could see it was Mendiola.

"Stop by the office if you get a chance," Mendiola said. "I got the report on the pawnshop deal. Something ain't right."

Cove threw his gear on, grabbed the Excel file, and headed down. Mendiola's door was shut, so he grabbed his coffee mug and joined Sarah at her console.

"You back on day shift?" he asked the dispatcher.

"Thank God," she nodded. "Graveyard was killing me." Sarah smiled. "I got a good laugh yesterday. Fred told me the guy you're chasing's a zombie."

"That's the word my informant used to describe him. Whatever he is, he sure seems to like the night. My source also said he's nuts. Said the guy 'was mumbling about worms—go figure."

Sarah nodded her head. "Probably crack bugs," she said.

Cove's squinted his eyes and twisted his head. "Crack bugs?"

"Yeah, crack bugs. The meth heads feel 'em," Sarah explained. "They think bugs are crawling under their skin. That's why they get all those sores. They scratch at whatever they think is crawling around in 'em. Crazy, eh? When I was going through the jailer's academy, the psychologist called 'em *delusional parasites* or something like that. Just thinking about it makes me shiver. We've had tweakers in the jail here complaining about 'em. They want us to take them to the clinic to get the bugs out." She rolled her eyes. "Give me a friggin' break, they don't go to the doc unless their skin's infected from scratching." She shook her head. "They're paranoid as hell; they think we're all plotting to kill 'em. They're just psycho until they dry out and then they get owly."

The front door opened, and Deputy Jeff Jenks walked through the door. He was middle aged, dark blond, and struggling to keep his weight off. He paused at Mendiola's closed door, looked over at Sarah and Cove sitting by the dispatch desk and continued back to the booking room.

Sarah nodded towards Jenks. "Fred's moving him up from Mackay. His wife's got a job with the phone company here."

"Fred got somebody in his office?" Cove asked her.

"Gabbro." Sarah said squinting her eyes. "Fred looked pissed. I don't know what's going on."

Jenks approached, holding a coffee cup. "Charley, ya staying busy?"

Cove frowned. "Yes and no. My boss has cut me down to forty hours and I've got some yahoo running around all night long shooting deer," Cove frowned. "If you see a silver Dodge with a roll bar that has a couple of spotlights mounted on it, get the plate for me. He's driving me nuts."

Jenks smiled and nodded. "I heard. Fred's got me looking."

Cove took a sip. "You worked the Holihan fatal, didn't you?"

"Yep, quite the mess. That's the worst one I've dealt with in a while."

"Did the passenger door pop open during the crash?" Cove asked him.

"I don't know," Jenks said. "Helluva hood ornament. I figured it was Gene, but I couldn't tell; I just wanted to get a frigging blanket over him; there were cars driving by. Gabbro shoulda got it done before I got there." He squinted at Cove. "Fred asked me the same damn thing. What's with all the sudden interest in that wreck?"

Mendiola's door opened. Gabbro squirted out and disappeared through the front door without looking up. Mendiola's red face looked out. "Charley, grab my mug if you would and come on in."

Cove walked into the booking room, grabbed the deputy's cup and filled it up. He took it in and set it on Fred's desk.

"Thanks," Mendiola said, and handed him a four page report. "They emailed it up."

He sat down, skipped over the synopsis and found the description of the suspect the pawnshop owner had given. *"Late twenties, unshaven, slender, and medium height."* Cove looked up at Mendiola and shook his head. "Too short to be my shooter, that's for damn sure."

"I thought the same thing," Mendiola said.

Cove flipped to the last page and looked at the photocopy of the driver's license the seller had presented for the transaction. He noted the guy's height and weight and shook his head. "Since Holihan was six-foot and two-fifty, we don't need to be looking for a dead guy. Obviously the guy selling the guns ain't him."

"Maybe they shrink in the ground after awhile," Mendiola said, frowning. "If you read the last paragraph, the pawnshop owner admitted to the detectives the guy that sold him the guns didn't look like the photo on

Holihan's license. What's up with that shit? Why's the pawnbroker even bother with it?"

Cove sipped his coffee. "Tells me why the crook went there to begin with–he knew the pawnshop buy was dirty." He flipped a page on the report. "And I'll betcha this guy's sold stuff there before, or at least some of his buds told him he'd need a phony ID. That's why he had Holihan's license."

Mendiola pointed to the description of the three firearms the guy had sold. "This is what'll blow you away, though. He sold these two shotguns with the rifle that came back as stolen." He reached over and pulled a two-page report out of a stack on his desk. "Now look at Gabbro's inventory from the Petersham burglary."

Cove took the burglary report and studied the list of stolen firearms. He looked back at the pawnshop report. The shotguns sold at the pawnshop were the same make, model, and serial number as those stolen from Petersham's. Cove's head canted and he looked up at the deputy. "Didn't the detectives run all of them for stolen?"

"Yeah," Mendiola said. "They ran 'em, but they don't come back as a hit. They're not entered in the fucking system. That's what I was trying to find out from Gabbro. Joey swears he entered 'em." Mendiola took a big drink of coffee. "Let me know when you get tired of chasing poachers. You'd look good with a bigger badge and maybe Erdos wouldn't be such an ass."

Charley gave him a smirk and shook his head. "You'd get tired of me writing speeding tickets for three over the limit," he said sarcastically. "You hear anything back from your drug snitches?"

"That's what I was going to tell you. One of 'em knows a tall skinny tweaker living in Salmon that fits the bill. Goes by Leo, but she doesn't know his last name and hasn't seen him for a while. Said he was weird." Mendiola opened the palms of his hands and shrugged. "I didn't bother to ask her why she described him that way. That shit'll eat holes in your brain after a while. I'll give Lemhi County a call and see if they know who he is."

"George is already on it. He's gonna hit up the deputies down there today." Cove finished his coffee. "Speaking of which, they worked the Pahsimeroi last night, saw a rig come down shortly after midnight with a broken taillight on the right side. Wasn't running overheads. I'm wondering if our guy broke his taillight the other night when he took out the road sign." Cove thought about telling the deputy about what he'd seen at Julie's, but let it pass. "Anyway," Cove said, standing up. "I'm going to go take a look at the busted sign."

On the way out of town, Cove passed Gabbro's patrol truck parked by the highway and waved at the deputy as he passed. Looking in the mirror, Cove didn't catch a response.

It had been warmer during the night and the river was no longer running slush ice. Thick clouds covered the peaks of the Lost River Range. When Cove got to the confluence of the Pahsimeroi, the sun was starting to break through the overcast. He pulled across the road from the damaged sign, grabbed a couple of evidence bags and his camera and told Annie to stay put. He was not optimistic about finding broken bits of plastic, since snow had fallen the night the sign had been damaged, and the plows had worked the highway over. He cursed himself for not getting out the previous day.

There was no damage to the sign itself, but one of the two upright wooden timbers had been sideswiped and it'd fractured, causing the sign to sag. Just as George had said, the damaged post had silver transfer paint from the impact. Cove photographed it, set his three-inch ruler on the post and took a second picture. Flicking his knife blade out, he took several scrapings of the paint off the wood, collected the shavings in an evidence bag and sealed it. He had no reason to believe the paint would be of any evidentiary value, or the lab would even bother with it, but he'd found that seemingly unimportant items sometimes grew in value through the eyes of a jury.

Cove started walking along the white painted fog line at the edge of the pavement, listening for oncoming traffic. Within a few yards, he started seeing tiny pieces of red plastic that had been skimmed by the plows working over the rough pavement. After fifty yards, he moved further off the road and scoured the broad ridge of snow the plows had kicked over. He found what he was looking for—a piece of red plastic taillight the size of his thumb, sticking up through the snow. He dropped it in a second evidence bag but left the seal open.

Placing his two fresh evidence bags in the box behind his seat, he pondered his find. He had no doubt now the blacked-out pickup he'd glimpsed at Julie's belonged to his shooter. What he didn't know was whether the vehicle Dax and George had observed was his guy.

Cove drove over the Pahsimeroi River bridge and turned up the county road on the east side of the valley where the two wardens had seen the rig come down. The sun broke through a blue hole in the clouds, caught his brown eyes and half blinded him. Dropping his visor, he caught Liz's eyes looking at him from the photograph. She was dressed in desert camouflage, her Kevlar helmet sitting on her lap. She was smiling back at him from the driver's seat of a sand-colored Humvee, her face blazed in middle eastern sunlight. He flipped the visor back up and leaned to the right. He grabbed his ball cap off the dash, and put it on, shading his eyes.

The Morse Creek sign came into view and Cove eased to the left side of the road, stopped, and looked out the window. A set of boot tracks led off the road to a fresh spot of yellow snow in almost the same place he and Julie had found. He didn't need to take any measurements to know who the tracks belonged to. He needed a last name. Studying the tracks, he realized the guy had walked over and back twice, once during the snowfall and once after. Another line of small egg-shaped tracks came in from the sagebrush and past the urine stain, without showing interest. The line of tracks beelined to the mouth of the culvert and then returned through the sage. "Coyote, I hope you're not hungry today," Cove said out loud and closed his eyes, massaging his temples, still feeling the edge of a headache.

Wild horses roamed south of Challis and Cove had seen where the studs horses dropped their turds in the same spot time after time, creating what were termed *stud piles*. A rancher had explained to Cove the horses used these spots to mark their territory, putting notice out for other studs to keep out. Coyotes and foxes did the same thing and he'd watched Annie sniff their markers. This repeated urination by Cove's shooter caused the warden to ponder, wondering if in some bizarre way, the guy was marking his territory—but it didn't make sense to him.

Cove continued up the road, knowing his shooter had driven past Julie's house with his headlights turned off. Knowing the guy must have seen his marked patrol truck sitting in her driveway. Knowing the guy had then turned behind Julie's house and driven down her alley. Knowing the guy had then headed up the Pahsimeroi and had been seen coming back down by his boss and the rookie. And he'd stopped at his same old pissing spot. He still didn't know who the shooter was or where he lived, but the more he learned about the guy, the more his behavior got under Cove's skin.

The cloud cover had burnt off, leaving the high desert valley glistening like a blue-capped gem. Fresh snow blanketed the sagebrush and the two mountain ranges framing the drainage were crystal white. Cove looked to the west and located the hill on the other side of the drainage where the two wardens had been parked. If the guy had done any evil, it'd almost have to be beyond their sight line, which was a still another three miles up the road. The valley had gotten another two inches of snow last night, but according to the footprints at Morse Creek, it'd stopped snowing sometime before the shooter had come back down the road.

Cove's cell phone rang. The display indicated it was Spark's. "Charley, George and I are headed over to the Lemhi Sheriff's office. He wanted me to get your suspect's description from you."

"He goes by Leo," Cove said. "Six-two or so, skinny, unkempt long hair, forty, cowboy boots. Mendiola believes he's a meth user. Somebody's got to have dealt with this guy."

"Just a sec, George wants to talk to you," Sparks added.

After a pause, Nayman came on. "Somebody complained to Boise about your owl feather hanging from your mirror."

"And?" Cove asked.

"That's about it, Charley. You've got a right to possess it 'cause of your heritage. I don't get involved in people's faith. I'd rather not have it hanging inside the state's truck, but I'm leaving it up to you. I just thought you should know somebody's whining about you."

"Thanks," Cove said passionless. "I just found where he peed last night. It was him."

"You sure?" Nayman asked.

"Yeah, I've seen his footprint too many times. He busted his taillight out on that sign too. It was him."

"Son of a bitch. He's changed his pattern," Nayman exclaimed. "Where you at now?"

"The Pahsimeroi, above Morse Creek," Cove answered. "I'm gonna drive up the valley and see if I can find some bird activity. Maybe he had another dry run, though."

"I'll call you after we talk to the deputies down here. Junior and I might have to take an earlier shift tonight."

*****

Leo was having a hard time with his DVD remote. The methamphetamine had taken his appetite and he hadn't eaten for two days. When he felt weakened, he'd gotten his vigor by sucking on his pipe. It gave him more energy than any meal could have delivered but lack of food had left him with the jitters; he was having a hard time pausing the video he was watching with his shaking fingers. Two naked blonde porn queens were making out on the TV. Leo managed to pause the movie while one of the actors was pulling on the other's perfectly round silicone-bolstered breast.

Shuffling to the yellow refrigerator, he pulled out a black can of Rockstar and a cardboard egg container. He put the two on the counter and grabbed a large plastic Big Gulp cup sitting next to the sink, dumped its old dark liquid out, cracked four eggs into the cup and poured the Rockstar over the top. He pulled a dirty wooden spoon out of the sink's dish pile and stirred the concoction up. Leaving the egg shells on the counter, he peered through the kitchen window, looked up the lane and around the yard. He could see nothing but the bright snow. Studying the line of cottonwoods that hid the trailer from the highway, he examined each twig and branch, looking for the Indian. Nothing caught his eye. He carried the egg mixture down the hall, opened the rear door. He peered out and looked at the river. There were no fresh tracks on the shelf ice along the river's edge. No eyeballs stared back from the rock cliffs on the other side. No curious odors struck his nose, and no birds called from the brush. Even the worms under his skin were quiet. Things were excessively still. Leo gripped his holstered revolver hidden under his black-leather vest and looked around; his paranoia notched up. It'd been five hours since his last bowl and he feared his meth-heightened senses were failing him. He decided to chase the dragon as soon as he'd eaten his lunch. He took a large chug and leaned into the doorway, feeling the slurry land in his belly like a cup of mercury. For a moment he felt dizzy and then felt saliva flooding his mouth that tasted like acetone. He knew he was going to puke. He set the Big Gulp on the floor of his trailer and stepped outside. He went to his knees and vomited into the snow. He squatted for a moment and stared at the yellow goo. His stomach knotted and he dry-heaved, leaving the taste of bile in his mouth. After a bit he felt better. He sat down in the doorway and sipped his meal, letting his belly get a feel for the stuff. He thought about Red and the Indian's truck parked at her house.

*****

Cove could see two golden eagles circling up ahead. As he got closer, he could see a flock of magpies clustered over a spot in the sage off to the right of the road. Watching the eagles reminded him of his father's Salish teachings, the belief that everything was connected in a circle; the earth to the sage, the deer to the sage, the birds to the deer, and everything back to the earth.

He parked short of the scene and let Annie out of the bed. He put her on a heel and walked along the edge of the road. The eagles cruised off towards the river and the magpies scattered. He found where a vehicle had parked perpendicular to the roadbed with its front wheels in the sage. A single set of boot tracks led towards what the birds had found and had returned on the same path.

Cove studied the tracks. They were fresh and crisp and revealed no surprises. The vehicle's tires had left the interlocking Z impressions. The boot tracks were the same-sized cowboy soles. They had originated and returned to the vehicle from the driver's side. There was no oblong hole in the snow where a hot freshly-fired shell casing had fallen.

Cove and Annie paralleled the tracks to the kill. They found the tracks from two other deer that had made their escape. The magpies had fed on the opened skull. Three feet behind the doe's head, he could see where the fine mist of high velocity blood spatter had settled on the surface of the snow, giving it a dark pinkish look. The night temperatures had remained above freezing and the animal's gut had started to bloat, lifting its two upper legs off the ground. Eagle tracks had yet to disturb the shooter's tracks, and Cove could clearly see the knee impressions left from his perp's puzzling behavior. He stepped behind the deer's back and studied the tracks, staring at the knee marks and letting his mind go into an almost trance-like state, imagining the shooter kneeling. Trying to understand. Failing, he looked back to where the shooter's truck had been parked and marked the kill by setting his hat on a sagebrush. He began walking towards the river bottom, following the line where the bullet must have travelled after it had passed through the animal's skull. He worked slowly with Annie at his side, studying the surface of the snow for any indication the projectile had come to earth. In the past, he'd found where bullets had cut long slashes in the snow before they'd come to rest and he'd been able to recover them with the aid of a metal detector.

The dark brown form of an eagle watched Cove and Annie from the line of cottonwoods along the river. Two magpies chattered two hundred yards away in protest of the interruption. Farther down the drainage a raven croaked out a deep gurgling call.

After three hundred yards, Cove gave up on the search for the bullet, believing it must have careened off at an unknown angle. He returned to the doe and stared at the killer's tracks, trying to feel what had taken place. He picked up his hat from the sage put it on, and thought about what he knew of his target. Forty or so years old. Leaving the meat. Killing at night by himself with a stolen rifle and doing it night after night. Tall and scrawny, Mendiola's druggie source knew a tweaker named Leo, a meth user. That was the only part of it making sense; meth users could go for days without sleep. The rest of it was a fog. There was no reason to kill a deer and leave its nourishment in the snow, at least no reason either of his ethnicities could logically explain. Neither his brain nor his blood could figure it out. *Maybe if I had my father's Salish instinct's,* Cove thought to himself.

Growing up on the reservation, he'd felt the tug of two cultures. His father had done his best to teach him the Salish way and his mother had tried to educate him on the ways of what seemed to be the rest of the world. It wasn't a conflict between his parents, but an understanding that they'd brought the two cultures together and tied a Gordian Knot with their love. Sometimes Cove felt as if he didn't understand either culture and this was one of those moments. Cognitively, he knew he didn't need to understand the motivations for the killings to put a case together against the shooter, but instinctively, he felt the need to know what was motivating this person in order to get ahead of him.

The game warden in Cove took over. He had to document the crime. He photographed the scene, starting with a full body shot of the deer, the trauma to its head and the knee prints in the snow. After measuring and photographing the boot tracks, he flipped his knife blade open and stuck it deep into the animals thigh. He placed his thermometer in the incision.

His cell rang. He flipped it open and heard Mendiola's voice. "Where you at?"

"Standing next to a dead deer in the Pahsimeroi," Cove replied.

"Same guy?" Mendiola asked.

"Yeah, happened last night. What's going on?"

"Jenks is over at Harris's place. Sarah sent him up there. Bob found a rabbit hanging from his fence and called it in."

The explanation didn't make any sense. "What'ya mean? A hanging rabbit?" Cove asked, wrinkling his forehead.

"Somebody tied a dead rabbit to his fence with a note attached to it," Mendiola explained. "Bob found it and called it in. Jeff just got there."

Cove looked at Mogg Mountain, thrusting its snowed covered mass into the nearly cloudless blue sky. "What's the hell's the note say?"

Mendiola paused and Cove heard papers being moved around. "Snitch me off again and it'll cost."

"You're kidding me..."

"I wish I were. Can you head over there and take a look? I'm starting to think you're right about your guy shooting Bob's cow."

"I've done what needs to be done here. It'll take me twenty minutes to get there."

"I'll call Jeff and let him know."

Cove hung up, pulled the thermometer out of the deer and read the temperature. *Eighty-five degrees.* He walked back to the truck with his dog beside him, leaving the doe in the sage. With bloat starting, it was not fit for humans, but the magpies, eagles, and coyotes would have a feast.

Annie jumped into the bed without a prompt. Cove closed the tailgate and got in the cab. He headed down the valley and turned off onto Furey Lane. He rossed over the string of cottonwoods marking the Pahsimeroi River and turned up the valley on the Custer County side. He found Jenks's parked across the road from the pole fence where the cow had been shot. Jenks and Harris were sitting in the county patrol truck with the engine running. Cove stopped on the road, shut his truck off, and glanced over at the wooden fence that set a few yards off the road He saw the big lanky jackrabbit hanging like a Ku Klux Klan billboard in Mississippi.

He got out, looking at the scene and felt the chill of colder air moving into the valley. Hearing footsteps on the hard packed snow of the road, he turned to see Jenks and the rancher walking towards him. "Hell of a way to leave a guy a note, eh Bob?" Cove asked.

"I wish the bastard woulda had the balls to knock on my door."

Bob Harris looked the same; gloved up, and still wearing his faded brown insulated coveralls and a gray short-billed hat with flaps half over the top of his weathered ears.

"When'd you find it?" Cove asked.

"Coupla hours ago." Harris took a glove off and rubbed his reddish nose.

"You see any rigs up here last night?" Cove asked.

"Mighta heard something," he said with an edge, "but shit, I sleep pretty damn good. If this prick'd find a job he'd do the same."

Cove looked at the flattened snow on the road. Traffic had rolled it smooth and was no help with tire tracks. He walked to the edge of the snow-covered sage. There were two lines of boot tracks leading to and from the fence.

Jenks pointed and spoke up. "Those are our tracks on the left of his. Fred said you were enroute so all's I've done is look at it and take a bunch of pictures. Figured you might as well's get a gander at it too. Kinda bizarre." He turned back to the warden. "Your deer poacher wear cowboy boots?"

Cove was looking at the tracks. "Yeah, and he killed another one on the other side last night. I'm sure these are his, a size twelve or thirteen."

"You getting anywhere with him?" Jenks asked, rubbing his bare fingers through his short blonde hair.

Cove looked at the heavy-set deputy. His eyes narrowed and he bit his lip. "From moment to moment, no. But it seems like I know this guy like he's my neighbor.

It's just a matter of time but he's driving me nuts." He paused and looked over at the rabbit. "If he lived next door to me, it'd be easy."

"Mendiola told Gabbro and me to keep our eyes open for this ass," Jenks said. "Shit, I been lookin', didn't need to be told. We need to hook this guy up." He glanced at Cove and squinted. "Sometimes I wonder about Gabbro though."

Cove started to reply but closed his mouth, and pulled his quarter-inch wide tape measure out of his pocket. He leaned over and measured the footprint, nodded and eyeballed the track's stride. "You get some pictures of the rabbit yet, Jeff?"

"Yeah, everything's documented."

Cove nodded his head towards the rabbit. "Let's take a look."

Jenks led the trio to the fence. It was a white-tailed jackrabbit that weighed about six pounds; in the summer, the long-eared hare would have been pushing ten-pounds with a grayish brown coat. But now, except for it's black tipped ears and bloody face, it was the color of snow. The cardboard note hung at an angle on the animal's chest and the scrawled half-inch high message was written with a shaky hand, using heavy black ink.

"He misspelled the word *again*," Jenks noted. It was spelled 'agin'.

Cove re-studied the note. "I didn't catch that." Cove nodded and read it out loud with a slow tempo. "Snitch me off again and it'll cost. He probably didn't graduate with a 4.0 but neither did I." He rubbed the back of his head and looked at Harris. "I wonder how he figured out you called in those shots the other night?"

"Gawd," Harris said looking down at the sign. "I didn't think of that. I just figured it was the license plate."

Jenks glanced at Cove with a question mark on his face and turned back to Harris. "What's this about a license plate?"

Harris explained how he'd called the plate from the silver Dodge into Gabbro.

Cove turned to Jenks and shook his head. "Joey lost it in the shuffle somehow."

Jenks started to speak, but the rancher cut him off. "He couldn't have found out about me calling the plate in, could he?" Harris asked, first looking at the deputy and then at the warden.

"No," Cove answered shaking his head. "He can't know about you calling in the plate." Cove squinted his eyes and pulled a pair of leather gloves from his coat, thinking about what he'd just said and wondered if and how it could have leaked. "George Nayman chased him two nights ago. They didn't try to blue light him, but he musta figured it was the law." Cove put the gloves on, recalling the night of the callout with Julie. "I think he watched me from across the valley. I found where he'd parked on a hill for a while. Probably watched my headlights. He couldn't have known it was me. I don't think I was ever closer than four or fives miles from him and it was dark out here that night—no moon."

"It don't make sense," Harris said.

Jenks looked at Cove and shook his head, twisting his lips in a slight smile. "You do this job long enough, you figure out that some *people* don't make sense."

Cove raised his eyebrows and turned his head, looking at Harris. "Somehow he knows we're on his trail and he's blaming you–and that's not making sense."

"He can stop by anytime," Harris said. "I've been keeping my thirty-thirty handy since I lost that cow."

Cove glanced at the snow-covered remains of the cow behind the fence and pulled his knife out of his pants, turned back to the rabbit. He used the blade to flip the cardboard around, exposing the Keystone brand name.

Harris had seen Cove look over at the dead cow. "This is too much of a coincidence, ain't it Charley?"

Cove met his eyes and nodded. "Yeah, but proving it is going to be a different deal." He turned to Jenks. "Tell you what, Jeff, you take the note and I'll take the rabbit. Maybe you and Fred can pull a print and if we ever find this guy's truck, it'll probably have blood in it. I can have the Fish and Game lab bump this to the head of the line for DNA." He flexed the hind leg joint with his gloved hands. "Rigor's just starting." He looked at the deputy. "Killed last night." Cove cut the animal off the fence and held it by the orange twine, and looked at it closer. "I don't think it's been shot. Must have been hit on the road." He cut the note off and handed the cardboard to the deputy, holding it by the twine. He turned to the rancher. "Bob, assuming we catch this guy, we might be able to charge him with witness intimidation, but it'll be up to the prosecutor."

Harris shook his head. "I catch this prick, I'll tie him to my fence, let the magpies have their way with him."

Cove gave him a tight-lipped smile and nodded his head. "You get him tied up, give me a call and I'll take my time getting here." He looked back at the deputy and gave him a half wink. "I really need to ask this yahoo why he's killing everything—what's his point." They walked back to the road. Cove dug a black garbage bag out from behind his seat, put the rabbit in it and stuffed the sack between Annie's kennel and the truck bed. She gave it a sniff and went back inside her box.

He turned to Harris. "You see that Dodge up here, you call me night or day."

"Not a problem," Harris answered. "I appreciate you guys coming out here on a jackrabbit. That cow of mine woulda been worth fifteen hundred bucks after she'd calved. It's not the money that pisses me off though. This crap with him sneaking around burning gas and shooting stuff in the middle of the night 'n leaving it, that's got me pissed off. If he needed the meat, that'd be another thing."

Cove got in his truck and started the engine. Jenks held his finger up and walked over to the open window. Harris was standing behind the deputy's truck, relieving himself.

"That thing I said about Gabbro..." Jenks paused. "I shouldn't have said it in front of Bob, but here's the deal, he can't keep his mouth shut. Be careful what you tell him about this guy unless you want it to get out."

Cove looked at Jenks for a moment. "Jeff, I appreciate you saying that."

"No problem," Jenks answered. "This jackrabbit thing. I'm wonderin' if this guy's gonna ratchet things up—escalate it."

"I hope not," Cove glanced towards the rancher. "Bob's a good guy."

"You think the note's about doing harm to Bob or shooting another one of his cows?" Jenks asked.

Cove shook his head. "It's probably just bar-stool bullshit. Middle of the night stuff." His face turned sour. "It's chickenshit."

Cove headed back down the Pahsimeroi, thinking about the dead deer he looked at in the past weeks and tapped his fingers on the steering wheel to count. *Six. Six deer in three weeks. Plus Bob Harris's cow—and now this threat.*

He crossed back to the other side of the valley, and turned down the Lemhi County road, his mind drifting from the drive, focused on the case.

Cove felt a tingling on his cheeks, like someone was watching him. Flipping down his visor, he looked at Liz's image, wondering if the feeling had come from her. He'd gotten the picture in the mail, five days after she'd been killed by a roadside bomb, mailed the morning of her death. It was an odd event, mixed into the horror of her loss. During the ten weeks of her deployment with her guard unit, she'd sent daily emails to him, but had sent one letter; it contained the photograph and had been mailed in an era where hand-written letters were a thing of the past. It had made him wonder if she'd had a premonition.

But Cove didn't feel Liz's presence. He looked down the valley and could see the Morse Creek sign. Studying the sage through his side window, he saw his watcher and stopped. It was a coyote.

In the Salish culture, there is a totem as old as earth– intertwined with the tribe's people and history. His name is Coyote. He's a mischievous trickster with a sense of humor and for the most part, he tries to help people out. For eons, many stories of Coyote have been told around campfires on long dark winter nights.

The canine was sitting and staring at Cove's rig two hundred yards from the road. Coyotes were not well thought of by the locals, even though they caused few problems with cattle and there were no sheep to predate on. But a coyote sitting within rifle shot of a county road in this part of the world was unusual. Normally, they were running at a full-out blur or at the ready, set to bolt if a vehicle slowed. Cove brought his binoculars to his eyes and discovered the coyote had shifted its attention towards the Morse Creek sign.

# *Chapter 14*

Charley Cove felt something pop from his Salish blood. It was as if Coyote had silently sent him an inspiration through the crisp Pahsimeroi air. His shooter wasn't marking his territory; there were no stud horses or canines challenging or competing for this guy's poaching turf. Cove pulled next to the road sign, looked back through his window and watched the coyote loping off towards the Lemhi Range. He realized his shooter was stopping at Morse Creek, but he wasn't doing it to empty his bladder. Something else was afoot.

He got out, stood on the roadway and looked down at the urine stain in the snow. He could see the shooter's old tracks under the recent snowfall along with the fresh set. The more he studied the patterns, the more he realized the tracks were focused on the opening of the culvert, not the spot he was peeing at. Cove walked off the roadbed and looked at the culvert's twelve-inch mouth. A piece of sagebrush plugged the pipe's opening. The bush's gnarled stem had been cut at an angle with a sharp blade. Reaching down for the sage, he hesitated, feeling his own foolish fear of snakes and knew if it was July this would have been a different deal. Pulling the vegetation from the opening, he looked in and felt the blood in his veins pop again. He knew exactly what he was looking at. He canted his head, thinking it through. Had it been summer, with no snow, he could have covered the hole back up with the brush and swept his foot tracks with his broom. He'd then

have to find a place to hide his truck and set up an
extended surveillance, waiting for the shooter to retake
possession of the evidence and then pounce, but now he
was stuck. His tracks marked his presence and there was
no going back. There was no way to take back tracks in
snow. It was a done deal. He had to take the rifle and the
seizure was going to throw cold water on the direction
he'd been going with the investigation. Cove's plan had
been to catch the shooter with the rifle, which would tie
him to the shell casing Annie had found, and the forensics
would pin the two deer associated with it to the shooter.
Cove believed the rifle would also forensically tie his
suspect to the killing of Harris's cow plus tack on
possession of stolen property—both felonies. But now Plan
A was down the toilet. The positive side of this discovery
was that the killing would hopefully come to a halt, and
the lab would accept the rifle for latent fingerprint
analysis, since it was tied to two crimes associated with
human victims. Any latents found on the rifle belonging to
his suspect would tie everything together.

Cove set the cased rifle on his front seat with the
muzzle pointing at the floor, unzipped it and looked at the
stainless-steel, bolt-action, scoped rifle. Without touching
it, he could see .300 WSM stamped on the barrel and the
serial number on the receiver. He removed an evidence
tag from a bundle that was clipped to the passenger-side
visor and copied the serial number to the tag. He attached
it to the padded case with a piece of fine wire. Viewing the
rifle's bolt, he could see the rear part of it was forward,
indicating it was in the fired position, and he knew he'd
find a spent shell in the chamber. Cove wouldn't have to

study the impressions on its primer left by the rifle's breech face with his eye loupe. The tiny star-shaped mark from the firing pin left in the primer dent would be as familiar as the face of a well-known foe.

He glanced out to where he'd last seen the coyote, but failed to locate his friend. He scratched his head and made the decision. Walking back to the culvert, he pulled a business card out of his wallet and wrote "*give me a call*" on the back of it. He placed a flat rock in the culvert, set the card on it and left a small rock on top of the message as a paperweight. He covered the opening with the sage. Cove didn't believe the shooter would be stupid enough to call, but the card would leave no doubt as to who had taken the rifle. It'd been his experience that when a suspect felt like a bee in a bottle, it would often cause the guy to stumble and break the case open.

Reaching for his phone, it growled and he knew his boss had beaten him to the punch.

"George," Cove said. "I was just calling you."

"He's the Tooth Fairy," Nayman said. "I think you're looking for the Tooth Fairy."

Cove scratched his ear and squinted. "What are you talking about?"

"Deputy Wade Hansen was in dispatch down here," Nayman explained. "I described your shooter to him, and he said it sounded like a guy they'd nicknamed the Tooth Fairy. They'd booked him on a DUI and possession of drug paraphernalia last summer here in Salmon. The guy had a big mountain lion tooth hung from his neck."

Cove stiffened.

Nayman continued with his revelation. "They wouldn't let him wear it in jail and he got all pissy and went ape, claiming it was his mojo. He threatened to sue. That's why they call him the Tooth Fairy."

"What's his name?" Cove asked, pulling a notepad from his seat console.

"Just a sec," Nayman paused. "William Leonard Terzi, his date of birth's 8-12-75. Wade said he's a real piece of work."

"Got an address?" Cove asked.

"Lived north of Salmon at Tower Rock in a trailer for a while, but Wade said he moved and they don't know where," Nayman replied.

"I got some news for you, too," Cove said. "I think you and junior get a reprieve tonight. I got his rifle. It was stashed in the drain culvert at Morse Creek."

"As sure as eggs is eggs!" Nayman spat. "How many damn times we drove over the thing? Sweet Jesus!"

Cove slowly shook his head while holding the phone to his ear. "I know. I feel like a dumb-ass. I can't believe I didn't figure it out the first time I looked at that spot. I thought I was better than that. I haven't run it for stolen, but it's a Winchester Model 70, a .300 WSM. It's gotta be the real deal. That's why he was stopping there. It wasn't to pee."

"Son of a bitch!" Nayman exclaimed.

"He killed another doe last night, too. She was bloated, and I left her for the coyotes. The only evidence he left were his footprints."

George Nayman congratulated Cove on his find. He asked to be updated and hung up mumbling something about sleeping with his wife.

Cove started to hit Custer County's speed dial and stopped. He put his phone back in his pocket and picked up the Excel printout he'd gotten that morning from Motor Vehicles. Looking down the list, he found William Terzi with an address of Ruby Creek, Challis, Idaho. *That's where he's been disappearing to.*

Cove pulled his phone back out, and speed-dialed dispatch. Sarah answered.

"I need you to run a guy for wants and history and get a driver's license photo emailed over from Boise if you would. I wanna see this guy's face."

"This your poacher, Charley?" Sarah asked.

Cove was tempted to tell her it was the Tooth Fairy. "Yeah, it's him. William Leonard Terzi, DOB of 8-12-75. Ring any bells?"

"I don't remember bookin' a Terzi, not one of our regulars," she answered, "but the name sounds familiar."

"I'll be there in forty. Let me talk to Fred if he's in."

"He's got Joey in his office right now and is wearing his do-not-disturb sign on his face."

Cove hung up, feeling the velocity of the case pick up like a train rolling down a hill.

*****

Leo Terzi's hands felt like rocks. They were no longer shaking, and he hadn't had any problem getting a dose into his crystal ball. He'd hadn't had a hitch feeding his worms, however no long-lost effigy had appeared from the pipe's fog. With the high came a sense that someone was watching his trailer; he was as paranoid as a cat in a doghouse.

Grabbing a handful of .357 rounds, he slipped them into his pants pocket, and took the loaded meth pipe down to the river for a second round. He found a cottonwood stump he hidden behind a line of tall willow brush. He kicked the snow off it and sat down. From this location, he could huff his second round of vapor, get higher than a cloud and catch some sun on his death-white skin, all while getting away from the beam that he could feel focused on his trailer.

*****

Cove turned onto the highway, driving towards Challis. He was focused on the Ruby Creek address. He knew of no private land in the drainage above the highway, but he was aware of a singlewide trailer set off the highway down by the river. It had to be the place Terzi had claimed as his residence when he'd registered his Dodge. He could think of nowhere to safely view the trailer without being seen, except perhaps in the cliffs across the river. They would take an hour to hike to, and he wasn't sure what good it would do. Thinking about his investigation, he knew he was close to having enough *probable cause,* or PC, for a judge to issue a search warrant. The trouble with a warrant was the question of what he could possibly find at Terzi's trailer linking him to the crimes. The only thing he could think of that had great evidentiary value was a fired shell casing. Terzi had killed at least six deer and one cow with the rifle. Cove had recovered the one spent casing and believed there was a second one still in the rifle's chamber that sat beside him. That left at least five unaccounted shell casings. One could be laying out in the snow where Harris's cow was killed, but Cove believed most of them were inside the Dodge where they'd been ejected when Terzi worked the rifle's bolt. Passing Morgan Creek, Cove decided he'd take a quick look at the tracks going down the snow-covered dirt road to the singlewide on Ruby Creek and see what the tire tracks looked like. With that fact added into an affidavit, he should end up with the judge's signature on a warrant. He was aware of a line of cottonwoods between the highway and the trailer; he hoped the vegetation would keep him hidden.

A half mile from Ruby Creek, Cove started to decelerate, lowering the noise of his vehicle. He'd been to the trailer during his rookie year on a complaint involving a dog that had been chasing deer, but couldn't recall how well the singlewide was hidden by the trees. He remembered the trailer was about three hundred yards from the highway and sat at an inside river bend next to its channel. When he got near the side road leading down to the residence, he pulled across the northbound lane and stopped perpendicular on the side road next to a rusty mailbox. He studied the imprints in the snow, with his head stuck outside his window. Cove found what he was looking for.

*****

Leonard Terzi sat on the stump, his eyes flared, and he froze. He listened to the truck easing away from his driveway. Widening his nostrils, he cocked his head back and drew in the cold river air. He flicked his tongue, but the only spice he hooked was the acidic packrat smell germinating from the cliff across the river. The breeze was wrong.

Standing up, he looked towards the highway, an eighth of a mile away. He glimpsed a dark-brown pickup truck flashing between the cottonwoods and caught the tale-tell shield on the vehicle's door. Shivering, he felt the worms quivering like little tuning forks vibrating in his veins.

*****

Cove pulled behind the courthouse and parked in front of the sheriff's office. Mendiola opened the front door and stepped aside. "Let's have a pow wow," he said frowning.

Cove sensed the deputy was not a happy camper, but interjected. "Let me grab what Sarah's dug up for me."

"I got it in here," Mendiola said, walking into his office. "I've been working on it."

Cove could see deputy Gabbro sitting in the booking room in front of the computer. Turning into Mendiola's office, he shut the door and picked up the pile of printouts sitting on the desk. Shuffling through the pile, he found Terzi's driver's license photo blown up to an 8x10.

William Leonard Terzi stared back at him with sunken hollow eyes. He wore a drunken smirk, exposing the few yellow teeth that still hung from his gums. His straggly unkept hair looked as if it had gotten long and just quit growing. His nose was bent to one side and around his neck hung a long polished canine mountain lion tooth, strung from a leather thong.

Cove checked his vitals. Six-foot-three inches, one hundred and eighty pounds. *Bones and guts,* Cove thought.

"I see he claimed a residence here on Ruby Creek," Mendiola interrupted.

Cove looked up at Mendiola and nodded. "His tire prints are on the road going down there. I just looked at 'em, but didn't drive down to the trailer."

The warden flipped to Terzi's criminal history. The last arrest was in Lemhi County for DUI and felony possession of paraphernalia.

"I called Salmon about the felony," Mendiola said pointing at the sheet. "It was dismissed when he pled out on the DUI."

"Meth pipe?" Cove asked, looking up.

"Yeah, the prosecutor felt he was going to have to dump it. Musta been something wrong with the search. Speakin' of which, he's sure got a case of meth-mouth, don't he?"

"Suspended?" Cove asked.

"Driver's license was reinstated a month ago."

Cove scrolled down to the next arrest on the list and saw two counts of stalking, both in Lemhi County. "How 'bout the stalking?"

"They went away," Mendiola answered. I didn't bother asking."

Flipping through the six-page list, Cove saw other arrests for narcotics, battery, telephone harassment, obstruction, and burglary.

"Any of the felonies stick?" Cove asked.

"No, all were pled down or dismissed. Sarah's looking for arrests in the surrounding states."

"They give you a risk assessment on him?" Cove asked.

"Not really," Mendiola said. "Just a typical paranoid tweaker. I'd guess it depends if he's on a runner and how far into it he is; he could be delusional as hell. We had that fruitcake in here from Mackay last fall that swore people were walking right through the cell bars."

"I found his rifle... or Petersham's," Cove said, looking at the deputy.

Fred Mendiola's frown left his face. "You shittin' me?"

".300 WSM. He was stashing it in a culvert up the Pahsimeroi. Looks like it's in good shape. Had it in a case. It's locked in my truck."

"Let's hope the lab can pull something off it," Mendiola said.

"I wasn't dumb enough to mess with it," Cove said. "I should have enough for a warrant now. There has to be fired casings in his truck cab. You got time to go talk to Pallid with me?"

"Absolutely," Mendiola said, standing up.

The two walked out of the deputy's office. Mendiola turned to Gabbro who was still sitting in the booking room. "Joey, hang around. We might need some help serving some paper in an hour or so."

"On who?" Gabbro asked.

"I'll fill you in later," Mendiola replied.

The two got in Cove's truck. Mendiola turned to the warden. "Gabbro entered the serial numbers wrong. It took me a while to figure it out. All of them with the exception of the .30-06, the numbers were entered one off." Mendiola shook his head. "He's blaming it on dyslexia."

Cove thought about it for a moment, raised his eyes and said, "A bit convenient."

"What are you thinking?" Mendiola asked.

Cove bit his lip. "I'm not sure."

Pallid's office sat on Main Street. The building was sided with rough-cut wood, stained brown with a false front. They pulled next to an older black Lincoln Continental parked in front of it. Above the door was a large white sign with the words "Mike Pallid, Attorney at Law" painted in blue.

Cove opened the door for the deputy and was hit by the smell of stale cigarette smoke. Pallid was on the phone and motioned the two inside. They walked in and sat down in front of Pallid's desk.

Mike Pallid was talking on the phone. He wore a long sleeved white shirt with a loosely knotted red and black striped tie. Gold cufflinks were clasped on the shirt's cuffs. He was middle aged with a red bulbous nose, a gut, and combed-over well moussed hair.

Pallid hung up the phone and smiled. "Greetings, gentlemen, what have you got?"

"We need a search warrant," Mendiola explained.

Cove set Terzi's 8x10 photo in front of Pallid and tapped on it. "This's the guy," Cove explained, feeling as if he were trying to sell the man a used car.

"Nice teeth," Pallid commented. He picked up a pack of Marlboro cigarettes from his desktop and pulled one out. He lit it with a gold Zippo, inhaled deeply and exhaled looked at Mendiola.

"What'd this guy do?" Pallid asked, taking another hit on the cigarette.

"I'm thinking quite a bit," Mendiola said. "Charley can explain it better than I can."

The warden began by articulating how his investigation had focused in on Terzi starting with the snowplow driver describing the Dodge, moved on to Gabbro getting the truck's color, and his informant coming up with the name of Leo along with the information about the tooth. He finished with the details provided by Lemhi County on his full name. Cove added the finding of the rifle and the recovery of the bullet from Harris's cow into his briefing.

"How do you know he's living on Ruby Creek?" Pallid asked.

Cove thumbed through the pile that Sarah had pulled off the computer. "That's what he claimed four months ago when he registered his truck."

Pallid frowned. "You know, Charley, that's not fresh enough for a warrant."

"I just eyeballed his tire tracks on the road going down to the trailer. Thirty minutes ago is fresh. He's left the same interlocking Z-pattern at the last three crime scenes. I've got photographs if you want to look at them." Cove explained.

"This informant—the guy that gave you his first name— can you document his reliability?" Pallid asked.

"No, this is the first time I've dealt with him," Cove answered. "But the information we got from Lemhi County corroborates the information he gave. My informant described him as wearing a tooth around his neck. When he was arrested in Salmon, they took one away from him when they booked him in." Cove pointed at Terzi's picture. "It's right there. My informant ties him to the Dodge, and Motor Vehicles has got one registered to William Terzi with no middle initial."

Pallid blew smoke out of his nostrils. "And all's you're wanting is to search his truck and look for fired casings?"

"Both fired and loaded .300 WSM cartridges. And blood," Cove explained. "I'm betting he's got a partial box of shells somewhere in there."

"This ain't Vegas, and I don't gamble on the law," Pallid said sourly. "Why do you think the fired casings are inside his truck?"

"That's where he's been shooting from," Cove explained. "Sitting in the driver's seat. When he works the bolt, they're going to flip up and to the right." Cove mimed the antics of manipulating a bolt-action rifle. "They'll bounce off the inside of the windshield."

"And you have a witness to this?" Pallid queried.

"No," Cove answered, feeling his face reddening. "I've looked at his boot tracks at the scenes. He's not standing beside the truck when he's shooting. He shoots from inside."

Mendiola leaned in. "Mike, I don't know how many crime scenes Charley's worked involving tracks, but for Christ's sake, if he says the guy was shooting from inside the cab based on footprints, the judge will take his experience into account and sign the damned thing."

Pallid turned back to Cove. "There's gotta be a hundred trucks with that tread pattern. You figure out what brand they are?"

Cove canted his head and glanced at Mendiola, seeing blood in the deputy's face and he felt his own skin deepening. He briefly thought about the level of proof he needed for a search warrant: *a fair probability of evidence of a crime.* "No," Cove answered, with his voice picking up a cadence-like pattern. "I have no idea what brand of tires they are and I don't see how it would increase our probable cause. It's the tread pattern that's significant, not the manufacturer. Also, at each of the last three crime scenes, the guy's left the same footprint. Big cowboy boots, consistent with a thirteen. He's got a stride of thirty-one inches, which puts him at six-two or so. His vitals show him at six-three."

"Stride?" Pallid asked, shaking his head. "I've never heard of that or foot size used in an affidavit for a warrant. I doubt it's good science." Pallid looked over at Mendiola and continued. "Weak warrants lead to suppression hearings and appeals. You know that. I don't want to jeopardize this case. I'd really like to charge this guy with Petersham's burglary and make it stick," he nodded, "and for shooting what's-his-name's cow, but you have to bring me more. Send the rifle off to the lab and let's see if his prints show up. Then we can get an arrest warrant for the theft, and maybe we can get a search warrant for the truck. We can use the deer charges as dealing material. Give me more cards to play with." Pallid rubbed his cigarette in a half-full ashtray on his desk and added it to a pile of cigarette butts. Despite his effort, it continued to smoke.

Mendiola looked over at Charley Cove sitting in the wooden chair, his back stiff and his head erect, staring into Pallid's eyes. Other than a darkened complexion, he looked emotionless. The deputy thought he'd travelled into the past, seeing something from some long ago meeting.

Both officers got back in the truck without speaking. When Cove pulled out, Mendiola growled, "When he hinted at dropping the deer counts as part of a plea bargain, I thought you were gonna count coup on the prick."

Cove shook his head, "My grandfather said one needs a worthy adversary for coup."

"I know we've got enough PC for a warrant," Mendiola complained. "You oughta just write it up and take it to the judge; he'll sign it."

Cove shook his head. "I thought about that. Pallid'd drop the case like a log."

Mendiola pulled his cell phone out of his coat pocket and pushed a speed dial key. "Joey, you can stand down, no warrant." He pocketed the phone and turned back to Cove. "How 'bout we run out there right now and do a knock and talk?"

Cove thought for a moment, twisting his head and nodded. "Works for me."

Mendiola pulled his phone out, punched a button and after a few seconds spoke into it. "Sarah, we're gonna go pay Terzi a visit on Ruby Creek. We'll give you a call when we turn off the highway and when we're clear. Have Gabbro and Jenks hang around until we're done."

The two came up with an interview plan. Mendiola would say Howdy-Doody. Cove would lean on Terzi by asking him why he was spending his nights in the Pahsimeroi. That would hopefully gain an admission of his habit. Cove would take it from there and see how far it would go. Cove would focus on the interview and Mendiola would watch for any indications of a boil-over.

When the Ruby Creek road came into view, Mendiola picked up Cove's radio mic, pressed the transmit button, and spoke, "Sheriff, three-two-one and seven-three-one will be on location in two."

*****

Leo jumped. His phone was ringing. He looked at the display and flipped it open. "Yeah?"

"Mendiola and the Indian are headed your way." And the phone clicked off.

Leo stared at the display for a second, bug-eyed. He grabbed his Crown Royal bag off the couch, turned his TV off and ran out the back door, headed for the willows. He sat down on the stump and drew his revolver. He set it beside him, facing back towards his trailer forty yards away, his view of it hidden by brush. Eyes, ears, and nostrils were wide open. He heard the truck coming, opened his revolver's cylinder and looked at the six cartridge bases. Things were as black and white as a piano's keyboard. Snapping the cylinder back inside the gun's frame, he thought, *five for you, one for me.*

*****

Cove pulled past the cottonwoods, and the trailer came into view a half-football field away. They were losing their light, with the sun now below the mountains to the west. Willows lined most of the riverbank behind the sixty-foot trailer.

The trailer looked like a poorly pitched tent. Its axles had been removed and cast off to the side, rusting away. The structure's lightweight frame sat low to the ground on a makeshift foundation of loose cinderblocks. The wooden porch consisted of old faded rough-cut wood that had never seen a coat of paint nor a carpenter's level. At one time, the trailer had a red trim-stripe painted along the roof line, but it'd turned pink from years of sun. A piece of wind-blown aluminum siding was peeled back, exposing yellow fiberglass insulation and skinny vertical two-inch wood studs holding up the shoddy walls.

"Doesn't look like he's here," Mendiola said.

"Might be parked in the rear," Cove replied, and stopped his patrol truck thirty-yards short of the trailer. Both officers exited in unison. They approached the singlewide, maintaining a ten-foot side-by-side separation, both studying the windows for movement. Both sensed an edge in the air.

Mendiola stood off to the right side of the door and Cove stood on the left, with his good ear canted towards the structure, his eyes looking at the drapes on the nearest window. Neither had spoken since they'd stepped out of the truck. They both knew the danger of standing in front of an unknown doorway. They listened for movement in the trailer. Hearing none, Mendiola reached over to the center of the door, gave three solid knocks and hollered out with a strong neutral voice. "Hello in there. Sheriff's department. Anybody home?"

Again, the two officers listened. Cove felt a cold breeze come down the drainage. He drew his Glock and concealed it behind his leg. Mendiola looked at him and whispered, "Hear something?"

Cove gave one short negative shake of his head and looked to his left, watching the corner of the building. He heard Mendiola's Colt come out of its holster and the soft click of the safety coming off. After thirty seconds, Mendiola hammered his fist on the door again. There was no response.

"Let's see if his truck's out back," Cove said quietly. He started easing towards the left corner of the mobile home, watching the covered windows as he moved with Mendiola following. Stopping at the corner, Cove took a quick look around the edge and continued walking along the short end of the trailer.

The silver Dodge was parked behind the building. The right rear panel was smashed in and most of the red taillight cover was missing. Beyond lay a jungle of willows with one opening, showing the river flowing some forty or fifty yards away. Cove glanced at the snow around the truck. It was peppered by old and new foot prints. They were all made with a set of large pointy-toed cowboy boots.

*****

226

When he heard the truck approaching his road, Leo had picked up his revolver and gotten behind the stump and knelt in the snow, hearing and feeling the worms vibrating in his body, not bothering to scratch them. He had a bigger itch. *Come on motherfuckers, let's party.* He started running his tongue back and forth along his lip. He wasn't trying to play the keyboard. It was time to feed.

*****

Mendiola looked at the damage to the truck. Cove glanced under its frame, looking for someone crouched under the far side. He shifted his focus on the line of willows and the open spot leading to the river.

"He's gotta be here somewhere," Cove whispered.

"Or with another tweaker." Mendiola added in a low voice, "They like to buddy up."

"No other tire tracks," Cove said, and glanced at the window near their back. "I don't think this guy's got a lot of friends." He looked into the truck's bed and saw the dark stain. "Two-bits that's jackrabbit blood."

Mendiola looked at the blood. "We never did tell Pallid about that note bullshit."

Cove moved up to the cab and looked in, with Mendiola watching his back. The interior was trashed with fast-food sacks and carpeted with dried mud. An open box of Keystone beer sat on the passenger's side of the seat. A small blue duffel lay on the floor. A box of Federal .300 WSM cartridges sat on the hump just forward of the shifter boot. "There's Petersham's shells," Cove said, studying the floor without seeing any spent cartridges. "The Keystone box has a flap missing. That rip's going to match the note." He paused. "There's gonna be a black felt pen in there somewhere, too."

Mendiola spoke quietly. "If that lazy bastard doesn't give you the go ahead for a warrant after this, I'm gonna go talk to the judge."

\*\*\*\*\*

Leo Terzi heard their footsteps, smelled their sweat, and caught part of the whispered words. He was tired of listening to these bastards walking on his roof at night and sneaking in when he was gone, watching his porn videos. Tired of them sneaking a huff from his pipe. And now they had the balls to come while he was home. It was time to close the deal.

# *Chapter 15*

Leo Terzi eased up from behind the stump in the darkening shadows, holding the .357 in his hand and watching the warden's truck disappear up his lane. He saw the vehicle come back into view on the highway and listened to it fade towards Challis. He was shaking, and it wasn't from fear or lack of food. Walking over to his truck, he put his Crown Royal bag back into its hide and moved to the corner of his trailer. He slid a loose cinderblock out from under the trailer. He reached in, recovered a dark-green military-surplus ammo can and took it into his bedroom. It was time to feed the worms.

*****

Cove sat down, feeling the weight of the case, turned on his computer and looked out his back window into the darkness. He thought about calling Ralph Petersham and telling him about finding his rifle, but he knew he would want to know who stole it and why he wasn't behind bars. Cove's email beeped. It was from Julie, and he opened the message up.

*Mr. Warden: Since you're too embarrassed to be seen eating breakfast with me at the restaurant here in Rumorville, why don't I cook us up some bacon and eggs in the morning along with a big pot of fresh coffee? Seven-thirty okay? -Julie : )*

Instead of hitting the reply button, he picked up the phone.

"I found his rifle."

"You're kidding." Julie asked.

Cove filled her in on where the rifle was stashed but leaving out the part of about the coyote. He told how his boss had figured out Leo's full name and where he lived along with the meeting with the prosecutor. He left out the methamphetamine indicators, the long criminal history and the rabbit hanging from the fence.

"In a culvert?" Julie asked. "How'd you know to look there?"

Cove hesitated. "An old friend showed it to me. Since there's still snow on the ground, I can tell you over breakfast."

"What's snow got to do with it?" Julie inquired.

"It's a Salish thing," Cove explained, feeling a blush. "We're not supposed to tell our stories if there's no snow on the ground. If we get a Chinook wind tonight and the snow's gone in the morning, you'll be out of luck for a while."

"Not happening, Charley. It's supposed to clear off and get cold tonight. I don't think you're going to have an excuse tomorrow."

"Good, I'll be happy to share it with you," Cove said. "I'll be there unless I get called out. If I do I'll drop you a text."

"If you get another callout, come pick me up!" Julie said.

Cove promised her he would and hung up, almost hoping for a midnight phone call.

*****

Fred Mendiola was sitting in his living room with his wife, watching the start of the Jay Leno show. Leno had just finished working the crowd, shaking hands and high-fiving when the deputy's phone rang. The display revealed it was his dispatcher, Sarah, calling from her personal cell.

"Fred, I hate to bother you at home, but I thought I'd better call ya."

"No, problem," Mendiola said. "What's up?"

"It just hit me where I'd heard Terzi's name," Sarah said. "Or at least his last name."

"Okay..." Mendiola said curiously, wondering why she wasn't waiting until morning to fill him in.

"Gabbro was married to a Terzi, wasn't he? Wasn't his wife's maiden name *Terzi*?"

Mendiola scratched his head. "Yeah, you're right... he was married to Suzanne Terzi, I dunno where she ended up."

"I just thought it's too strange a name. He's got to be related to Gabbro's ex," Sarah exclaimed.

"Gotta be related. She left town after they split, right?" Mendiola asked.

"She's been gone since they had the fight."

"Do me a favor in the morning." Mendiola's face was as serious as a car wreck. "Get Gabbro's driver's license photo from Boise and email to those Pocatello detectives. Have them show it to the pawnbroker."

"You think he's involved?" Sarah asked.

"I sure as hell hope not," Mendiola said massaging his forehead. "Cove figured out the guy's using Petersham's stolen rifle." Mendiola hesitated. "I know I don't need to tell you this, but keep this between the two of us. Maybe I'm blowing smoke, but the description the pawnbroker gave them's been grinding on me."

*****

Leo Terzi picked his reading glasses from the dresser, put them on and squatted on the bare mattress that sat on the floor at the end of his trailer. He looked up at his pet watching him through the terrarium's glass. The snake's eyes were starting to glaze over, signaling it was time to shed its skin. He popped open the ammo can and pulled out a brown leather zippered shaving kit. He took off his shirt, revealing his drug-skinny chest. The inside of each of his forearms were tattooed. The one on the right arm sported a marijuana leaf imprinted with dark blue ink. On Leo's left arm there was the tatt of a skeleton playing a red piano and smoking a cigar. The image was faded and sagging on his lose pale skin.

He unzipped the kit and pulled out a plastic bag containing two tiny meth crystals. Bringing it up to his face, he stared at the Ziploc for a moment. He tilted his head and placed the dope back in the kit. Standing up, he reached beside the dresser and found his snake stick. It was cut from a three-foot willow sapling about a half-inch in diameter with two forks on the business end that were just shy of an inch long. Terzi slid the plywood cover off the glass box. The snake began clacking its tail and felt his

presence with its two infrared pits set between its nose
and eyes. Terzi slowly brought the stick into the terrarium
and moved it within a few inches of the serpent's head. He
paused and then pressed the snake's neck into the gravel.
The animal's rope-like body flipped around and settled
into a slithering rhythm trying to worm free while
furiously shaking its tail, clamoring like a snowball on a
hot stove. Satisfied he had his friend under control, Terzi
reached into its lair and dug around in the gravel until he
found his treasure, two small Ziplocs clasped together
with a rubber band.

Each baggie held an *eight ball* of crystal
methamphetamine, or an eighth of an ounce. The
combined volume of the small crystals was about the size
of a walnut and resembled elongated pieces of course salt.
He pulled the stash out, set it on the dresser and released
the snake. Without taking his eyes off the viper, he
replaced the plywood cover on the top of the terrarium.

He sat back down on the mattress and separated the
two Ziplocs. He put one in his shaving kit. He brought the
other up to his eyes and flicked it with his middle finger,
admiring the contents like a jeweler sizing up a trove of
diamonds. Laying the dope on the mattress, he fished
around in the shaving kit and pulled out a length of nylon
chord, a rubber-topped dropper bottle, and a loose
syringe, its needle covered by an orange cap. The cord had
a loop tied on one end. On one end of the mattress sat a
pile of rumpled blankets. He dug around in the pile, found
a ragged King James Bible in the bedding and set it beside
him. He reached back into the shaving kit and found a
spoon and a cigarette filter. The spoon's handle had been

bent back under itself so when it was placed on a flat surface, its bowl sat level. He used it to scoop out a thumbnail sized pile of meth crystals from the Ziploc and set it on the Bible. He pushed his glasses up his nose and took the dark brown dropper bottle, unscrewed the cap, and carefully squeezed the rubber bulb over the meth. He watched eight drops of distilled water fall into the spoon. He took the cap off the syringe, stirred the liquid around with the needle and watched the crystals disappear. Holding the syringe in his mouth, he tore off a small piece of cigarette filter and laid it in the liquid. He put the beveled needle tip into the filter and drew the sweet brew into the syringe, being careful not to suck up any cotton. He set his now-loaded baby back on the Bible.

Leo stood up and looked out the window and saw nothing but the night. He went down the hall and looked back towards his couch. He paused, rubbing the tooth hanging from his neck. He opened the back door and stuck his head out. The cold air stung his bare white skin as he stepped into the night. He closed the trailer door and listened, folding his arms tight to his chest. The icy river made a rippling sound. His tongue tasted the manure of his neighbor's far off horses. The acrid smell of packrat urine soaked into his nostrils. He looked across the river up into the cliffs, and let his eyes adjust until he could see the little gray-haired rats watching him, lit by moonlight that only he could see. An owl hooted from the cottonwoods and a coyote yapped, but he sensed no enemies and stepped back into the trailer, shivering.

He sat down on the mattress and wrapped the nylon cord around his bicep. He tightened it up, holding it in place with his molars. He pumped up his fist and watched his vessels grow through the tatt of the dead pianist. Picking up the syringe, he paused over the vein protruding from the inside crook of his arm, and slowly pushed it into the vessel. He brought the plunger back and a dark flash of red hit his candy. He popped the cord loose and watched the blood mixing with the liquid meth in the syringe. His face looked dead serious. "Bombs away," he whispered, and pushed the payload home, with the snake watching from above.

It smacked him fast. One moment he was sitting on the mattress, needle in his arm, and now he was riding on the hood of his Dodge, doing a hundred miles an hour with the ice-cold wind blowing across his white-hot skin.

The snake looked down through its cloudy eyes and watched his keeper rolling back and forth on the mattress, moaning in an unrecognized language. The reptile opened its mouth, flicked its tongue, and sensed the euphoria snapping in the coils of Leo's twisted brain.

*****

Julie Lake had changed from her work clothes into her sweat pants and a light green T-shirt. She was prepping tomorrow's breakfast. She'd been on the phone talking to a source about the effect climate change was having on the forests of Central Idaho. Much of the Douglas Fir above Challis was turning red, dying from a pine beetle infestation. She'd decided to chase a story on it, believing it had regional if not national appeal. Her source had explained the relationship between the outbreak and the lack of subzero temperatures that once kept the insects in check prior to the current climate change. She was tired. She turned her computer off for the night and felt the need to escape by slicing and dicing. Neil Young was singing "Heart of Gold" in the background and she was humming along.

She'd chopped up half of a white onion and sliced a red bell pepper. The onions had opened up her sinuses and she was now finely chopping a small Serrano pepper to give the meal some zing. A fresh loaf of bread was baking in the oven. Earlier she'd fried some sliced sausage links. Between the bread, the links, the onions, and the peppers, her house smelled enticingly homelike and felt warm and friendly. She dumped the concoction into a stainless bowl, put it in the refrigerator and pulled out a gray cardboard egg container. She cracked a half dozen eggs into a round clear glass mixing bowl, added some ground pepper and chopped garlic, and placed it next to the stainless bowl in the refrigerator. She pulled the bread from the oven, bringing forth a stronger homey aroma to the room and turned the stereo off.

She was tired and content, ready to snuggle in bed with her book, drift into a deep night's sleep, looking forward to a companionable morning meal.

*****

Leo's worms were well fed. He'd ridden the rush from his needle slam and he was ready for a young doe, but he still sensed a sinister focus on his trailer. Somebody was

thinking about him and he figured it was the Indian. He
could feel it. It had to be him.

He drove up the Pahsimeroi with his overhead lights
off, stopped at Morse Creek and killed the engine.
Grabbing his flashlight, he dropped off the side, saw the
Vibram boot tracks and froze. He shined the light down to
the culvert and confirmed the brush covering its mouth
was still in its place. Sensing a trap, he turned the light off
and listened. No engine idled in the distance. He could
smell the lingering exhaust fumes from his truck and the
ammonia coming from his breath, but sensed nothing
from an unseen engine. He stood, letting his eyes adjust to
the darkness. It was dead quiet on the sage flats. The air
was frozen. No owl hooted from the bottoms and the
coyotes were silent. He watched the Lemhi Range emerge
from the darkness. With the meth in his brain, it was
another two-moon night lighting the valley up in bright
blacks and whites, as dazzling as midday, but without
color. No threat as far as his crystal-enhanced eyes could
see.

Pulling the brush from the culvert, he reached in and
felt the rock. The worms recoiled in his veins. He shined
the light into the culvert, saw the business card, and
pulled it out, fingers trembling. He read the note on the
back of the card and then flipped it over and saw the
Indian's name. His skin turned a dark purple. A flush of
sweat oozed out of his pores, smelling like the chemical-
laced urine he'd left in the snow during his last visit. The
coyotes along the river cocked their ears and tested the
air, pumping it in with flared nostrils.

Leo got back in his truck and turned around. His head throbbed and his eyes watered. Near the highway junction he pulled over and fished a marijuana blunt from his Crown bag. Placing the fat cigar-looking joint in his mouth, he lit it with his Bic. He sucked a deep lungful of smoke in and held it, letting the THC get his mind back on track. He sat in the darkness of the truck, thinking about the Indian. He took another hit and the blunt's tip cast a red glow across his face.

When he got to Ruby Creek, he pulled in and checked around his trailer. He shined his flashlight in the snow and examined the tracks from the two bastards. Pulling his pistol, he shined the light up on the roof while pointing the revolver. Nothing. Entering through the front door, he put his hand on his TV and felt the warmth. He knew they'd been back.

He drove into Challis, pulled into his hidey-hole and shut down the engine. He sat listening to the town's quiet, smelling the air and catching the taste of wood smoke emanating from the sleepy houses. He could clearly see the eyeballs staring at him from the knotholes in the fence. Looking behind him, heads emerged from the trashcans. He didn't care; he had enough juice in his veins that the evil bastards couldn't touch him. He'd worked out a plan and it was past time to get it rolling. No traffic travelled Main Street. He started his truck, eased out onto the road and idled down the alley, parking a quarter block from Red's house. He reached down and grabbed his duffel. He eased his door open, got out and listened. A dog barked a block over. He walked slowly towards the back of her house to her bedroom window and looked along the edge of her drapes, trying to see inside. Nothing stirred. No lights were on. Flaring his nostrils, he thought he could smell her inside. *Goddamn!* He eased around to the front door and set his duffle on the porch. He took out a circular glass cutter, licked its black rubber suction cup and listened. Still nothing. He placed the suction cup on the door's window and drew the cutter's wheel around, the cutter making a scraping sound as it scored the surface of the glass. He gently pushed and pulled back and forth, flexing the glass until he heard a quiet snap. He pulled the glass circle out of the door still stuck to the suction cup. Sticking his nose up to the eight-inch hole, he sniffed and came close to having an orgasm.

Reaching through the hole he gently unlocked the door, hearing a quiet-dull thud from the mechanism. He opened the door and stepped inside the house, smelling the food and smelling Red. *Goddamn!*

*****

Julie was dreaming, but felt a cold draft. She snuggled deeper into her blankets. The dream took her back to her college days when she had taken a photography class and was learning to develop black and white prints in a darkroom. The small room was lit by subdued photo-safe lights and had a strong odor of chemicals. Charley Cove was her lab instructor, wearing his uniform and gun belt in the red-hued darkroom. In the dream, his hair was long and he wore it in a ponytail, clasped by a beaded ring. The feather from his mirror hung from the beadwork. They were the only two in the lab and were developing black and white photos of the deer they had found dead in the

Pahsimeroi. She was standing next to Charley and they were watching an image appear on the 8x10 paper submerged in the clear developing liquid. Julie held the corner of the paper with plastic tongs and was gently moving the sheet back and forth in the chemical. The image of the doe became sharp and clear. The pool of blood at the deer's head turned dark red, looking odd on the black and white photo. The lab smell became vivid.

Her bedroom light snapped on and a hand slapped across her mouth. Her eyes were wide open. She screamed through his fingers, but only a muffled noise escaped. She grasped his corpse-like skin, shook her head, and tried to pull his boney grip from her face, but it wouldn't budge as he pressed her head deep into the pillow. She looked up at the skull-like face that grinned back at her, exposing a handful of yellow teeth. She felt the ice-cold barrel poke into her cheek and she stopped her muted scream.

Terzi took his hand off her mouth and brought his crooked finger to his lips, losing his smile. "You scream once, and you'll never see the fuckin' Indian again. I promise."

She tried to ease her hand under the pillow, but Terzi grabbed her by the throat. He yanked her from the bed, slammed her to the floor, and tightened his grip, blocking the air from her trachea. He relaxed his grip, letting a little air choke into her lungs. "You fight me, no air."

Julie froze on the floor, still smelling the chemicals from her dream-turned-nightmare. The gun's barrel was now jammed into her throat. He was digging around for something beside him with his free hand. "If you wanna breathe, shut up." He took the gun away from her throat and she heard the sound of duct tape being peeled off its roll. The tape went over her mouth and jammed over her nostrils, blocking her air. She flared her nose and found some air, breathing around the tape's edge. That's what she focused on—inhaling and exhaling. He rolled her over and painfully squeezed her wrists together, jammed a sharp knee into her back and joined her arms with a plastic zip tie and then rolled her back to her side. She lay, arms bound behind her, facing out her bedroom door with tears running down her face, thankful she'd gone to bed wearing her sweat pants and T-shirt.

"You're gonna need somethin' on your feet," he said, and stuffed a running shoe on each foot, leaving the laces loose. Terzi stood up and started going through her dresser, picking up panties, bringing them to his nose, testing them. "Too goddamned clean," he mumbled. Leaning over, he grabbed her by the waist and threw her over his shoulder and grabbed his duffel. "We're gonna party, Red. We're gonna party real good."

He went to the back door, opened it and stepped out into the cold night, carrying his booty. He stood on the porch, listening to the air rasp around the duct tape on her nose. The dog was still barking. He packed her to his truck, no longer walking with stealth, but striding out. When he reached his truck, he opened the passenger door and threw her down on the floor, knocking her head on the dashboard. Julie Lake passed out.

# Chapter 16

Cove was dreaming. He was a boy riding bareback on a white and brown horse. His mount had a black-painted palm print on its white rump. Except for a loincloth and moccasins, he was naked, with long black hair flowing in the wind. He was no longer light-skinned, but was full blood Salish, and had gained his grandfather's nose and broad face. He was at a full gallop, grasping his horse's chest with his thighs, riding with two other young boys, rolling across a never-ending hill covered in deep green grass under a cloudless blue sky. Holding hard to their horse's long manes and woven rawhide reins, the three were laughing and yelling war whoops, hoping to count coup on some imaginary enemy. They were as unencumbered as the brown-spotted young eagles riding the wind above them.

*****

Julie could recall being carried into the trailer, but she didn't remember being bound to the chair's arms with duct tape. She realized she was in the chair when Terzi had ripped the tape off her mouth. She'd screamed at him to let her go, but he just laughed in her face with breath that smelled like a janitor's mop bucket. He took another length of duct tape, covered her mouth, wrapped it around her long red hair and back across her mouth. At least her nostrils were clear and legs were free.

Leo Terzi stared at Julie and scratched his face, grinning. He glanced at the TV and turned back to her. "We can git high and watch a video." He laughed and walked down the hall rubbing his mojo tooth and went out the back door.

Julie took the opportunity to try to stand up, but it was clear, even without the chair, she wasn't going to be able make a run for it, let alone open the front door. She had no idea where she was. She remembered Charley mentioning Ruby Creek, but she had no idea where it was and she had no knowledge of how close the creep's neighbors were, or even if he had any.

Terzi pulled his Crown Royal bag from his truck. He walked back into the trailer and sat down on the couch in front of Julie. Sober as a preacher, he looked at her. "Red, I'm going to give you a gift." He pulled out his glass pipe and Ziploc of meth, fingered two crystals into the bowl and found his Bic. Standing up, he flipped the lighter on, holding the flame under the bowl, feeling the heat on his ring finger that sealed the bowl's vent. Looking into Julie's wide eyes, he brought the stem up and slowly inhaled the vapors, rolling the pipe back and forth, turning the crystals to steam. Without looking away, he sucked the fumes in. After a bit, he leaned over and exhaled the thick foggy vapors into Julie's face. Seeing it coming, she closed her eyes and held her breath. The smell permeated her nostrils. It reminded her of smoke from a garbage fire. When it'd subsided, she looked up at Terzi, her eyes narrowed, face bright red, and kicked him in the balls harder than a high school punter ever smacked a football.

Terzi went down hard, dumped like a sack of spuds, breaking his glass pipe, rolling in the fetal position and grasping his groin with both hands and moaning.

Julie hadn't thought through the move, it'd been a visceral reaction to what he'd done to her–starting with the invasion of her home, the abduction, and finally the drug smoke he'd blown in her face.

Terzi slowly got to his feet still bent over and glared at Julie. "Bitch, now you're gonna have to..." His head wheeled around and he looked down the hallway. "Huh?" He grunted and jerked his revolver out of his cross draw and fired two quick rounds down the hallway into his bedroom, the explosions rattling the trailer's walls. Holding his gun out with one hand, he shuffled slowly down the hall and stopped in the doorway of his room. He looked around inside, bug-eyed, with his head cocked at an odd angle. He knew he'd heard them and had seen a shadow, but whoever it was had escaped. He looked at the fresh bullet holes staring back at him from his bedroom wall and turned around to see Julie staring at him from the chair.

*****

Cove awoke, recalling bits and pieces of the dream. It'd felt real. Easing back into his world, he could smell the earthy odor of horse sweat.

He jumped in the shower and shaved yesterday's beard off. He still felt the propulsion of the investigation and despite Pallid's negative attitude, he was motivated to push the case. After the plain view sighting of the cartridge box and blood in Terzi's truck, Pallid would be hard pressed to come up with an excuse to not support a warrant. Although Cove hadn't seen any fired casings on the floor, the trashed interior indicated Terzi didn't iron his underwear and he believed he'd find at least one of the casings in the mess.

Cove threw his uniform on, thinking he was going to start the day off with a good meal and good company. He had plans of grabbing Mendiola and selling Pallid the used car. Then going to the judge to get the warrant signed. By afternoon he'd be coordinating a multi-officer visit to Terzi's trailer.

He loaded Annie and drove down to Julie's house with the sun breaking over the Lost River Range. The sky was clear and the air was cold. Cove pulled in behind her Subaru. *She'll want Annie inside*, Cove thought, and dropped the tailgate. Ten feet from the door, he saw the hole in the glass and his blood turned cold. Without processing it, his Glock was in his right hand and his eyes scanned the windows. A glow hinted from back in the bedroom. He eased up to the door, paused and listened. He pulled his cell out of his coat pocket, punched in 9-1-1 with one hand, and dropped the phone, still on, back in its pocket. He held his gun pointed forward, keeping it close to his chest, and eased the door open. Clearing the doorway, he silently stepped into the room, moved laterally away from the bright entrance, stopped, and motioned for Annie to search. She went forth eagerly, nose down, and hackles up. Cove switched to a two-handed isosceles grip, looking over his front sight, weapon pointed to the edge of the bedroom wall. He leaned his good ear towards the lighted room. Annie disappeared into the room and after a moment that seemed more like a day, she came back out. She glanced at Cove, sniffed at the back door and sat down. Her behavior told him there was neither friend nor foe in the bedroom. Cove moved at a fast walk, down the hall, cleared the second bedroom, the bathroom, and then through the kitchen, checking the washroom. Finally, he looked into Julie's bedroom. *No blood.*

"Sheriff, coming in!" Mendiola's voice boomed from the front door.

"In here!" Cove yelled back from inside the bedroom. Half the bedding was on the floor. The bed's headboard had been pulled from the wall and was set at an angle from the wall. The top two drawers on the dresser were open and underwear lay on the floor. Cove leaned down and picked up a black plastic wire tie. "He's taken her. It's Terzi... I cleared the rest of the place." Cove felt the deputy next to him. "I was supposed to meet her for breakfast. Annie was interested in the back door. It's got to be Terzi."

Mendiola's eyes scanned the room. "Looks like there was a struggle."

Cove saw the butt of the Glock under Julie's pillow, stepped over to it and pulled it out. He dropped the magazine into his hand, looked at the cartridges showing through the view-holes and confirmed it was fully loaded. Slamming the mag in place he stuffed the gun in the small of his back and looked at Mendiola. "Unfired."

"Lake's gun?" Mendiola asked, squinting his eyes.

Cove met his gaze. "No, it was Liz's. I loaned it 'cause of the stalking."

Mendiola looked confused. "Your phone still on? Sarah thought you'd butt-dialed 9-1-1. When she said it was your phone and when her screen showed where you were at, I figured something was up."

Cove pulled his cell out, snapped it closed and noted a missed call. "That's what I was hoping, thanks for rolling," Cove said. "I didn't know what I'd find."

"That hole in the front door," Mendiola said. "The glass. It's the same MO as Petersham's burglary. You might be right, this might be Terzi." He shook his head, frowning. "Sarah figured out he's Gabbro's ex-brother-in-law; there's some kinda bullshit going on."

Mendiola pulled put his cell and looked at the display. "He's gotta have her at his trailer." He paused and looked at Cove. "I wish I had somebody to sit on this scene. He's got to have left some prints unless he's using gloves."

"Let's leave Annie." Cove suggested.

"She ain't a bite dog," Mendiola said, looking at Cove as if he were crazy.

"Nobody else knows that," Cove said.

Mendiola nodded still frowning. "Better'n nothing, let's look out back."

The two exited the front without touching the rear doorknob, moved around to the rear of the house and confirmed the boot tracks in the snow.

Cove studied the footprints. "It's Terzi."

Are you positive, Charley?" Mendiola asked.

"Yeah, I am." He pointed at the tracks. "Longer stride here—he was in a hurry when he left."

Cove's eyes followed the tracks and found a white running shoe laying on the snow. He picked it up and confirmed it was a woman's seven and a half and set it back down. He followed the footprints to where he could see down the alley. "Son of a bitch!" Cove mumbled and stared down the empty passage chewing his lip.

"I'll get the cavalry rolling," Mendiola said, looking at his phone. He punched in one number and put it to his ear. "Sarah, we've got an abduction, Julie Lake. Call Lemhi, tell 'em we're gonna be dealing with a barricaded subject. Tell 'em I need at least four to help form an entry team and their two snipers too." Mendiola pinched the skin between his eyes. "Call Stanley and Mackay. Get 'em all rolling, code. We'll stage at the pullout at milepost 253 on highway ninety-three. Get Jenks moving that way and I'll call Gabbro," Mendiola paused. "He's suspended as of right now. Call the state police. Tell 'em I want two units. I want the highway shut down either side of Ruby Creek." Mendiola hung up, frowning, and looked at Cove. "We'll get this asshole."

Cove glanced back down the alley, noting he'd made no such promise for Julie Lake.

Mendiola jolted him. "Let's get moving."

The two officers dashed to their trucks. "I'll grab a coupla tear gas canisters," Mendiola said. "Meet me at that pull out. Jenks should be there soon. I'll be right behind you. Try to come up with some negotiation plan."

Cove jumped in his truck. When he turned on Main street, he hit the switch turning on his flashing light-bar and cranked the siren's yelp button on. Passing the courthouse, he heard another siren and glanced in his mirror. He saw Deputy Jenks's rig with its overhead blue lightbar flashing. He felt Liz's Glock in the small of his back, pulled it out and placed it in the console.

Cove's radio chattered with noise. He heard officers from Mackay and Stanley transmitting they were in-service and responding. When he hit the highway, he turned his siren off, focusing. At the staging area Mendiola had designated, he pulled off, looked into his side mirror and watched Jenks follow him in.

Cove rolled his window down when the deputy walked up.

"This the guy you been chasing?" He asked.

Cove reached up on his dashboard and grabbed a large manila envelope. He handed Terzi's photograph to Jenks. "Yeah, he's got a long history, but no felony convictions." Cove heard a vehicle coming fast. He looked at his mirror and saw Mendiola approaching in his lit-up SUV.

Jenks handed the photograph back to him. "A real beauty. Meth head?"

"Sounds like it," Cove nodded.

"Any idea what he's got for weapons?"

Cove shook his head. "No, I think there's a .270 that's unaccounted for from a burglary."

Jenks nodded. "I'm gonna make sure my AR15 mags are topped off, in case Fred says we gotta go in." He handed the picture back to Cove and hurried back to his patrol truck. Cove looked around, struggling with what had happened. *Coyote, where are you?*

\*\*\*\*\*

Julie stared down the hallway into the room where Terzi had fired. Terzi picked up a shaving kit from the floor in the far bedroom and walked towards her. From the corner of her eye, she watched him work around the living area, looking out of each window, his eyes wide and paranoid. He opened the front door, stepped out on the porch and glanced back in, looking at her with his nostrils strangely flared. She'd never seen a rabid dog, but she thought this was what one must look like.

Terzi stepped back in, set the shaving kit on the table, and sat down. He slid a plate to the side, picked up an empty .357 shell casing and flicked it towards the sink. Julie watched, not wanting to make eye contact, but she felt as though she was riding a train with a half-dead conductor at its helm, and she was searching for a sign of what lay ahead.

Terzi glanced across his stained couch and looked at his toy taped in the chair. "You don't like me right now, but that's gonna change." He wasn't smiling. "I'm gonna share something with you, then you'll be my woman." He reached into the shaving kit and pulled out a syringe, his lips parted and his tongue started sliding back and forth along his lips. "I'm gonna teach you how to play the piano too. I'm real good." Terzi stared at the table, pushed his paraphernalia out of the way and began using the table as his keyboard, nodding with the music in his head. Julie stared, watching his behavior, unsure if the creep was delusional or miming like a kid playing an air guitar. After a minute, Terzi froze and looked around with a befuddled face, as if he'd misplaced something. Finally, he focused on his shaving kit, picked up the syringe and looked inside its barrel as if he'd lost something.

Julie saw the needle and shuddered, knowing where the conductor was taking the train. She looked down at her feet. Her left foot was bare and she could feel the cold coming through the trailer's floor. Her other foot still had its unlaced running shoe on it. She brought the bare foot up, placed it on top of the shoe and felt a tear slip down her cheek.

*****

Cove started to get out of his truck when his phone growled.

"Charley," Nayman said. "What the hell's going on? I hear Mendiola's asking for lotsa help?"

"It's Terzi. He's kidnapped somebody," Charley explained. "Fred'n I were poking around his trailer last night. Musta struck a nerve."

"You're shittin' me. Who'd he snatch?" Nayman asked.

"Grabbed Julie Lake from town. She's a reporter," Cove explained, and heard a siren coming from Nayman's phone.

"Dax and I are headed your way. See you in fifty."

Cove closed the cover of his phone and approached Mendiola, who was talking on his cell. Jenks was standing next to him. Mendiola looked at Cove and closed his phone.

"We need to keep him contained." Mendiola said. "We will not allow him to drive off. I'll get a rifle team on the cliff and one in the cottonwoods. State police will block the highway."

Cove took a deep breath. "It'll take at least an hour for everybody to get here and briefed, and another forty-five for the snipers to get in the rocks."

"I know," Mendiola said. "This might run through the night. I've got the state SWAT team rolling. They'll be here by dark, but let's hope we can talk him out before then."

Cove scowled. "He can cook her for dinner by then." His phone rang, he looked at the display, but didn't recognize the number. "Second time this guy's called," Cove said shaking his head as he opened it up.

"Yeah?" Cove asked curtly.

An unfamiliar voice laughed. "Geronimo? I got your squaw."

Cove turned to cold stone. "Terzi," he said, lowering his voice and breathing deeply. "Don't..."

"I already have, Indian. Now, we're gonna play lets-make-a-fuckin' deal. You and me. You for her. Ya know where I live, and keep the fuck off my roof. Red and me is already started the party. See you soon." And the phone went dead.

Cove stared at the cell's display. "He wants a swap."

"What?" Mendiola asked.

"Terzi–that was him," Cove said, still looking at the phone. "Me. He wants to trade me for Julie."

Mendiola glared at Cove and rolled his head. "You're shittin' me. What the..? Why you?"

Cove shook his head. "I don't know... I left my business card in the culvert. That's how he musta got my number."

The two officers stared at each other; both their faces had turned cold.

Mendiola spoke first. "We ain't gonna do no damn swap. Ain't gonna happen. We gotta get control and I ain't trading him anything but a sack lunch. He's not running this show." Mendiola looked downriver towards Ruby Creek and turned back to the warden. "Gimme his phone number."

Cove opened his cell and read the number while Mendiola wrote. When Fred was done he looked at Cove. "I'll give him a call in a sec and see whether I can't get some kinda dialogue going."

Mendiola's phone rang and he looked at the display. "It's the lab," he said, and brought the cell to his ear. The oversized deputy listened, thanked the voice on the other end while looking at Cove and hung up. "Jesus Christ, they got an AFIS hit on your latent print. It came back to William Leonard Terzi," he said shaking his head. "That takes the frigging cake."

Cove canted his head, bit his lip and caught movement across the river. A Bald Eagle had just landed in a cottonwood tree on the far bank. He could see its curved yellow beak and its white head swiveled towards the officers. Below the bird, shelf ice marked the river's far edge. There were two lines of tracks imprinted in the snow on top of the ice. Each track had two side-by-side paw prints with an intermittent scuff from a thick tail and they disappeared into the slush of the river. *Otters,* Cove thought, and looked up at the bird now acting anxious. The eagle swooped from its limb and cruised downriver, swinging its broad wings towards the mouth of Ruby Creek.

*****

Leo Terzi pulled the bent spoon out of his hype kit. He laid it on the table and found his Ziploc bag of meth. He set it on the table and dug around inside his kit for his cigarette filter and dropper bottle.

Julie was watching Terzi, denying what she was watching, but knowing who the syringe was for. Her heart was pounding and the tears were rolling down her cheeks. Terzi walked over to the kitchen counter and turned on a portable CD player. An electric guitar twanged a rhythm back and forth. Hank Williams Jr. began singing about his rowdy friends.

"Can't party without Hank," Terzi said, making eye contact with his redheaded captive. He pulled a piece of cotton off the filter, laid it on the table and spooned a portion of meth crystals from the Ziploc. He studied the drug for a moment and glanced at Julie. He mumbled to himself, "I'd better go easy on this first one." He dumped half of the crystals back into the plastic bag. The lump in the spoon was about the size of a dried pea, about half his normal payload. He picked up the dropper bottle and counted out five drops of water. He pulled the cover off the syringe's needle and began stirring the juice, watching the crystals turning to slush and finally disappear into the syrupy water. He picked up the pinch of cotton and dropped it into the liquid. He looked up at Julie, his face as sane as a school bus driver. "You're about to ride the

needle, honey. Don't be afraid. I know what I'm doing."
He put the syringe's metal tip into the filter and started to
pull the plunger. Nothing happened. Terzi set the hype
down and fished around in the kit for his reading glasses.
Once on his nose, he picked the syringe back up, and tried
to suck the liquid up into the device, but the needle was
plugged. "Shit," Terzi said, and stood up. He grabbed his
lighter and walked to the sink. "Goddamn it." He turned
the faucet on and held the flame under the needle until he
saw a whiff of smoke escape out of its point and stuck the
hot metal under the running water.

*****

Fred Mendiola dialed Terzi's number and gave up after
several rings. "Cove, let me try your phone. Maybe he's
screening his calls."

The warden handed his cell to Mendiola. The deputy
toggled up the call history, found the number and turned
to Jenks. "Get your recorder out and hold it up to the
phone. I want a record of this." He redialed the number. It
was picked up on the first ring.

"Geronimo, you're gonna be late. Get your fuckin' red
ass down here!"

"Mr. Terzi, this is acting sheriff Fred Mendiola," The
big deputy said with a subdued voice. "I wanna work with
you on this thing. Let's talk. Is there something I can do
for you?"

"Fuck off." The phone went dead.

Without getting his cell back, Cove walked to his truck,
and opened the door. He sat rigid behind the wheel,

looking through the windshield without seeing anything. He held his head slightly twisted, listening for a sound he didn't hear. Waiting for something to come to him. The feather hanging from his mirror caught his focus; two of its barbs had separated. Reaching over, he straightened them with his thumb and finger. The surfaces reattached like two pieces of Velcro. The feather was from the tail of a Great Horned Owl. To his father's people, the owl was respected for its silent hunting skill and it represented wisdom, but the Salish also considered it to be a harbinger of death if seen in a dream or a vision.

He stared at the feather and slowed his breathing. Its outer surface was whitish with five dark gray crossbars. At the base of the flight surface was a cluster of white downy plumes. Its centered quill was a dark shiny gray. The feather reminded him of a story his grandfather had told him after they had taken a sweat bath together on a cold winter night. The sweat lodge was behind his grandfather's cabin. It was dome shaped, constructed using long willows stuck in the ground and lashed together with twine–similar to the old wikiups the people had once lived in. Several pieces of old faded canvas covered the structure. His grandfather had heated large river rocks in a nearby fire and moved them into the lodge with a shovel. The two had sat quietly inside while his grandfather took a rusty coffee can and splashed creek water on the hot rocks. The water turned to steam and instantly heated the lodge. The splashing was repeated every minute or so. Cove remembered it being so hot he had a hard time breathing. After the sweat, the two had run and jumped briefly into the icy creek and had quickly dried off with towels. It was during the toweling that his grandfather quietly told him the story.

It was a tale of conflict with Blackfoot warriors. His ancestor was with a hunting party in buffalo country east of the Bitterroot Valley. The Salish had discovered the war party preparing to raid their camp. Cove's grandfather explained how *his* great grandfather and several other tribal members—at great risk—performed a preemptive attack on their age-old enemy. Cove recalled that an owl had been hooting in the darkness during the storytelling.

Cove's eyes narrowed. He started the truck's engine, buckled the seat belt, and pulled out onto the highway.

Mendiola's voice crackled through his radio. "Seven-three-one, where you headed?"

Cove reached to the radio and turned the volume all the way down, while stepping on the accelerator. His hand moved to the truck's dashboard and engaged the four-wheel drive. At the Ruby Creek road, he slowed enough to maintain control and powered through the turn.

*****

Julie felt her heart striking her chest. She was watching Terzi. He had managed to clear the dried blood plugging the needle and had filled the barrel of the syringe with the liquid from the spoon. He tapped the air from the syringe's barrel. He stood up, put the syringe sideways between his lips and walked around the couch to Julie. He pulled the device from his mouth . "Nothing to be scared of, Red. This is gonna be one hell of a ride." Staying clear of her feet, he put the syringe back in his lips, wrapped the cord around her bicep, and started tapping for a vein.

\*\*\*\*\*

The trailer came into view as Charley Cove's truck cleared the line of cottonwoods. Forty yards from the building, he reached down and turned his siren on, it gave out a hundred decibel scream. His foot floored the gas pedal. It was a simple plan hinged on three tons of audacity.

He caught the left side of the building with the right half of his truck, hoping like hell Julie was somewhere else in the trailer. Halfway through the shattering crash, the truck's airbag exploded, throwing Cove's head back against the headrest. The momentum carried the six thousand pound missile through the building, ripping the trailer's entire end wall off. Cove's truck stopped when it impacted Terzi's parked Dodge. Torn aluminum siding, broken lumber and bits of ragged yellow fiberglass insulation covered the hood and roof of his patrol truck.

Cove rolled out of the truck door, clenched his Glock and jumped into the gaping hole of the trailer. The impact had knocked the singlewide part way off its block foundation and the new entryway was scrambled with debris. Cove found himself standing on a mattress, peering around the left edge of a wall, down a hallway too choked with dust to see anything. He held his Glock up, with his eyes looking for Terzi over the gun sights. Finally the air cleared enough to see Julie, wide eyes staring at

258

him, her mouth covered with duct tape. She was strapped to a chair on the other end of the trailer in the line of fire.

She looked over her shoulder and Cove saw a bright orange flash of flame above her head. A bullet tore past his face, careened off the far side of the hallway and zinged out through the opening with a buzzing sound. He ducked back behind the wall in time for another explosion to burst through the sheetrock next to his head, spitting dust in his eyes. He leaned back out into the hallway, looking for a clear shot. He saw Leo Terzi behind Julie with his gun up. Just as Cove found his front sight on the shooter's face, what felt like a sledgehammer hit him in the chest and put the warden to his knees. Gasping for air, he reached to his sternum, struggling to breathe. He knew he'd taken a bullet to his torso, but failed to understand what was happening. He touched his chest with his hand and felt the lump of lead and copper smashed against his Kevlar. It brought his brain back into the fight. He started to roll out from his knees when another one hundred and fifty-eight grain chunk of lead slammed into Cove's right thigh and blew out the back of his leg muscle. A flash of white-hot pain burned from his toes to his brain, grinding through his teeth. Cove reached for the wound, feeling the sticky wetness, and looked at his hand dripping with dark blood. He realized he was lying on his side, and his Glock was gone. He felt his life pumping from his torn leg. *I shoulda run in,* Cove thought, while trying to find the strength to look for his gun.

*****

Julie Lake was yelling through the duct tape, making a muffled howling. She stared at Charley Cove at the end of the hall, laying in a growing puddle of blood. Her eyes were wide open and her skin was flushed. She was trying to stand up while taped to the chair. She watched as Leo Terzi walked towards the downed warden, revolver in his hand.

*****

Cove rolled over and searched for his handgun. A coiled rattlesnake came into focus. The snake's scaly head was pulled close to its body, ready to strike, the two tips of its slate colored tongue flicked out, tasting the air. Half of Cove believed he was having a vision and the other half told him it was the real deal, but whichever it was, it didn't make any sense. He turned his head and found the Glock lying a few feet from the snake and struggled to reach for the gun. Cove couldn't comprehend why his arm was so heavy and where his strength had gone. His body had always been strong and now it was flawed. He heard the pounding of his heart and managed to raise his head, only to see Terzi walking in slow motion towards him. Cove's brain had slowed time down. Perhaps it was a mechanism to prolong his last minutes. Perhaps it was his rapidly dropping blood pressure or his veins still flushing with adrenalin. He tried to reach for the Glock and felt himself rising upwards. A bolt of pain ran through his leg. Tiny bright spots were spiraling around in his eyes, and he suddenly felt weightless. The smell of cat-piss hit him in the face and Cove was jolted back to reality, as if a nurse had popped an ammonia capsule under his nose. His eyes focused. He was face to face with Terzi. The tweaker had grabbed him by the shirt and pulled him up to a sitting position. Terzi opened his mouth and Cove was struck with another belch of the stench. The smell was replaced by the taste of the oily muzzle of a gun barrel being pushed into his mouth.

"I thought maybe you weren't coming," Terzi said, his bloodshot eyes drilling into Cove's. "We're just startin' the fuckin' party. You can watch Red's first needle slam..."

Drums pounded in Cove's ears. His bloody fingers touched his pocket, grasped his knife, flicked the blade open, and with all of his father's Salish strength, he buried the three-inch blade into the back of Terzi's thigh, cutting through the sciatic nerve and hitting the femur. Cove twisted the handle and felt the tip snap off in the bone. He watched the spark fade from Leo's eyes and heard a far off scream. Time was like a stretched rubber band. From outside his body, Cove watched Terzi, still holding him by his shirt, still holding the revolver's barrel in his mouth. He watched Terzi's finger turn white as he pulled on the trigger and saw the .357's hammer being drawn back. The cylinder rotated so slowly he thought he'd taste the bullet before it took his head off. At twelve pounds of pressure, he saw the hammer break and watched it start towards the firing pin, finally slamming home. Cove heard a snap echo from the gun's empty chamber and he felt himself falling, pulled by Mother Earth, feeling himself absorbed into the warm darkness of her soil, and then he was gone.

# EPILOGUE

Charley Cove was laying in short green grass, looking up at Liz, framed by blue sky and white cumulus clouds. She was smiling and naked, her bare breasts a deeper tan than Cove had ever seen. She was sitting bareback on a bay-colored horse, holding its black mane and rawhide reins, looking at him and talking in a language he couldn't understand. She started to ride off. Cove shouted at her and struggled to get up, but failed. Liz stopped her horse, turned it broadside with a rein, and looked back at him with one hand leaning on the animal's rump. Her smile was gone, but her eyes still twinkled like stars. She looked at him and slowly shook her head. She said something in the same unfamiliar tongue. Her smile returned and she made a clicking sound. She put her bare heels into the horse's flank and took off at a fast canter, her hair bouncing with the horse's lope, her body flowing with the animal's movement. He saw her take a quick glance back and then watched as her mirage disappeared into the clouds.

He felt a stickiness on his hand, and found his fingers covered in fresh bright-red blood. It made no sense. Turning, he discovered a doe laying beside him, its head smashed open.

Hearing something behind him, Cove turned. It was Coyote, sitting on his haunches a few feet away with his tongue hanging out of a toothy grin.

"Where am I?" Cove asked.

Coyote laughed like a human. "Looks as though your ass is in the grass, Charley," he said smiling.

Cove looked at his bloody hand.

Coyote lost his smile. "Stop feeling guilty. You didn't let them down. You did the best you could."

Cove glanced back at his hand and the blood was gone. Confused, he looked up at Coyote. "Where's Liz going?"

Coyote's grin returned. "Don't worry about her. She's in the circle." He laughed again and took off running towards the sun.

Cove frowned, stared at the little gray canine, wondering what he'd meant about the circle. When he could no longer see Coyote, he tried to get up, but had no strength. He glanced beside him and discovered the deer was gone, but a puddle of blood remained. Looking into the sky, he focused on a cumulus cloud, its top boiling up from the heat rising off the rolling green hills. The hard grassy ground of Mother Earth became softer, and he felt himself being pulled down into its comforting depth.

Cove sensed pressure on his hand. He felt lips on his unshaven cheek. His eyes eased open, like sunlight on a dawning morning. The sky was gone.

From far away he heard a voice. "Charley, can you hear me?"

He tried to move his head, but couldn't summon the strength. He moved his eyes and watched as Julie Lake came into focus. She seemed to come from far off. He watched her lips move.

"Hey, Mr. Warden, you're finally with us."

The voice was closer, and Cove's mind flashed back to Julie strapped to the chair, duct tape around her mouth and head, with Terzi's gun stuck in his mouth. He studied the image near him and saw her smiling. He wondered if they were in the afterlife.

"Where are we?" he asked weakly.

"In the hospital in Idaho Falls," She explained, and Cove felt another squeeze on his hand. "You were life-flighted down last night."

"Terzi?"

A deeper voice answered. "He fell in the river after you stuck your knife in him. Fred's got Search and Rescue trying to recover his body, but they're fighting the slush ice."

"George?" Cove asked.

"Yeah, Charley, it's me," Nayman answered. "You didn't think you could drive one of our trucks through somebody's house trailer without me being around to chew your ass, did ya?"

Cove groaned and felt another squeeze from Julie's fingers.

Nayman coughed. "You stuck him good, Charley. He left a hell of a blood trail in the snow. Fred got there in time to see him go in the river. 'Said he could see something sticking out of his leg, but we couldn't figure out what had happened until Julie filled us in. Junior and I got there after the shit hit the fan. Fred said he watched you drive off. They heard the shots and they rolled in."

"Gawd," Charley whispered. "He's gonna kill me."

"You'd better hope that's all he does," Nayman said. "He was cussing your ass up and down when we were loading you in the helicopter. I wish I'd had my recorder going."

Another grip from Julie's hand gave Cove the energy to roll his head towards her. "You okay?" He asked.

"Yeah, Charley, I'm fine." Julie said. "You just got out of surgery."

"Where's Annie?" Cove asked.

"She's in my Subaru out front," Julie replied. "She's fine. I was so happy to find her in my house..."

Nayman spoke up, continuing to fill Cove in. "Fred's got a warrant out for Joey Gabbro—he's in the wind. Fred had the detectives down here show a photo of him to the pawnshop guy, and he positively ID'd Gabbro as the perp who sold those guns. Fred thinks Gabbro screwed up on the one serial number. It was the rifle that came back stolen. He and Terzi were in cahoots; their phone records prove it. Gabbro called Terzi right before you guys went out poking around his trailer."

"Terzi went in the river?" Cove asked, still confused.

"Yeah," Nayman said. "Between you sticking your knife in him and the icy river, he couldn't have lasted a minute, unless he's Superman. He's probably down there wrapped around a submerged cottonwood somewhere. Even a blind man coulda followed that blood trail."

Cove moved his head back to Julie. "Surgery?"

"The bullet broke your femur. They had to pin it. If Fred hadn't put a tourniquet on you, I don't think we'd be holding hands."

Cove looked down at her fingers interlaced with his.

Julie leaned in. "I lied to you, Charley," she said, her bright green eyes meeting his. "I don't have a boyfriend." Hesitating, she continued, "I don't know whether you're ready for a girlfriend, but you've got yourself a nurse."

# *A Note to the Reader*

First of all, during my law enforcement career, I worked with numerous first-class deputies, so it wasn't hard to create Fred Mendiola and Jeff Jenks. Joey Gabbro was a different challenge and my sincere apologies to the fine staff of the Custer County Sheriff's Office for creating a dirty cop and putting him under their roof.

There is no Ruby Creek in Custer County and there are no alleys in Challis, but there is a Pahsimeroi Valley, and it is a wonderful place. I hope I did it justice in my attempt to describe it.

Some people believe they can feel "crack bugs" crawling under their skin; this is a common delusion with methamphetamine users. The chemical produces *stimulant psychosis* and it explains Leo Terzi's behavior. Paranoia is the norm for tweakers; the farther into their run, or binge, the more paranoid they become. Terzi's belief about cops walking on his roof is not an exaggeration–they get that crazy. His enhanced night vision and olfactory senses came from my imagination– the drug doesn't do that for the addict. However, meth users frequently believe they have enhanced senses or powers, and thus I'll claim that Leo actually thought he had two-moon nights while sucking on his pipe. It's not much of a stretch for a meth user.

*I hope you enjoyed this story. While it's fresh, please take a moment and give it a quick review. -Tony*

266

Made in the USA
San Bernardino, CA
13 May 2020